MAKING MUSIC WITH THE DELICIOUS TWINS

BRETT DAVIS

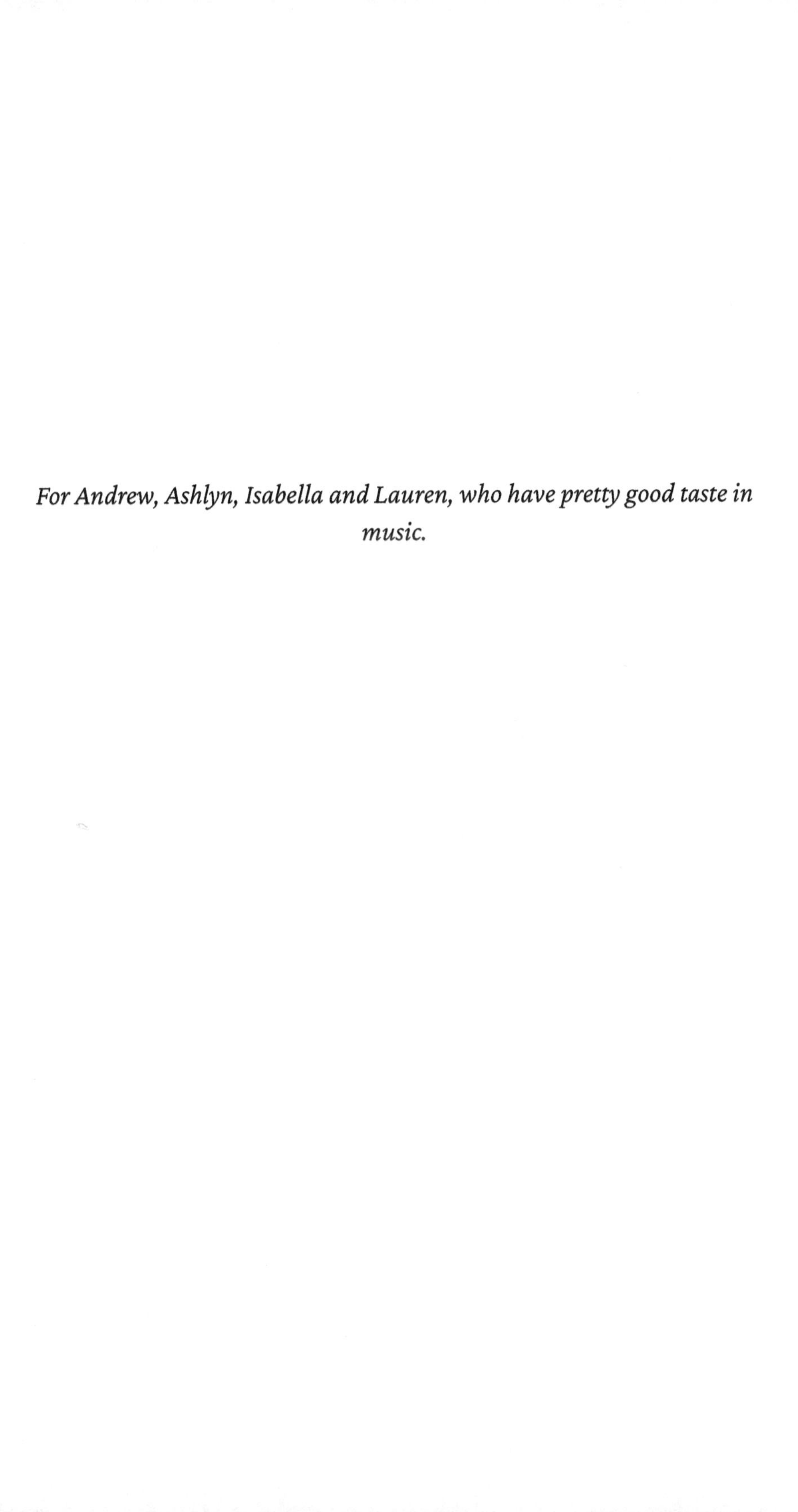

For Andrew, Ashlyn, Isabella and Lauren, who have pretty good taste in music.

Music is like a snowflake. Every note is unique. Some smooth, jagged, but—like snowflakes—they merge to form something more beautiful and infinite than the parts. She floats on the music. She *soars* on the music. There is a light above, and she heads for it, and the light is the music, and the music is the light—

CHAPTER ONE

The piano player at Grace Tabernacle Baptist plays in a nice, low, churning style. The other choir members lay back and let her take the lead. Her bright hair reminds Margaret Deener of the brightly colored clothes so popular with the dancers on Soul Train. The styles have become slightly more subdued in the late seventies, and she secretly misses the flashier colors. The pianist is nearly seventy years old, and she's shepherding a guitarist and a bass player—whippersnappers in their fifties—through a respectful but upbeat version of "Amazing Grace."

The congregation sings along, especially Margaret's two little girls standing with her and her husband, John, near the middle of the church. The church roof soars overhead, and the girls' voices soar with it. This is their favorite song. One starts to sing loud, and the other tries to outdo her, only to be topped again. Their father frowns down at them, urging restraint with his eyes. The girls have pretty voices that swirl and twirl like cords in a rope, a rope rising to heaven.

Others in the congregation make out where the sound is coming from. The sound is much better than the drone around it, a faceted diamond in a field of rough stones. Heads turn, some with frowns at the volume, some with smiles for the harmony. Their mother pokes at them with a knee, but they don't quit. This is their favorite song, and they are coming to their favorite part.

Once the song is finished, and the congregants leave, the girls get stopped by congregation members several times on the way out, walking between their mother and father.

"Margaret, you certainly are raising two little songbirds there," says Mrs. Anderson.

"It was one of the prettiest things I have heard," says Mrs. Evers. "John, why can't you sing like that?" Mrs. Evers, tiny and wizened, isn't too wizened to flirt.

Their father grimaces. No one stops them to complain, everyone is too polite for that. Most people don't say anything. The girls can tell their father is upset by how he grasps their arms and shoulders and moves them along steadily. He smolders in the driver's seat on the way home, and their mother makes nervous small talk, pointing to things they've seen a hundred times. They stare at the low houses of Percival, which seem to hide away under the trees. The foothills of the Ozarks are a child's blue scrawl on the horizon. The girls hold hands, certain punishment is on the way.

"If dad slows the car down, we can jump out and run away to the mountains," Barb whispers.

"We can be mountain women," Bet agrees, nodding vigorously.

"We can eat, like, nuts and berries to survive, like that old guy on TV," Barb says, getting into the fantasy now.

"You girls shush," their mother says, indicating it's not a suggestion.

They approach their own house, a two-story white box in an older subdivision, sheltered under regal oaks that tower above it and its neighbors. The girls exit the car and wait for their father to unlock the front door. They run upstairs to take off their stiff, starchy dresses and put on play clothes.

"Let's go climb the tree," Bet says.

"Let's just get out of the house," Barb replies.

When they close the door, their mother is behind them, her voice shaky with unspent emotion. "Girls, I do not appreciate it when you act up in church."

"Mama," the girls say together.

The tension breaks, and tears stream down their cheeks. Their mother's chin quivers.

"It was not right to sing the way you did. That wasn't praise. That was showing out."

"But, Mama," the older one says. "Was it any good?"

Their mother looks down at them, one at a time. "Yes," she says. "It was very good."

"God wanted us to sing," Barb says. "It was to praise."

"Maybe," their mother says. "Maybe." She gives them a little smile, and their tears begin to dry. "Just don't sing quite so loud tonight."

She shuts the door. Their father doesn't come in, but they can hear him talking down the hall. The door is not thick enough to keep out his voice.

"Margaret, where did those girls learn to sing like that?"

"I don't know, John. It was loud. But wasn't it pretty?"

"Little girls don't sing like that. Have you been giving them lessons?"

"No," their mother says.

"Margaret, have you been giving those girls singing lessons?"

"No, John. I have not."

With ears to the door, the girls learn their mother can tell a lie. Or at least not tell the whole truth.

CHAPTER TWO

The piano lessons are a gift. A secret gift.

Margaret Deener watches her daughters in the rearview mirror. She can't believe how much they've grown in the last year.

"Where are we going, girls?" she asks.

"To the store, mama," they say in unison.

"Now, you know it's not right to lie, right? This is just a story we're telling so you can get some piano lessons."

"We know it's not right to lie, Mama," Barb says. "We'll just tell daddy we went to the store."

After the incident in church, Margaret suspended the singing lessons and opted for piano lessons instead. There was only one piano at the church and that job was already taken, so she considered it a safe compromise. Margaret Deener is friends with Velma Ludvigsen, who offered an excellent rate on the piano. Barb and Bet had asked for guitar lessons, but Margaret was practical.

"The school has a piano they can use for practice," Mrs. Ludvigsen said. "People who don't need to know about the lessons won't have to know."

Margaret drops them off in front of the school and waves a furtive goodbye, although no one is watching.

Mrs. Ludvigsen waves them in, gives them both an awkward half-hug and ushers Barb to the piano. She gets to go first, one of the benefits of being the eldest. Bet grabs a dogeared Cricket magazine from a small table and relaxes on an overstuffed chair in the hallway. She looks down the hall. Large, glass doors open up to the back yard where the Ludvigsen dogs roughhouse on the grass. Bet appreciates the secret lessons but would also like to go play with the dogs. Smooth piano music flows through the door.

"Very nice," Mrs. Ludvigsen says. "But please play the song that's right here before you. "What you're playing is not 'Turkey in the Straw.'"

"It's *better* than 'Turkey in the Straw,'" Barb insists.

And it is, Bet agrees, not being a fan of that particular tune.

"But we're not here to play something better than that song," Mrs. Ludvigsen taps slowly on the sheet music. "We're here to learn how to read music and play it. If you just come in here and make things up, you're not learning. You already know how to do that."

Bet approaches the piano as a mathematical problem. A certain key, when pressed, emits a specific sound. It is only a matter of keeping track of which key emits what and playing them in that order. To Barb, the piano is a trackless jungle in which to roam.

Mrs. Ludvigsen sighs and gives up.

"Okay, Bet, your turn. How are we today?"

Mrs. Ludvigsen, tall and fit, is the only woman to jog through the roundabouts and cul-de-sacs in her neighborhood. She's older and just chops off her hair to show she is done with artifice.

"Your sister has favored us with a new composition again," she says.

Barb plops down on the chair and picks up the Cricket magazine. She doesn't look at the dogs at all.

Mrs. Ludvigsen gives Bet a very polite smile. "Let's see if *you* learned the song."

Bet accompanies her into the piano room, puts her sheet music on the stand and arranges herself on the stool. She plays "Turkey in the Straw." She is slow and halting at first but then picks up the pace and finishes with a flourish.

"Very nice," Mrs. Ludvigsen says. "But your timing is a little off. That's a hard thing to get right."

Barb has good timing, Bet thinks.

Mrs. Ludvigsen pushes the metronome's metal arm to begin its robotic cadence. Bet starts the song again, poking the keys with her tiny fingers. The metronome ticks and ticks, relentless, and she realizes she's out of time with it. She glares at it, but it won't stop, won't deviate from its relentless rhythm. She misses a note, then another.

She starts shaking with frustration. She can't read the notes because she's crying. She would really like to be out in the yard with the dogs.

"Oh, honey," Mrs. Ludvigsen says. "Don't cry. It's not worth crying about."

"But I can't do it," Bet says. "She can do it, and I can't."

"That's not quite true," Mrs. Ludvigsen says. She leans in close and whispers, "she can play. But she can't play like you can. You can read music. You can play anything that's written down. She can only play what's in her head."

"But what's in her head is good."

"Ah," Mrs. Ludvigsen says, tapping the music, "but what's written down is better."

CHAPTER THREE

Bet is slightly impressed. But only slightly. Stan Swinea is a talented kisser. Even at sixteen, Bet knows enough to recognize that he doesn't slobber on her face like a dog licking a bone. He's slow, smooth, kissing her like he wants to know her. They break only to breathe. Bet sucks in air. While they share breath, he looks into her eyes. His are icy blue and slightly bloodshot eyes.

"Hang on, let me flip the tape," he says, his voice husky.

Sixteen songs of love, from The Police to Howard Jones. They've already heard it twice, and they'll hear it again.

Bet wears a blouse and a summer sweater. Stan wears a Yellow Jackets shirt, which Bet slides off his hairless, muscular chest. Now it's her turn. Stan's hand moves under her sweater, sliding it off like an orange peel. Then there's pressure at her waist, and his hand slips beneath her blouse. In a single, smooth motion, his fingers slip over her ribs and across goosebump skin. His hand slides over her bra, lingering. She kisses his neck and nibbles his earlobe. His hand wends up her spine to unhook her bra.

She slides her blouse and bra over her head. They rub bare

chests together and then Stan's mouth descends on her breasts like a starving child. Bet sucks in air and cups the back of his head, moving him closer to her heart.

She stands and unzips her jeans. Stan shoves them to the floor, and her panties follow. They move faster. Stan unzips his jeans and shucks them off, taking his underwear with them. The cool air between Bet's legs is replaced by Stan's finger. She holds on to his muscular arms as he pushes his middle finger inside her. Her own fingers find his erection. She drops to her knees, hard enough to make her wince, and takes him into her mouth. She's aware there's still music playing, but she doesn't listen. He tastes like a salty sponge. Stan's hands rest on each side of the back of her head.

He jerks. "Ouch. You're biting."

She doesn't know how to move her teeth out of the way, but she gets her tongue more involved. Stan's breathing grows ever more ragged. He lets out a little cry, and suddenly her mouth is flooded with hot salt water. She pulls away, and another blast hits her cheek. Bet falls back on her naked butt with a thump and hot drip rolls down her stomach. She swallows.

"I'm so sorry," Stan says. "I couldn't help it."

"It's okay. Could you get me a Coke?"

She drinks half the Coke before she can swallow again without being sick. They lie on his bed and kiss. After about fifteen minutes, she feels he's ready again. She's ready, too, as a preliminary expedition from his finger discovers. She pushes her hips against the finger, enjoying the pressure as he moves it as deep as it will go. He stretches above her, arching his back like a cat. She reaches down to help him, guiding him.

She winces and gives a little grunt of pain, then smiles. At first, it hurts more than it feels good, and then the order reverses. His movement is awkward, and their hips bump as she tries to move with him. Her hands tingle as she moves her fingertips over his back, occasionally digging in her nails. Her fingers urge him to continue. With a groan, Stan pushes inside her as far as he can go and stops. She feels a burst of wet warmth. Bet clutches his back with one hand and his butt in another. Stan only twitches. He kisses her sweaty forehead.

"How was it for you?" he whispers.

"Good," she whispers back, and it's true. But it could have been better.

They lie there for a while, tired, motionless, scared. Bet looks at her watch, which sits atop her pile of clothes. It's time to go home.

Fifteen minutes later, Bet parks her battered Camaro beside the driveway and gets inside the door to her home. Her parents are watching TV in the living room. Her mother turns her face toward the door and smiles when she sees Bet. Her father's favorite show is on, a cop show set in New York.

"There was a ballgame on. It delayed my show," her father says. "You could have stayed out another thirty minutes."

Bet stares at him in amazement.

"I'm kidding," he says, deadpan.

Bet sniffles and stalks upstairs.

"What did I say?" her father asks her mother. "Should I go after her?"

"No, that sounded like a minor boyfriend sniffle. She'll be all right. Barb's back there, anyway."

Bet passes Barb's open door. Barb's in bed, the covers up to her neck. Bet doesn't feel like being sociable, but Barb cries out for help.

"Bet! Bet! Can you get me some orange juice? I'm out."

A hand appears from under the covers and shakes a small glass smeared with pulp.

"All right. Give me a second."

She gets the juice glass and heads downstairs to the kitchen.

"See?" Margaret whispers to John. "In the fridge already."

Bet carries the juice back to Barb, who slurps it down, holding the glass with both hands like a child. She finishes with a loud swallow.

"Would you please, please, get me some more juice? I feel like a desert."

"More? What am I, your slave?"

"Aren't you crabby tonight. Please?"

Bet brings back the whole carton of juice, pours Barb a glass, and sits on the edge of the bed.

"Barb, can I ask you something?"

Barb sucks down more orange pulp. "Sure."

"Did you enjoy it when you first had sex?"

Barb spews orange juice across the floor.

"Don't do that," Bet says, annoyed. "I just brought you that juice."

"I'm just—I just—I don't know what to say."

"What do you mean?"

"Bet—I've never *had* sex. I'm a virgin. Why do you ask?"

Bet turns as red as one of the dots used to mark chords in Barb's old guitar songbook.

"Nothing. No reason."

"Oh my god. You had sex."

She says it a little too loud. Barb, still holding the glass, brings the covers up to her mouth to muffle her words.

"You had sex! With Stan Swinea!"

Bet nods. She feels like smiling and crying at the same time.

"I can't believe it! You have to tell me *all* about it."

Be shrugs. "I thought you already knew."

Their mother appears in the doorway. Barb freezes. Bet sucks in her breath.

"My two little angels," she says.

Barb relaxes her face and rolls her eyes, and Bet lets out a loud exhale.

"Bet, you better let Barb get some rest." Their mother nods at her. "Barb, why don't you take some more Nyquil? It's been a while since you had any."

"My mother, the drug pusher."

"Medicine pusher. There's a difference."

"We'll talk later," Barb says, and her eyes show she means it.

Bet heads to her room and gets ready for bed, moving as if in a dream. She is terrified that she has headed into the realm of sex before her sister. She wonders if she has doomed her soul to Hell forever. For a second there, when she came home and saw her mother and father, and they saw her, their innocent daughter, she wanted to go back, back to the time before she had sex. She wonders if she has caught a disease, and her mind conjures the oozing pus and gaping sores that will no doubt be her fate. She wonders why she had sex at all. She wonders when she will do it again.

After a couple of hours, she sneaks down the hall to Barb's room. Barb is asleep on her back, snoring gently. Bet steals some of her Nyquil, drinking directly from the bottle to avoid germs on the cup. It's cherry flavored.

CHAPTER FOUR

THE SCHOOL GYMNASIUM IS SHEER CHAOS AT HALFTIME. THE BAND IS playing, vibrating the metal bleachers. Bet slouches in her seat up in the nosebleed section.

"Go Yellow Jackets!" the cheerleaders shout, dancing and waving pom-poms. "Defang the Wolverines!"

The dull roar of dozens of conversations almost drowns out both the band and the cheerleaders. The band calls it quits, then sits down on the front bleachers and doffs their sweaty hats. The cheerleaders jump and shout their exhortations.

Four students, three boys and a girl—Bet's sister, Barb—drag amplifiers, a microphone stand, bass guitar and two electric guitars to the center court from the home dressing room. Bet debates leaving. She looks to her left, then the right. The bleachers are packed full. Leaving would certainly draw attention to herself. Could her sister see her from the court where she and the boys were setting up? One of the boys plugs in, emitting a squeal of feedback that gets the crowd's attention. One of the boys, tall and scrawny, taps the mike. The cheerleaders cede the court, kicking legs and scissoring arms as they go.

"Are you ready to rock?" the kid says into the microphone.

A rock band at halftime is unusual, so many in the crowd pay some attention, although they don't stop talking. The band launches into the Cars' "My Best Friend's Girl." The singer, Rob, even looks a bit like a young Ric Ocasek but with a better haircut.

Janice Reagan leans close to Bet and says loud enough to be heard over the music, "Isn't that your sister?"

"Yes," Bet says, embarrassed. The band isn't good, and they're playing in front of Stan and everybody.

"Do you think Stan looks like he's limping?" Bet asks in an effort to shift the conversation from her sister to her boyfriend. "Man, the Wolverines are killing us. Stan's going to be in a pissy mood for sure."

"Why isn't she singing?" Janice asks. "She has a pretty voice. I've heard it."

"Because it's Rob's band, and Rob is the singer."

"Rob is a dork, though."

It is irrefutable. Rob is a dork.

"You have a pretty voice too," Janice says. "You sound just like Belinda Carlisle, but better."

Bet shrugs. "Thanks. I do think Stan is limping. I wonder if he's hurt, and that's why he's not making many points."

"I don't know. I hope not. Rick is having a good night, though. Sort of. He would be if we were winning."

Janice has gone out with Jeremy from the tennis team, but no one except the tennis team and their mothers care about the tennis team. Rick, the team captain, stands tall and golden.

Janice is dreaming if she thinks Rick even knows she's alive, Bet thinks.

"They're going to do another song," Janice says. "I hope Barb sings."

"This is an original song," Rob says into the microphone. "I hope you like it." He adds, almost as an afterthought, "We're the Yellow Derringers,"

"She's not going to sing," Bet says.

Rob starts wailing over the amplifiers, cranked up to drown out the ambient noise.

Janice listens for a few seconds. "This is really bad. Your sister should be singing."

"Or they should at least be playing the Cars again."

The players come back onto the floor, waving and looking happy, although they face near-certain defeat. A couple of them try to dance to the strange, slow song until they give up and wave to the crowd again. Stan bobs his head a little, looks at Barb, and laughs.

"Oh my god." Bet slumps on the aluminum bleacher like she's about to melt into a puddle beneath it.

Barb doesn't notice how bad things are going. She plays on, nodding in time to the somewhat jerky beat, doing her best. The song shudders to an end. A few polite claps are audible among the din of the ongoing conversations.

"At least they're not getting booed," Janice says.

Bet nods. "They should be."

CHAPTER FIVE

"Mom, I want to ask you something." Barb fills out her college application at the kitchen table while her mother empties the dishwasher and cleans the counters.

"Okay. What?"

"I wonder if there's a mistake here." Barb stares at her birth certificate. The number 3 is typed in the space for the number of previous children.

"Where?"

"Here. I knew that you and dad had a little boy before me, and he was born dead. But this says three."

Her mother doesn't look at the paper.

"It's no mistake. We had the little boy, and then we had twin girls. They only lived a little while."

Barb stares at her mother, who doesn't meet her eyes. "Oh, Mom. You must have been...just crushed."

"It was very sad. They were so sweet. I've told you about them before."

"I don't remember." Barb imagines her mother and father,

trying to have children for years, feeling joy and hope and then despair. Twice. And then trying again.

"You must have wanted children very much."

"We did, dear." She rests a hand on Barb's shoulder for a second. But she's busy and resumes stacking plates. "You."

The number 3, typed in black ink on white paper, bespeaks a certain steel. Her mother is tough, Barb realizes. She wonders if she is as tough as her mother. She and Bet have called themselves the Delicious Twins for years. Her mother hates the words.

CHAPTER SIX

"Twins. I still can't believe it." John Deener says.

His daughters, Susan and Sarah, wriggle in their tiny cribs, arms and legs flailing at the world, eyes tight shut. He puts his own fingers on the glass. Of course, they can't see him, but he feels a connection. Margaret's difficult pregnancy after the death of David, their little boy, worried them. Margaret spent half the day in labor. But the proof of the value of perseverance waves its chubby, wrinkled arms and legs and announces its own life. In duplicate.

His younger brother, Ted, older brother, Reggie, and sister, Pat, stand behind John, their reflections all tall, skinny, and proud. John is grateful, but they're ghosts in its reflection. The future is ahead, just beyond that glass, just out of reach.

Two nurses and a doctor, Dr. Derban, come in, all in white with white masks. They flit from child to child and spend extra time above the wriggling, wailing twins. Another doctor and more nurses come in to continue the rounds, but Dr. Derban is gone with John's twin daughters. They wheel Susan and Sarah away, to a room deeper in the bowels of the hospital.

Derban comes out a few minutes later. He stands before the Deener family in the hallway, his eyes as baggy and red and tired as theirs.

"Where did you take the girls?" John asks. "Is something wrong?"

"I'm sure it's nothing to worry about," Dr. Derban says. "They seemed to be having a little trouble breathing."

"But they're all right, right?"

"They seem to be, John. Just some trouble breathing. We're checking that out now."

Dr. Derban delivered David. David never had trouble breathing because he never got a chance to breathe. That was two years ago, but Derban remembers.

"It's not as bad as David, John," he says. "Just relax. Wait a little while, and I'll come tell you more. Now, I better get back in there."

"Yes, please, go ahead," John says. "Thank you."

John stands with his family in the middle of the hallway. Pat puts a small hand on his shoulder, guiding him to the chairs. They slump into uncomfortable seats.

"If you guys need to go home, go ahead," John says. "I'll stay until I find out how things are."

"We'll stay with you," Ted says. "I can go in a little late tomorrow."

"So can I," Reggie says.

It's not true for either of them. Reggie runs the family farm, and Ted is a mechanic at the Stan Johnson car dealership, and both needs early starts even if they're sick.

"Thanks, I appreciate it," he says.

It's a long time before Dr. Derban comes out again. John stands to shake his hand. Dr. Derban meets John's eyes but won't speak until John is seated again on one of the metal chairs. He keeps a hand on John's shoulder. A sense of *Déjà vu* passes through John so violently that he shudders.

"John," Derban says, then and now. "John, I have some bad—awful—news."

Pat sucks in a breath. Reggie and Ted shift heavily in their chairs. John looks at the floor. The same floor he saw two years ago. His eyes go out of focus the same way they did then, blurring the black and white tiles into a gray puddle.

"John, they didn't make it," the doctor says. "It was their lungs. There was a problem with their lungs. I don't think they developed properly. There was nothing we could do."

"Did they—suffer?"

He shakes his head. "No, John, they didn't suffer."

John stares at the gray floor. Dr. Derban puts his hands on John's shoulders, calling him back to the world.

John looks up at Dr. Derban. "Doctor, do you think we'll ever be able to have children?"

Derban shrugs, then seems to catch himself. "I believe so, John, I really do. The problem was different this time. It's not symptomatic of anything. There's nothing that can keep you from having children."

Derban talks for a while longer, offering people John can talk to. At some point, Derban finishes and clasps a final caring hand on John's shoulder before he walks off.

"Come on, John," Pat says. "Let's go home. Come back and stay with me and Mom and Dad."

"No," John says. "Margaret is still here. I'm going to stay with her. I want to be with her when she wakes up."

Pat walks John to her room, and he collapses on a chair.

"I love you," Pat says, and leaves the room.

Ted and Reggie nod with solemn expressions and leave too.

John rests his head on the back of the chair and watches Margaret sleep. Her tousled brown hair wraps around her face and pillow. Her mouth is open, and she snores slightly. Her eyes move under her lids. She dreams of her daughters, watching them grow into little girls, go off to school, then move away to start lives and have families of their own. Their son is with them, first teasing his little sisters, then caring for them. He grows into a tall, strong man who carries the Deener name into eternity.

John wishes she could sleep forever so he would not have to tell her the news.

He falls asleep. Someone comes in during the night, but John can't rouse himself to look, and the person doesn't wake him. When he opens his eyes again, Margaret is in bed, awake, a faint smile on her face.

He can't smile back, and Margaret, although groggy, seems to notice, and frowns.

"John? Are they going to bring the girls in later?"

There is nothing to do but look at her. It sinks in, and she pushes her head back into the pillow.

"What happened?" She clamps her lips to stifle a sob that tries to escape behind the words.

"Something with their breathing. They lived a little while, but they stopped breathing."

Margaret strokes her right arm. The movement almost looks like she is cuddling a baby. "I only saw them for a few minutes. I was hurting so bad—I shouldn't have let them knock me out."

"You couldn't have saved them, Margaret. No one could save them."

"I know that. But I could have been with them to the end."

"Don't do that to yourself, honey."

John reaches out, and she grabs his hand and holds on as if to keep from sinking. They look into each other's red, watery eyes.

"What are we going to do now?" she asks.

"We'll just do what we've always done. We'll keep on going."

"We'll be alone," Margaret says. "I didn't think we'd be alone at this point."

"Is that such a bad thing?" he offers a weak smile.

"No," she says, failing to smile back. "It's not."

Two days later, they stand on a hillside at Edgewood Cemetery. Edgewood Cemetery is not at the edge of a wood but at the edge of a road. Cars move in the distance, life going on, not even slowing down.

It's warm, and the wind is fierce. Brother Harlan from Grace Tabernacle Baptist clutches Margaret's arm to steady her. He's a big man with a big head of thick hair cut down to stubble. His booming voice used to raise the roof and bring a sweaty crowd to the edge of religious ecstasy, but he is old now, and the wind nearly takes his words.

"For men are not cast off by the Lord forever, the Lord tells us in Lamentations three, verses thirty-one to thirty-three," he says. "Though he brings grief, he will show compassion, so great is his unfailing love. For he does not willingly bring affliction or grief to the children of men."

But it comes, John thinks.

"Blessed are they that mourn, for they shall be comforted," Brother Harlan says. In his own words, he adds, "I am here for you whenever you need me. You should also lean on your family." He looks Margaret straight in the eyes, and then John. "Please don't ever be afraid to ask for help. No one can get through such a tragedy alone."

"Thank you," John says.

The service is brief, reflecting the short lives commemorated by it. John's family stands behind them, all in a row; his short, round father, tall mother, and equally tall siblings. They are not burying children. They bury plans, dreams, hopes.

Susan and Sarah are buried next to David. They have lots of

room. Their tiny coffins fill less than half the space allotted for eternity.

CHAPTER SEVEN

Barb lived her entire life on one side of the Missouri River, and now she's crossing to the other. She pictures pioneers crossing it on rafts, or Mark Twain floating along it on his way to St. Louis. She's crossing it in her green 1973 Volkswagen Super Beetle. The car is seventeen years old but runs like a dream. Her father made sure of that.

"It's muddy." Bet stares out the passenger side of the car. "This is the worst scenery I've ever seen. How much longer?"

"Not too far. Quit bitching. Just relax."

Bet fiddles with the radio, but it developed an affinity for country. "Don't they listen to anything good up here?"

"We're driving right up the middle of the state. You know you won't get anything good."

"I wish you had gotten the tape player fixed," Bet complains.

"We'll just have to sing."

"Ha."

"We used to sing," Barb says.

"Don't remind me."

"You're so high school now, Bet."

Bet rolls her eyes. "Thank you, oh student of higher learning."

"You're welcome. You're going to miss me when I'm gone."

"I'll have the house all to myself."

"Only if you kill Mom and Dad."

Bet shifts her focus out the window as if considering it.

The pile of junk in the back seat clogs most of Barb's view in the rearview mirror. More of her precious belongings are crammed in the station wagon behind her. Her mother in the passenger side of the wagon gives a little wave. Bet rocks in her seat, bursting with boredom and energy that won't get any better as the night goes on. They'll stay in a motel in a double room and watch cable until their father falls asleep.

"So, what are you going to do now that I'm out of the way?" Barb asks.

"Same old thing."

"Going to keep seeing Stan?" Barb asks.

"I don't think so."

"Have you started thinking about college?"

"Nope. Dad and Mom haven't given me the college talk yet."

"Matter of time."

"I'm not going," Bet says.

"Are you sure?"

"I'm sure. I'm not going to give in, like you."

When did she get so nasty? Barb wonders. *Was I ever like that?* Their mother hinted she would like to ride with Barb. Barb wishes she had let her.

"I didn't give in. Maybe I'll learn something. And it beats going to work."

Bet rolls her eyes. "You didn't pick this place to learn anything. Journalism? Please. You picked that because it's not hard."

"I won't argue."

"And somebody told you because the place is between St. Louis and Kansas City, they get good music."

"Oh, come on. If I wanted decent music, I'd go to Austin or something."

Bet shakes her head. "It's too hot there."

And too expensive, with out-of-state tuition, Barb thinks. Her parents couldn't help much, and Barb didn't want to go broke just to learn something.

"So...what do you think the nightlife is like at the U of Mo?" Bet can't hide her envy. Whatever it is, it will be superior to what Barb is leaving behind.

"I'm hoping to find out. Why don't you come visit me? When school's out. Maybe I'll get a summer job and stick around, and you can stay with me."

"Maybe. They've been looking up churches for you in Columbia, you know," Bet says with an evil grin. "Apparently, there are quite a few. I'm sure they've found some good ones. You are expected to attend services three times a week."

"My studies will no doubt interfere."

"Your studies. Two words rarely found together. Are you really going to be a journalist? Or is that just something you told Mom and Dad?"

"I might be." Barb imagines herself at a press conference. She sticks an invisible microphone under Bet's nose. "Your house is on fire and your dog is dead. How do you feel?"

"I'm going to Disneyland," Bet says. "I never liked that dog anyway."

They laugh until the car swerves, and their father gives them a warning honk from behind.

"It sounds like a cover story to me, so you can be in a band," Bet says. "Do you think you'll be in a band?"

The Yellow Derringers broke up after their disastrous halftime debut. The Pencils played together three times and called it quits. The Fleshtone Crayons never even held a practice.

"I don't know. They've all been working out so well," Barb says.

"Yeah, but you brought your guitar."

She does have that squirreled away on the floor of the Bug. Her father made her promise to leave it behind, but she hid it under a pile of bras and panties he would never examine. She could no more go away to college without her guitar than she could go without shampoo or tampons.

"That's just for me," she says more to herself than Bet. "I'll see what I have time to do. The classes are supposed to be pretty tough, or at least the catalog says so."

"Are you nervous?"

"Yeah, I am." She's leaving home. She has no idea what she's going to do.

"I'm kind of nervous too."

Barb glances at her. "You are?"

"I am. I mean, you've always been around. I'm not used to the house without you. It will seem kind of weird."

"Thanks." Barb keeps her eye on the cluster of cars approaching on the opposite side of the road. "So, what are you going to do? You're halfway there. Two more years to go."

"I don't know what I'm going to do. I've thought about some different things."

"Yeah? Like what?"

Bet shrugs. "I don't know. Sales, maybe, just to get some money. I don't really have any plans beyond that."

"Time's coming up, though."

"Ugh. You sound like Dad."

"Dad's not always wrong." Maybe she is growing up. Maybe she is losing her mind. "Hey, Bet—did you know that Mom and Dad had twins?"

"Yeah, us. The Delicious Twins."

"No." Barb shakes her head. "Before us. They had a little boy who was born dead. Then they had twins who died shortly after birth."

"Really?" Bet frowns. "I remember hearing about the little boy. I don't remember anything about actual twins."

"I didn't either. But it was on my birth certificate, and I asked mom about it, and she told me."

"That must have been tough. I'm glad they kept trying. They got their practice run out of the way with you, and then they achieved perfection with me."

Barb gives her a sidelong glance but decides not to rise to the challenge. "I've been thinking about it ever since. What if there's like another universe, and in that one, they lived? What if they're living the lives we should have had?"

Bet snorts. "You aren't even at college yet, and you're already on drugs?"

"I'm not on drugs. Yet. And don't you be getting on any."

"Like that's possible on the mean streets of Percival."

"Anyway, I was just thinking about it." Barb glances at the car passing them on the left. "What if those twins formed a band, and their parents actually encouraged them?"

"That would be a better universe than ours, I guess. So, that's what the twins would do in your perfect universe?"

"I guess so."

"They wouldn't work retail in Percival?" Bet asks.

"They would. If that's what they wanted to do."

"What if they didn't know what they wanted to do?"

"Then they'd be living in our universe, wouldn't they?" Barb replies.

They're silent for a moment, then Bet says, "Mom did get us those piano lessons."

"Yeah," Barb murmurs. "But why was Dad so against it?"

CHAPTER EIGHT

St. Louis is an oven, especially backstage at Club Bandstand. On the way to the club, nineteen-year-old John Deener had noted the kids milling around on the street, sweat pouring off their heads. Old ladies sitting on stoops, uselessly fanning themselves. Dogs sitting in the shade of parked cars, too hot to chase the kids.

Dickie leans close to him and says in a high-pitched, excited voice, "I heard a guy from 'American Bandstand' is here tonight,"

John waves his hand at the floor as if to smack down his words. "I heard that too. That's not true. Some of the guys are just saying that to make us nervous."

"I bet KATZ radio is here," Dickie replies.

"Yeah, they probably are," John agrees.

They wait backstage for the show to start. John and Al hold their guitars upright and lean on the necks like old men with canes. Dickie leans on his standup bass, which towers above him. Hugh leans on the wall with his drumsticks casually tucked int his waistband.

"Welcome to Talent Night at Club Bandstand!" the announcer shouts from onstage. He's dressed like a carnival barker.

"Man, there are some really good bands here," Al says. "Dexter Peterson is over there with his group."

Dickie nods in Dexter's direction, but John doesn't look, doesn't take the bait.

"They'll probably get the recording contract," Dickie whines.

John shakes his head. "I read the fine print. Decker Records says the winner will get a contract, but it doesn't have any details. We'd probably just end up on the B-side of someone else's single or a compilation record."

"Do they say anything about paying us?" Hugh asks, and John shakes his head.

"I'll still take it," Al says.

Dickie nods, head bouncing like a bobblehead.

"Me too," Hugh says.

"Oh, me too," John says. "A record and some airplay? That's why we're here."

The dancers shuffle around the floor. Boys grin at the girls. The girls stare at the stage. Cops approach some kids who try to sneak in beer. A few people walk in, fanning themselves.

A skinny kid who works at Club Bandstand walks up and hands John a run sheet for the evening. "Here you go, Percival members," he says. "This is the order for the night. Three songs each. Be backstage in fifteen minutes. The door's right around there."

"Oh, man." John scans the run sheet. "We're up third."

"Aw, shit," Hugh says. "I was hoping we'd go later."

"Me too," Al says. "I'd like for the crowd to be loosened up a bit."

John looks at his fellow bandmates. Dickie isn't flashy but he's solid and tall. The girls seem to like that. His black hair is combed in a swoop over his eyes. Hugh is the opposite of Dickie. He's flashy but thin as a rail, and his brown hair looks like wheat in a field. Al, who plays guitar and sings, is stocky but with long arms that wrap around his guitar, making it look almost like part of his body. He has an amazing voice. John plays guitar and sings, too, but he's better at playing guitar than singing, so his voice is limited to harmony.

Their band, Percival, a rock band mix of Chuck Berry, Bill Haley and the Comets, appeals more to the guys in the crowd. The girls prefer the doo-wop bands. Dickie, John, Al, and Hugh all wear sport jeans or creased khakis and shirts freshly washed and pressed by their mothers.

The opening bands get the night off to a stumbling start. The first band, a rock n' roll group, launches its set with a cover of "Rock Around the Clock."

"Aw, shit!" Dickie says. "They're doing our song."

"Half the bands tonight are going to do that song," John says. "It's ok."

The organizers mix things up and throw a doo-wop band for second; the girls in the audience approve, judging by their cheers.

The doo-wop band staggers backstage, sweaty and relieved its set is done. Percival is up. John pushes any thoughts of airplay or records out of his mind and focuses on his fingers and the fretboard. Al starts a cappella singing the opening to "Tutti Frutti," but it's a fake-out and the band cranks into "Rock Around the Clock." The crowd gives a brief cheer and then dances enthusiastically, even though they've already heard the song once already.

John eyes the crowd as best he can without messing up his finger-work, but he plays the wrong chords several times. Al gives John a warning glance, which John ignores. Dickie's hair has come loose from sweat and covers his face, which the girls in the crowd like. They shamble to the end of the song.

They do an Eddie Cochran cover next. It's not horrible, but John fumbles the chords and sings off-key. He isn't the only one who makes mistakes during the song—Hugh doesn't quite have the beat down. Al's singing could be better, but John feels his own failings like actual wounds. His armpits grow cold with sweat, and he stares at his fingers as if he can send them scurrying to the correct locations through willpower alone.

"Pearl of Great Price" ends the set, a song John wrote himself. It's the only original song of the night, so this will set Percival apart. The song opens with a simple guitar riff that expands into a complicated tune with subtle bass fills and a danceable beat. Or at least it did in rehearsal. On stage, in front of the Club Bandstand crowd, KATZ and Decker Records, John can't quite play it, and Al suddenly can't find the right pitch. John can tell the song is a disaster, a plodding, amateurish mess. The crowd is polite, but most kids stop dancing and watch like vultures eyeballing a staggering cow.

John plays louder, hoping to cover his failings with sheer volume. Al sings, glaring at John with annoyance as he matches the volume. John's E string breaks. It curls up from the pickup and strikes him square in the eye.

"Son of a bitch!" he shouts into his microphone.

It occurs to him much later that if he had just waited a decade and a half to shout an obscenity into a microphone, no one would have thought much of it, or might even have welcomed it. But on this night, in the club that Chuck Berry built, rock and roll is still too young to hear such obscenities.

The crowd gasps. Percival stops playing. John, cradling his stinging eye, runs into the wings, nearly knocking over the next band's bass player. Percival won't be heard on KATZ this night, nor will they be chosen to grace a Decker Records B-side—ever.

CHAPTER NINE

Music floats down the dormitory hall. Barb goes to the dorm to borrow notes from a friend, and a different kind of note echoes by as she leaves. It's guitar, acoustic, good enough to make her stop. Not the usual folky guitar stuff you expect to hear on college campuses, but hard, driving, urgent. It flows from a room down the hall. The singing, a high-pitched voice crooning a love song, starts as she gets closer. She leans on the wall, notes in hand, and listens.

"I wind you round my fingers—Pier 1 had you on sale. If they catch me with you, I'll surely go to jail," the voice says.

As she listens, she realizes it's a love song to a wicker basket. *Now that*, she thinks, *you don't hear every day.*

Another door down the hall opens. An Asian student, bleary-eyed, stomps up to the room emitting the music. "You know this idiot?" he demands.

Barb shakes her head.

"Singing, playing all the fucking time. Very rude. Goddamn communist bastard." He bangs on the door. The guitar gets much louder, just for a second, then stops. The door opens. "I have to sleep," the student says. "Please."

"Sorry," the singer says. "I didn't realize how late it was."

The student stomps away, muttering. The singer is thin, with straight black hair in a Moe Howard bowl cut. He's pale as spilled milk in a snowstorm.

"Hello," he says in a thick accent that sounds like all the Russians she's seen in James Bond movies.

"Hello," Barb says. "I'm sorry to be standing here, but I heard you singing."

"I'm sorry about that."

"No, I liked it. I thought it was good."

"You did?" He doesn't appear particularly surprised. "No one on this floor does."

"It's—unusual."

"That's good, though, is it not? But where are my manners? Would you like to come in?"

The place is beyond neat, a far cry from the usual college mess. It's almost empty. Just the standard issue two single beds, two desks with chairs, two chests of drawers, and night tables with lamps. Beyond that, there is a guitar and virtually nothing else. No clothes hanging out of drawers, nothing on the walls, no stack of dead-soldier beer cans. It looks more like a hospital room than a dorm room.

"I had a roommate, but he left," he says.

She sits on the edge of the departed roommate's bed.

The man sits in his chair with his feet on the other bed. "Would you like a beer?"

"Um, no, thank you."

"Just as well, I don't have any. Permit me to introduce myself. I am Pavel Karash."

"Barb Deener. It's nice to meet you. Are you from Russia?"

"What gave it away?" A smile flickers across his face. "Yes, I am."

"Your playing. It didn't sound—"

"Russian?"

"Right. I guess. I don't know what Russian playing would sound like, but that's not what I expected."

"I grew up on the shore of the Caspian Sea, hearing Western music. I liked it very much. That is what I learned to play."

"So, what do you study here?"

"Everything. So, nothing, really. I take a few classes but am not trying to learn anything. Just staying in school so I can play music."

That strikes her as a good plan. She regrets she hadn't thought of it.

"Do you play around here?"

"Not yet. I don't want to play by myself. I am trying to form a band."

"Any luck?"

"Not yet."

"I—" Barb hesitates. She should be concentrating on her studies. She spent too much time exploring the few clubs of Columbia, not enough time exploring the history of journalism or the methods of its current practice. "I can play guitar," she says. "And sing. And do both quite well, if I do say so myself. But I can't read music."

"Who can?" he says. "That is why it is rock and roll." He looks at her for a second, then reaches for the guitar, a Gibson battered like he's been fighting off muggers with it.

"Here. Play something. And sing."

She pauses to think a bit before she launches into the Cure's "Just Like Heaven," doing the rhythm first, then the lead, then layering her voice on top of it all. The lead is suited to an electric, and the strings seem tight on the Gibson, but she concentrates and does a nice rendition.

Someone bangs on the door, and she stops playing.

"Shut up!" the Asian guy shouts. "I beg you!"

CHAPTER TEN

"ALL RIGHT, GUYS, WE'VE GOT TO WRAP IT UP. MY ROOMIES HAVE TO sleep sometime," Barb says.

"How can they sleep when art is being made?" Pavel asks, but he's already unstrapping his guitar.

She can't believe it's been a year since she met Pavel—who they now call Crash.

The basement is full of old boxes and paint cans and has its fair share of spiderwebs, but still has plenty of room for a four-piece band to rehearse. They can even leave their instruments behind. The drum kit is tucked into the corner, and three guitar stands sit in the middle, forming a rough triangle. They trudge up the stairs, Crash first, then Ben, then David.

Ben Jones looks like a drummer should, squat and muscled. He once finger-drummed on a desk so relentlessly that Pavel couldn't concentrate during a statistics test. Pavel failed the test but found a drummer.

David Kennel stands by chivalrously to let Barb go ahead of him up the steps, extending his arms dramatically to usher her past. He has an impressive wingspan and his fingers are as slim as the tines on a rake. He cracks his knuckles loudly as he walks behind her, the knuckles of fingers that have spent the last two hours tugging on bass guitar strings.

Barb's housemates watch TV and fight over the remote as she emerges from the basement. One of them glances up as the band members head out the door.

"Oh, hi, Pavel," she says.

He turns. "Hey, Amber. How are you?" His accent flickers and is gone.

"Good. I didn't know you were in this band."

"I'm afraid so."

"Cool. Take it easy."

"You, too."

Pavel sets off down the road, hands in his pockets, shoulders hunched against the cold. The dreaded Missouri winter is on its way.

"Hey, Crash, you want to ride with us?" Ben calls after him, but Crash just shakes his head and continues walking.

"See you Thursday, Barb," Ben says, and he had David head for Ben's Dodgy-looking Dodge.

"Amber, I didn't know you knew Pavel," Barb says once all her bandmates have gone.

She's giddy. The practice went well and they nailed a new song. Pavel's words matched a tune that she helped perfect. It snapped together like an easy puzzle.

"Sure. I went to high school with him."

"High school? You went to high school in Russia?"

Amber laughs and surrenders in the remote war.

"No, and he didn't either. Is he off on that Russian bullshit again? He's not from Russia. His parents are. He was born and bred in Centralia, Missouri."

"That sneaky son of a bitch."

"Oh, don't worry," Amber says. "It makes him seem more

exotic. Hey, I don't want to encourage you or anything, but you guys sounded good tonight."

The housemate with the remote control turns away from the TV. "Yeah, for a minute there, I thought you just had the radio on loud. It sounded very professional."

"Thanks, guys," Barb says. She feels even giddier than before.

"Listen, I know a guy who works at the Blue Note. It's this club, and they get a lot of great bands," Amber says.

Barb knows more about the Blue Note than she knows about libel law.

"If you guys want, I can see if he can set up an audition. Maybe you can open for some bands sometime."

"Oh, man. Am, if you can do that, I'll be in your debt forever."

Barb calculates the band could play a twenty-minute set without embarrassing themselves and maybe half an hour after another week or two.

"Just thank me when your first album comes out. What's the name of the band, anyway? Or do you have one yet?"

They'd been arguing about it for weeks. Barb and Pavel like one name, Ben and David another. But Ben and David weren't here to defend themselves, so Barb decides it's time to make the call.

"Yeah. Pod."

CHAPTER ELEVEN

Just thought I would drop you a line. Hope you're doing well. Mom says you're working at the mall. That's great, sounds like you're having fun.

I thought I might come home this summer but now may not. I told you about the band I'm in now, right? Pod. I know, goofy name. But we're getting some notice. The St. Louis Post-Dispatch did a little write-up on us. I'll send it along. I'm a blonde bombshell now (you'll see when you read it). Do not show this to Dad!

Anyway, we opened for Plastic Master at a club here not long ago. It turns out there playing at a festival in London. As in England! They invited us to come along. I was hoping to get to see you, but I really think we should go to this. It could be a big break for us.

Have you started thinking about what you want to do next? I think it's great you moved out and live with Lisa, but you can do more. I know, I know, I sound like Dad. I'll stop.

Come and see me now that you're a working girl and making some money. Classes aren't too bad. And I'm really excited about this band. This is the best one I've been in, by far. The guy in it with me is pretty weird, but he has some great ideas. He's the one in the story, Crash Pavement. His real name is Pavel Karash, and he's sort of Russian. Anyway, hope you're enjoying yourself. Talk to you soon.

Love,
Barb

St. Louis
Out and About

Pod

If you're blasting down I-70 toward K.C. and decide you need some entertainment, you could do worse than to exit at the University of Missouri and catch the band Pod at the Blue Note. Pod may consist of Ol' Mizzou students, but they don't sing about girls and beer. They sing about spaceships, talking dogs, and one man's love for wicker products. Lead singer Crash Pavement twitches onstage like the ghost of Ian Curtis, and blonde bomb-shell guitarist Barb Deener, who looks like she could snap Crash in half, adds vocals so sweet you'd think they were imported from Heaven. Sometimes they both just shut up and let their guitars do the talking. Add a concrete-solid rhythm section, and you've got music worth remembering.

CHAPTER TWELVE

This massive, outdoor London crowd is similar in some ways to the crowd that shows up at football games; lots of guys, lots of girls, lots of beer, and lots of shouting. The difference is that back in Missouri, Barb was among the crowd shouting at the football players on the field. Now she stands on stage, and the crowd is shouting at her.

"Look at that mob!" she says to a sweaty Pavel as he fidgets with nervous energy.

He just shakes his head, taking in the enormity of it all.

It's Pod's largest audience. They're used to clubs the size of closets, now they're standing before a field full of people somewhere outside London. Barb's fighting ferocious jet lag and is a little bit hung over. It'd only been a few hours, with some local bands starting things off. Pod isn't at the bottom of the bill, but they can see bottom from where they are. The crowd is done with the local bands and ready for something new, an exotic band from America that plays weird music.

"Ladies and gentlemen, if there are any of you here, let me introduce a band from the plains of Missouri by way of Red

Square," shouts the emcee, a skinny comedian Barb has seen before. "They're mad. They talk to aliens. They're taking over!"

"All right, guys," Pavel says. "No pressure, but let's play the show of our lives."

The emcee has been in commercials, art house movies, or both, but it's too late for Barb to figure out where she's seen him because he's waving for them to come onstage.

"They are none other than Pod!"

Barb's hands shake so hard she can't even smoke, but she stuffs her hands into her jean's pockets so Crash won't see. Ben is nervous, too, tapping his sticks against his leg. Crash's nervous excitement is contagious. Only David looks cool, almost bored, but Barb notices he's cracking his knuckles more than usual.

A kind of soccer chant booms when they take the stage, a looping, shapeless sound that echoes back and forth across the field. Crash stomps to the center of the stage and grabs the microphone stand like he needs it to withstand a gale-force wind, his guitar slung behind his back. David picks up his bass and gives a couple of strings an idle thump. Barb straps on her guitar and gives the crowd a little wave. The resultant roar tells her they're paying attention. Crash turns around and looks at Ben. Reliable Ben starts pounding away. They're playing a short set list, one that consists only of songs that have gone over well in a couple dozen club dates. The songs were well received in Columbia, Missouri.

"There I was, there I was in my cage," Crash shouts as David fills the air with droning bass lines to accompany Ben's urgent tribal stomp. "The aliens were blue. They told me what to do. I bit my tongue, but I was in a rage!"

Barb and Crash argued for the opening song to be "Out of Here," the story of an alien abduction from the inside. Barb doesn't have much of a vocal part in it, but it's by far their loudest, rowdiest tune, and Crash thought it would be best to lead off with it, to get everyone's attention. Ben and David favored "Sticking to Me," a quieter song about a lovesick tape dispenser.

Barb and Crash were right. The crowd bobs, weaves, and jumps up and down, writhing like a giant organism. She wishes she could enjoy the moment for longer, but Crash's character in the song has escaped from the spaceship, and it's time for her guitar to represent his mad dash through the woods to freedom. She steps away from the mike and tears into the six strings, pushing them so hard against the frets she worried she'd draw blood.

The crowd moves with her. She raises the neck of the guitar, the crowd surges up. She slashes down, and the crowd falls back. It's intoxicating. And natural. It doesn't distract her from her playing but drives her further into the song. She's playing her part better than ever before.

She reaches the end of the solo and steps back, the spell broken. The crowd shouts for her. She flashes a smile and flicks her hair out of her face. The stage is wide and broad, the better to accommodate the larger bands to come. Speakers line the sides, followed by banners and display ads touting Coke, various kinds of tobacco, and weird British products she's never heard of. The rest are people, all people. Looking at them, listening to them—*obeying* them. *I want to remember this,* Barb thinks. *It may never be as good as this again.* She wants to remember the smells: sweat and tobacco. The light: overcast but bright. The vibe: rock and roll, all the way.

"Yeah!" she shouts, though no one can hear her over the din.

David continues his bored-man routine like he's playing an accountant's convention at a Holiday Inn. He nods to the crowd now and then in a cool Frank Sinatra way. The women shout their approval every time he does it. Ben is sweating like a caveman, even though it's a chilly day. Crash is going berserk. He grips the mike stand like it's electrocuting him, only it's not killing him. It's giving him even more energy.

Crash can't dance. But he can twitch. He has energy. He is the anti-James Brown. Crash's head is shaking one way, his legs another, and he flails his arms like he's signaling an airplane. First one, then the other, never letting go of the microphone stand. His guitar bangs around his back like a giant piece of jewelry.

His high, scratchy voice is hard to ignore. He sings for all he's worth, shouting like wants the crowd near the beer stands in the back to hear every syllable. When the song crashes to a halt, he hangs his head and arms, crucified. The crowd goes wild. Or at least jumps up and down, which is all there is room to do.

They let the pandemonium die down and begin the second song. This one starts slow. Crash wanted to begin on a high note, throttle back, and then slowly build again. Crash's barking seal imitation is no good for slow songs, but Barb can sing anything. She steps up to her mike. There is no music at the opening. She hears only the inchoate rumble of the throng. She closes her eyes, and it fades and becomes as distant as thunder.

"I missed you. I missed your airrrrrrr."

She lets the last note hang, feels it flow over the crowd. This is a love song, but not the usual sort of love song. Crash wrote it so that you can't even tell if it's a male or female inflatable lover, but the doll is lonely because its lover has been away. Barb thinks it's beautiful. She sings it so the crowd will think so too.

She worried that the crowd would get restless during the acapella first verse. The more she sings, the quieter they get. David's bass begins to thrum, and Ben starts the backbeat. The crowd claps along. Crash's guitar issues a series of chiming notes that bob and swirl around her words. They add a sense of menace when the doll expresses anger at being left alone and joy when it remembers the nights spent in its beloved's arms.

"You filled me up. You made me believe I could breathe."

The crowd, arms raised to heaven, sways along. Crash looks back and Barb detects a slight smile.

We can do this, Barb thinks. *We can do this.*

Pod carries the crowd on a rollercoaster ride, up, down, up, down. They end with "Keep the Chains," a song about Harry Houdini communicating from beyond the grave. Ben pounds out a triple-time spine, keeping the energy to match the crowd. Crash flails his arms and legs like a scarecrow in a tornado, and the show is over.

They stagger offstage. Barb feels sorry for the band coming next, some sensitive British folkies who will have an amped-up crowd on their hands. Barb is exhausted. A roadie hands her a beer and she chugs half of it, then wipes the cold can against her forehead.

"That was a bloody great show," Crash says, dripping sweat, already picking up the local lingo.

"Group hug," Ben says.

It is sappy, but they're feeling good. They put sweaty arms around sweaty shoulders and smile at each other. David steals Barb's beer.

"How heartwarming," says a voice. "A pod of Pod." A skinny man with a long ponytail that hangs over his shoulder like a pet snake stands behind them. He's in black from bottom to top—black hair, T-shirt, jeans, and trainers. He smiles, revealing bad British teeth. Not black, but on their way. "Excellent show. I don't think anyone will top it for the rest of the day."

"That's nice of you to say," Crash says, fake Russian accent in place.

"Allow me to introduce myself. I'm Colin Exeter, president of Senses 5. Have you heard of us?"

"You guys signed Stack Six and the Severed Little Fingers," Crash says. Turning to Barb, he explains, "A great label. You have some of their stuff. You just don't know it."

"Glad word's gotten around," Exeter says. "You guys are better than both of them. Have you given any thought to recording?"

They all nod and three of them speak at once.

"Of course," Crash says.

"Many thoughts," Barb says.

Ben only says, "Duh."

"So, you've signed with a label already?"

"No."

Exeter looks around the cavernous backstage.

"Not very private here, but maybe we can get something preliminary going. I don't suppose you have any lawyers with you?"

Crash shakes his head.

"Pity. But do you have a little time?"

They look at each other, hope lighting up their eyes.

"Man, we are done now," Crash says. "We have got all day."

CHAPTER THIRTEEN

"So, what do you think?"

John jumps at the sound of his daughter's voice and rustles the paper in his hands. Barb leans in the doorway and shifts her gaze toward the square black object propped up against the stereo. She sent it in advance of her arrival, a flat vinyl emissary.

"I haven't listened to it yet," John says. He *has* listened to it, five times. He doesn't like it but recognizes it's good.

The album jacket is black, with white tentacle-like strips converging in the center to spell a word. Pod. It's fragile and lightweight, with grooves that could easily be scratched, wrapped in cheap, colored paper, and yet it is something John couldn't create. The picture of the band on the back cover is small, grainy, black and white, and out of focus. It is meant to look like an old tourist snapshot dropped on a sidewalk, and it succeeds. There is no caption or names of the band members on the sleeve. Their faces are hardly recognizable.

If his band Percival had ever recorded an album, his face would have been on it as clear as an engraving.

"Are you going to listen to it?" she asks.

"I am. I've just been busy. But I want to talk to you about it. I think it's quite an accomplishment, even though you clearly ignored me when I said you should stick to your studies. But now I think you should do that. You need to get your grades up."

Barb crosses her arms.

"Sit down, please." He nods at the couch

Barb ignores the request. "You won't have to worry about my grades."

"You're giving up the band?"

"I'm giving up school."

He shoves the paper off his lap onto the carpet. "Barbara, you are *not* dropping out of school. You have invested time and money in it already."

"I have invested one year in college," she shoots back. "That's long enough to know I don't want to go back. Pod is a great band, Dad. You would know that if you would get over your pig-headedness and play the record."

He stands up so fast he sees black spots in his eyes. She glares, but he's so angry he can barely see her. "Barb, it's a mistake. You're making a mistake, and you're smart enough to know that. Throwing your education away these days is the stupidest thing you could do."

"I can think of one thing that's worse."

"What's that?"

"Throwing away my dream."

He rolls his eyes. Barb gives him a look of utter disgust.

"Oh, Barb, you don't know what you're talking about," he says as she stomps up the stairs, then disappears from view.

But he's not so sure she's wrong. After all, he knew something about giving up dreams.

CHAPTER FOURTEEN

"Come this way, boys," the man in the gray suit says.

John Deener notices that the man's jacket is buttoned up like a suit of armor, and his hair is slicked back to a metallic sheen. He looks sharp, almost like he's from the future. He's a deejay and a record producer looking for the next Chuck Berry. Shoot, when Chuck Berry got arrested last year for transporting a fourteen-year-old waitress across state lines for immoral purposes, everyone went on the lookout for a new Chuck Berry.

"Nice to meet you," the man says. "I'm Jeremy Rod."

"John Deener. This is Al, Hugh, and Dickie."

"Gentlemen," Jeremy Rod says. "I understand you're a rock and roll band."

"Yes, sir," John says.

"No horns, piano?"

"No, sir. Just guitar and bass, Bill Haley style."

"Just the basics, then."

Arbor Records on Belmont put out a couple of good 45s but haven't spent much on the decor. The office is spartan, with one fake plant that looks dead. A woman with a swooping hairdo sits in front of a typewriter reading a magazine.

"Good luck," she says, without giving them even a glance.

Jeremy leads them into a small recording studio. A set of battered acoustic guitars and an acoustic bass lean on stands. A tiny drum set, just a hi-hat and cymbals, sits forlornly next to a baby grand piano on the losing end of a battle with a paint stripper.

"This stuff is not much to look at, I know," Jeremy says. "But it'll let me hear what Percival can do."

As if by agreement, John and Dickie, take up places as far away from each other as possible in the small room. They share little more than glares. Al and Hugh nervously get between them. Jeremy takes a seat on a stool pushed against the wall.

"Are you all okay?" Jeremy asks.

"We're okay," John says with a dry laugh. "Just a little nervous, is all."

"You're not the first to be nervous," Jeremy says. "But don't let it take over. I've heard some good things about you."

Hugh starts the beat. In lieu of a bass drum, he taps his shoe on the floor. "Pearl of Great Price" is jinxed, so they play something else, something simple. Al wrote "My Angel." It's crap, but Al wrote it when drunk so it's easy to play and sing. Given the battered equipment, that's probably a good thing.

Hugh's beat is solid, but Dickie's bass line is shaky. The small acoustic bass and his long fingers gave him trouble with the strings. His fumbling makes John angry, so he plays guitar too fast. By the time Al begins singing, the song is nearly shaking itself apart. They soldier through, John and Dickie shooting daggers at each other now and then. Al tries to end the song on a high note, but the performance takes a toll on him, and he brings "My Angel" down to earth, wavering, uncertain. Jeremy Rod's face is telling.

"I think you boys have some talent. I do. But you need to work on your presentation."

"Mr. Rod—" Hugh begins.

"No, no. Look, I said I heard some good things about you. I also heard some bad things about you. I heard what happened at Club Bandstand, and I saw what just happened here. I have to tell you, you don't seem able to deal with pressure. I've heard literally hundreds of bands that can play well in rehearsal but don't have the salt they need when it is time to play for the public. I have to put Percival in that category."

"But we've played county fairs and some dances at home without any problems," Dickie says, the whine shining through his voice.

Jeremy's face remains stuck in a frown. "That's good. But let me tell you what separates professionals from talented amateurs. Talented amateurs can have good moments and they can have bad moments. But professionals must be perfect all the time. Every day. Every show, no matter what happens or who's there. Percival might be able to play the occasional county fair or dance, but if you can't do a good job at Club Bandstand or in front of me, you're not professionals. And I'm only looking for professionals."

"So—what does this mean?" John says.

"Boys, I'm afraid you won't be heard on vinyl anytime soon. Not my vinyl, anyway."

"Well. Thank you for your time," Hugh says.

"I'm just telling you what I'm hearing," Jeremy says. "And I'm not hearing professional."

They trudge back outside. The receptionist is not far along in her magazine, John notices miserably.

"Sorry," she says without looking up.

"Nice going," John says to Dickie when they reach the sidewalk.

"What do you mean?" Dickie says, the dejection on his face instantly replaced by anger. "You were playing like crap."

John steps closer, pushing his face closer to Dickie's.

"I was forced to play like crap to cover your crappy playing. We were finished the minute you wrapped your Frankenstein fingers around that bass's neck. You played like you were strangling a goose."

"Guys, look, you're going to scare her," Al says.

He points through the window to the woman reading the magazine. She doesn't look up.

"I don't care if she sees us," John says. "I hope she sees who screwed things up for us."

"Oh, *I'm* the one who screwed things up. I didn't hear Mr. Jeremy Rod in there mentioning *my* screwup at Club Bandstand. That wasn't me, John."

"You shut up," John says. "That was an accident, and you know it. It could have happened to you. I was playing well up until that happened. But you were playing like shit in there from the instant we started."

Al pushes between the combatants.

"Guys, just cool down."

"Ah, let 'em fight," Hugh says. "Maybe we all would have done better if we ever practiced anymore."

"Shut up," John and Dickie say in unison.

"It's true," Hugh says. "When's the last time we practiced? We can hardly get you guys in the same room together. What's going on?"

"Nothing," John says.

"You guys used to be friends." Hugh shakes his head. "I don't get it."

"John just doesn't understand some things." Dickie says, his eyes on John.

John grabs Dickie by his jacket so quickly that a zipper slices across his finger like a serrated knife. "I understand one thing. You're fucking my sister, and you've knocked her up. And now you're running away."

"She dumped *me*, man," Dickie says.

John shoves Dickie back so hard that his head smacks against the glass. A long crack appears in the window, running from the bottom to the top. The woman inside finally interrupts her reading, her eyes widening as the crack spreads.

"Oh, shit," Al says.

"Let's get out of here!" Hugh shouts.

John glares at Dickie, ignoring the crack and the woman's frightened eyes.

The woman shouts something inside.

"John!" Al says. "You can beat Dickie up later. Let's get out of here!"

John relaxes his grip, and Dickie straightens his jacket, retrieving some dignity. The band members scramble down the street. Jeremy Rod appears in the doorway and yells after them.

"I know where you live!" he shouts. "Somewhere down south! You'll pay for this!"

"Keep going," Hugh says. "We still have time to make Marcia's party."

"How much is she supposed to pay us?" Al asks.

"Enough to fix that window. If we can keep the Rock 'Em Sock 'Em Robots off each other."

John's sister Pat isn't speaking to Dickie, and John worries about her. Running down the street with his bandmates away from a shouting record producer should be fun, a lark, something to tell the grandkids, but he can't focus. His lungs and legs burn.

Percival may play at Marcia Tilden's party, but it's not a band anymore. He runs away from his future, from his bandmates and friends. They'll play the party, get the money and then...*I will kill Dickie. Dickie drinks a lot, maybe I can make it look like an accident.*

"What do you guys say?" Al asks when they've gotten far enough away from the scene of the crime. "We have plenty of time to get back home and play at Marcia's. Can you try to avoid killing each other that long?"

"Sure," John says. "I'm up for it."

Dickie looks at him, surprise evident on his face.

"Uh—me too," he says, not taking his eyes off John.

"You are?" Al says.

"Sure," John says, affable. "It's a paying gig, after all."

"We better hit the road, then," Hugh says.

MARCIA TILDEN LIVES IN A LARGE, ANTEBELLUM SOUTHERN STYLE HOUSE. A circular driveway leads to white columns under a massive porch. Light blares from every window, illuminating the yard to rival the noonday sun. Inside, the light hurls itself against glittering crystal chandeliers and shatters into its component parts, dying beautifully along the white walls and ceilings. John has never seen anything quite like it.

Al called Marcia when Percival crawled back into town inside the belly of the massive Buick. Marcia's graduating party from Percival High is a party bigger than prom. The band wouldn't be invited if they weren't the entertainment. Their frayed cuffs and tattered seams are barely good enough to wear if they hide behind their instruments.

"Hey, guys, how are you?" Marcia asks at the door.

"Hey, Marcia," Al says. The place looks great."

Everyone else nods agreement.

Marcia's father, Milton Tilden, owns a string of prosperous department stores across the Midwest and is rumored to be pondering a run for governor. Milton, a huge man with coarse features and a barrel chest, is everything Marcia isn't. Marcia is tiny and pale with perfect features. She could have been carved by Michelangelo.

"Come on in," Marcia says. " I'll show you where to set up."

She leads them through one cavernous room after another. They stop at the back of the house in a room; workers string up lights and extension cords.

"Right there." She points to a small, elevated stage.

A permanent performance stage in her house. That's a first, John thinks.

"I've got to finish getting ready," Marcia says. "If you need anything, just shout. People should start showing up in about half an hour."

Hugh's drum set takes the longest to set up. Percival does not have much in the way of equipment, just two amplifiers. They plug them in and stand around, tuning up. Hugh's drums have a paper cover proclaiming the name Percival, which he painstakingly drew in art class before his high school graduation a year before. John feels like ripping it off the bass drum and tearing it up. It's just a cruel joke now.

The audience shows up just when Marcia said it would. Her friends gravitate to the back room, some discretely sipping alcohol from flasks. The older family members and friends of Mr. Tilden mostly stay in the front, but some, curious, come to check out the rock and roll band.

The frustrations and disappointments of the day fade as soon as Hugh's beat starts. Al takes up a position between John and Dickie. All the awkwardness of the morning session is gone. They're playing their own instruments, standing up, in their hometown.

If only Jeremy Rod could have come down here tonight, it might have been a different story, John thinks. Percival sounds good.

The kids respond with shouts and smiles to "Rock Around the Clock." They follow with "Jailhouse Rock" even though they lack a piano. John plays the piano part on his guitar. He hunches over the neck, squeezing out the thin, spidery notes, exciting the already excited crowd. Flasks pass between the kids.

The acoustics are excellent and work in their favor despite the large size of the room. Marcia breaks from dancing to watch the band and bobs up and down. Her face is broken by a huge smile.

"Pearl," John says after a couple songs. He wants to play it once more while they are good.

The sweaty crowd cheers for them.

"Are you sure?" Al asks, worry evident on his face.

The Club Bandstand show had been such a disaster that they have sworn never to play that song again.

"We can do it," John says. "We're hot right now. We can do it."

The rest of the band exchanges worried glances. John gives Dickie a quick nod with something other than malice in his eyes.

The crowd shouts for them to play *something*.

"All right," Hugh says. "Take a deep breath, everybody. Let's do this one up right."

"I have a little treat for you," Al says, drawing cheers. "This is an original song."

The beat is like a metronome, Dickie and his standup bass pound out the notes like an unstoppable heavy machine, and John's fingers move with divine guidance. Al's voice rises to the occasion, hitting all the right notes. An excited adrenaline rush pulses through John like never before.

Jeremy Rod is wrong. Percival *is* a professional rock band.

The space is packed with beautiful people, sweaty and drunk but still beautiful. The girls are not quite as sweaty and drunk as the boys, but they are into the music. The crowd looks up at the band with rapturous faces as "Pearl of Great Price" continues.

John smiles at a few girls, including a couple he recognizes from school, and they smile back. He met a new girl—Margaret Black—but he hasn't written her. Maybe he'll leave this party with a few telephone numbers.

Dickie also attracted the attention of one of the dancers, a blonde girl three or four years younger than him. Too young to be at the party, and she shouldn't be drinking. Dickie smiles at her, pleased at the attention. He points his fingers at her as he plays as if releasing the notes just for her.

The edges of John's vision begin to dim. Pat Deener once looked at Dickie like that. She met him at a couple of Percival rehearsals. John didn't notice at first, but after rehearsals they would disappear. Dickie later admitted they were dating. John always liked Dickie, and he and Pat looked happy together. And now the son of a bitch is making eyes at another girl.

Without thinking, John unplugs. Al keeps playing. John swivels his guitar around, holding it like a baseball bat, giving it a couple of test shakes. The crowd looks at him as he steps behind Al, managing to avoid tripping on wires.

He steps up for a good swing. Dickie's head starts to turn, but the white wooden body of John Deener's Les Paul catches him square in the back of the head. John puts some muscle into it and follows through, nearly catching a stunned Al in the face. The music stops. Dickie's arms shoot out, pushing his standup bass on top of the blonde girl, who screams and falls, not so much under the weight but from the surprise. Dickie staggers forward and collapses face-first into the crowd. John looks at the audience, a sea of gaping mouths and eyes. His anger fades and disappears. Dickie lies motionless on his face, blood pooling under his jet-black hair.

"Oh, shit," John says.

Two men grab John's arms with hands so big that the finger-tips nearly meet when wrapped around his biceps. The men step off the stage carrying John with them, moving him inexorably like a stick caught in a flood.

"I told you not to have a rock band for your party!" Milton Tilden yells at his daughter. "That stuff is no good!"

The goons throw John in the front yard. He stays face down in the grass, sobbing.

I killed my friend, John thinks. *Now the band is as dead as Dickie.*

CHAPTER FIFTEEN

 Barb stands on the upper floor of a Manhattan warehouse, holding a tattered piece of paper with a proposed list of songs for their upcoming album written on it.

"The set list for Sub Rosa Scarecrow." Crash says.

He doesn't look as weird as he used to. He has a haircut with some style, and his ripped black jeans and T-shirt came that way from a trendy gallery in SoHo. His black sneakers cost more than he used to spend in a semester at Columbia.

"Ugh. You know I don't like that album title." Barb had argued for something simple, and functional, like Pod #2.

David sided with Crash. Ben had no opinion, so Barb loses.

"I just don't think we should give the critics any ammunition," Crash says. "I can see that #2 thing coming back to haunt us."

"Critics?" Barb says. "They love us. Rolling Stone loves us. Spin loves us. You read the reviews."

"They won't always love us."

"I just want to remind you, Crash, that I wrote five songs for the next album. I don't see any of them on this list." Her voice is steel, with a razor's edge.

The warehouse floor is mostly empty, housing only a drum set, several guitars, a piano left over from someone else's rehearsal, and a big refrigerator full of premium beer and vodka. The members of Pod agree on one thing: No pianos. Ben and David fiddle with some electrical boards on the other side of the floor but escape to the streets of Manhattan once Barb ramps up.

"That's right." Crash sits on an amplifier and begins tuning a guitar. "I'm sorry, but they just don't fit the flow of the album."

Barb pours her second beer of the day down her throat, then slams the bottle down on a nearby table. "Oh, excuse *me*. Crash, I don't remember you telling me anything about the flow. You said if I wrote some songs for the album, you would consider them."

"I did. And I didn't want to use them."

"Because of the flow thing."

"Right."

Barb scoops up the bottle and throws it toward the dormant piano. It smashes against the floor, and green glass shards plink off the dusty windows.

"Great," Crash says. "No going barefoot during rehearsals."

"I guess I should have asked you if I could throw the bottle since you're now the boss of the band."

Crash stops tuning the guitar and looks at her. "Barb, I'm not the boss of the band. But I'm usually the public face. The label thinks our albums work better if they have a sort of consistent theme. I wrote the songs on the first album. They want to continue that."

Barb stalks over to the fridge and reaches inside for another beer. There's really good beer in there, and it's five o'clock somewhere.

She spins to face him. "Look, Crash, you and I talked about this a long time ago. I don't want to be just a hired musician. I don't want to be just Pod's guitarist. I told you I wanted to write songs, and you said we would record them. Ben and David don't give a shit about songwriting, and that's fine, but I do."

"I know you do. I remember our talks."

He had once told her that their beer-fueled musical rants at Shakespeare's Pizza were the most time he'd ever spent in a woman's company. He is truly a geek, but now a geek with power.

"There are only a dozen songs on this list," she continues. "We could easily add a couple of mine."

"We're back to the flow problem."

"You and that fucking flow."

"Maybe we could do a couple of B-sides—"

"B-sides," she cuts in. "No one does singles anymore, Crash. Give me a break. Don't talk to me like I'm stupid. You know, the Police put out a bunch of albums before Sting stopped letting Stewart Copeland and Andy Summers record their stuff. You're shutting me out after only one."

Crash makes a face like he's sucking a lemon. "Jesus, Barb, I'm not like Sting. You'll get to record your songs. But first—let's get Pod where it needs to be. The way to do that right now is for me to write the songs. Later, we'll loosen up, try different things, like the Clash did with 'London Calling' and 'Sandinista.'"

She chugs the third beer, wipes her mouth and holds back a belch. "All right, Crash. I'm going to keep writing songs, and I'm going to hold you to your words."

CHAPTER SIXTEEN

The tour bus sounds like an elementary school playground, and smells like a frat house. Barb figures being in it must be close to what it's like for the crew of a submarine. You see the same people daily, get to know their many quirks, share their various intestinal distresses, and watch as clean clothes become dirty laundry. Of course, the musicians get off the bus now and then to eat and play but, otherwise, she figures the analogy is apt. The bus's windows are so dirty and obstructed with wadded T-shirts and assorted junk that it's nearly impossible to see outside.

Pod is on tour across the upper-upper Midwest and parts of Canada, funded by a beer company. They travel, eat, and play with the Frothing Weenies, Code Blue, and Salvation. Salvation has a song on the soundtrack to "Last Rites IV", the horror movie series about a sexy but murderous priest. Only Pod has had a song that cracked the alternative chart Top 10, so they're the tour stars.

Crash is getting sloppy in his singing and playing. The Weenies are no threat, and Code Blue is good but inconsistent, but Salvation outplays Pod almost every night and has more fun doing it. It doesn't help that Crash's bedside manner onstage, while always aloof, has gotten downright cold. He won't talk to the audience, and half the time won't even look at them. Barb likes to chat. It's just rock and roll, and she thinks it should be fun, but Crash grouses that she's messing up Pod's mystical reputation.

Crash plays cards and drinks beer with Todd Runyen of Salvation and Jim Stacker, who insists on being called the head Weenie. They laugh like old war buddies. On stage, Crash is a remote, silent beast. On the bus, he chatters and gossips like a Florida retiree, at least with the guys.

"Checking out the boys' club?" Rebecca plops down onto the padded seat next to Barb. Barb's headphones are slung under her chin like a doctor's stethoscope and she pulls them down. "Sorry, I didn't notice you were listening to something."

Barb shakes her head. "That's all right. I was listening to you, actually."

She shows Rebecca the CD cover. One of the limited benefits of the tour is that Barb got copies of the entire catalog for Salvation, Code Blue, and the Frothing Weenies, which translates to a grand total of four CDs. Only Salvation has been around long enough to put out two.

"The first one's better, I think," Rebecca says. "But what do I know. I'm just a girl."

Rebecca Hannifin is one year younger than Barb at twenty-one. She's short, pretty, and fit. She'll drink a beer now and then, but she also goes for a jog every chance she gets. Rebecca makes Barb feel like a slob.

"I like them both," Barb says truthfully. "Although, now that you mention it, the first one is probably my favorite."

"You know why that is?" Without waiting for an answer, Rebecca provides one. "I had two songs on it, and Jerry had one," referring to Jerry Fortica, the lead guitarist.

"Let me guess," Barb says. "On the new one, it's all Todd."

"All Todd, all the time. He says recording only his songs gives the album a better consistency."

"I've heard that before."

"Unfortunately, enough critics agreed with him to make his case. Rolling Stone liked the new one better. I won't get any songs on any more albums unless Todd breaks a leg or something."

"What is it with these guys?" Barb pouts. "I thought music was supposed to be fun."

"I know. I'd almost rather be in the Weenies at this point. But at least Todd is still pretty fun to be around. Crash is such an asshole half the time. I don't know how you put up with that guy."

"Sometimes I don't either."

"Hey, you want to jam sometime?" Rebecca asks.

The bus is occasionally prone to outbursts of jamming when someone has had too much beer and picks up one of the ratty acoustic guitars floating around.

"I don't mean on the bus," she quickly adds. "Maybe one night when we're stopped, an off night. I've got some songs I've written that I'd like to hear performed, and I don't think I'm going to accomplish that with Salvation."

"Sure," Barb says. "I'd like that." She's written some songs she knows Crash won't play, much less record.

The next night, bands are booked into low-rent motels that sprouted up beside highway offramps like square mushrooms. They're encouraged to bunk up, but Barb gets her own room, even if it consists of little more than a bed and a bathroom. She's laid out on the bed, idly surfing channels on the TV bolted to the white wall. The roar of trucks from the nearby highway is interrupted by a knock on the door.

"Come in," Barb calls.

Rebecca enters, carrying an acoustic guitar even more battered than one of the bits of stringed driftwood on the bus.

Barb raises an eyebrow at the guitar, which seems to consist of duct tape as much as wood.

"I keep it in the luggage hold, or whatever they call it, but I didn't pad it very well," Rebecca says. "Plus, it was pretty beat up to begin with. It's my first guitar. Anyway. You wanna play? You look kind of comfortable."

Barb intends to sleep until her head falls off, but she doesn't mind staying up a little later. She falls back onto the bed but manages to prop herself upright.

"Sit down," Barb says. "Play something. I don't have any beer."

Rebecca smiles and sits in the lone chair, a stark wooden sculpture with some padding tacked on. "I don't want a beer. I thought the show went well tonight, but while we were up there, I was thinking of my songs and how the crowd never gets to hear them. So, I thought you might want to hear one."

"I do," Barb says.

Rebecca plays. She hits the first chord with no hesitation, no fumbling. She's a professional even when she's just playing for a pal. And then she sings, just a sad little love song, head and shoulders above the crap on the radio.

"I have your collar, but I don't have you," Rebecca sings, and her voice makes it sound less ridiculous than it should.

Rebecca stares in Barb's direction, lost in the song while she plays the chords and sings. Barb has a theory about songwriting. She feels every word and note should sound inevitable, like nothing else could come next. Truly great songs shouldn't depend on gimmicks, like an echoing guitar sound or a pounding drum machine but should be something that could be played on virtually any instrument, even an old, duct-taped guitar, with little loss in the translation. Barb rarely reaches these goals in her own songwriting. Rebecca, she notes with a bit of chagrin, comes close with this one.

Rebecca strums the last chord and sings the final words. "So, there it is." Her face is a little flushed.

Barb claps. "I liked it."

"You did? For real?"

"For real."

Rebecca gets out of the chair, hands Barb the guitar, and sits beside her on the bed. "Don't you have one or two?"

"I've got a bunch. But we don't have that much time."

"We've got time," Rebecca says with a smile.

Barb nestles the guitar into the hollow of her hip and gives the strings an introductory strum. She's not as precise a guitar player as Rebecca. She's sloppy and doesn't mind extraneous string noises sounding alongside the notes she wants to play, which drives some people, including Crash, nuts. Barb decides to play a song without a title. It doesn't have a bridge yet, just a verse and chorus, so Barb plays that. The transition from verse to chorus is jarring and breaks her songwriting rules, but Rebecca nods along. Her bare knee touches Barb's.

"So that's it," Barb says. "It's rough, you can tell."

"It's rough, but I liked it. Crash wouldn't play that?"

"No. It's too ordinary for him. If I threw in something about aliens attacking her, he might be interested."

"It's about life on the road, isn't it?" Rebecca says. "The disconnect from everybody. You did a good job of capturing that."

Barb realizes the song is about her ongoing cold war with her mother, who insists she comes home for a visit, as if Barb just works at a K-Mart up the street. She feels stupid writing about something so obvious, and not noticing it until someone points it out to her. She vows she will get a better grip on her subconscious.

Rebecca reaches across for the guitar and draws it slowly across Barb's thighs. Their faces are close. Through drowsy eyes, Barb studies the reigning sex symbol of alternative rock. Rebecca looks good up close. No suddenly noticeable scars, no discovery of different-sized eyes. Rebecca is just a good-looking woman, no matter how close or far away she is. And now she is very close. She leans in and gives Barb a kiss, full on the lips.

Barb is a little surprised, but her slow reflexes, which have kept her from committing many a social faux pas, keep her from pulling back with a jolt. Maybe she should give this a try. She kisses back, feeling that familiar smothering sensation. Rebecca moans softly. Rebecca cups Barb's breast, and she sits up a little straighter. She follows suit and feels Rebecca's small, firm breast through her shirt, slightly sticky with sweat. Rebecca moves her left hand up to cup Barb's chin, which is when Barb breaks off and takes a deep, gulping breath.

"I can't," Barb says. "I'm sorry. It's just me. I'm sorry." Barb is a little surprised to feel her Southern Baptist upbringing rising within her.

"It's okay," Rebecca says. "Really. I knew you are straight, I just thought—I don't know, I just thought I'd give it a shot. I really like your music, and I respect you a lot. I'm the one who should apologize."

"Don't. That was one of the best kisses I've had in a long time."

Rebecca laughs. "I heard you weren't having much luck in the romance department."

"So, my love life is the subject of gossip," Barb says. "That's comforting."

"I thought I might help you spice up your reputation a little," Rebecca says.

Barb laughs. "Well, all right. That makes me feel better, to know that you care about my reputation."

"Another thing that would make you feel better is some sleep. You look tired. I think I'll head on back."

Barb nods. "All right. I'm planning some serious crash time."

"Me too." Rebecca grabs the guitar and heads for the door. She looks over her right shoulder at Barb, a lovely, golden, lesbian, punk-rock goddess, all the more beautiful for being slightly disheveled. "You sure you don't want to come back to my room?"

Barb almost wishes she could reach inside her head and change her mind. "Nah. But feel free to dream about me."

"Maybe I will. You still going to talk to me tomorrow?"

"Oh, yeah. You haven't seen the last of me."

CHAPTER SEVENTEEN

 can imagine her cupping her mouth in secret conversation.

"You haven't called home in a *month*," her mother says in almost a snarl before her voice dissolves into a burst of coughs.

Barb groans. Pod had a great show in an Austin nightclub the night before, and she's still feeling the effects of the after-party. She pops a third aspirin and washes it down with a shot of Jack Daniels. She called home tonight, a Sunday night, because she thought her mother would be at church. Just a nice, brief chat with her father, hello to Bet if she's around, then pass well wishes on to her mother and be done with it until her guilt catches up with her.

"I'm sorry, Mom."

"I suppose being a rock star means you no longer have time for your family."

"That's not what it means at all. But it helps if family doesn't nag me to come home every time I call."

"Well—"

"I mean, Mom, this is the most exciting time of my life."

Barb looks around the ruin of her hotel room. Magazines, half-eaten pizza escaping from soggy cardboard boxes, crinkled beer cans in a line, and valiant dead soldiers litter the space. The throb in her head from the margaritas and the rasp in her throat from the cigarettes, yelling, and singing are part of the adventure.

"I'm doing what I love. Very few people ever get to do that. You don't seem to understand what that means. This is the time that I have, and I've got to make the most of it."

Her mother pauses. "I understand a lot more about that than you think I do."

Barb waits for her mother to explain this cryptic remark, but she doesn't.

"And I'm not asking for you to come home just to be nagging you. There's—there's something you should know."

"Well, what is it?"

Her mother hesitates. "Your sister needs some help. I think it would be good for you to come spend time with her."

"Help? What kind of help? Professional help? Mom, I'm not a shrink. I doubt I can help Bet."

"She could use her big sister around just a little bit."

"She's probably just bored in Percival. I know I was. She's a kid living in a small town. She just needs to figure out what she wants to do."

"There's plenty to do around here."

"Not really, Mom."

"Well—it's not really that, Barb."

"Then what is it, Mom? What is it?"

Her mother doesn't reply for several seconds, and Barb wonders if they lost the connection.

"She could use a role model," she finally says. "Someone she respects."

Barb laughs, a deep, raspy cigarette laugh. "I'm no role model, Mom."

"Maybe you are, and you don't know it," her mother says. "Barb Deener—you aren't on drugs, are you?"

Barb issues another laugh, a sharp, shocked one. "Mom! No, I'm not on drugs."

It's the truth. She has marijuana in her system, but she's not *really* on it. Barb isn't really a fan of drugs. Alcohol, yes, drugs, no. Marijuana's high is like she's running a second or two ahead of herself. Cocaine makes her excitable and she doesn't find that enjoyable, and heroin is just stupid.

In that sense, Pod is the perfect band for her. None of the guys are big druggies. Ben and David are beer-swilling guys from the Midwest, and Pavel is terrified drugs will make him more normal.

"Well, good, I didn't really think you were, honey, but you know, you read so much about people in rock bands being on drugs. It scares me sometimes, I have to admit."

"Don't be afraid of that. I'm in the band for the creative part, Mom. Anything else is just secondary."

"That's good. How are things—how are things going?"

Barb isn't sure how to answer. Pod is still touring behind the second album and making plans to record a third, and expectations are high. Weirder bands than Pod have been doing all right, getting big play on MTV, being asked to contribute to soundtracks. This could be the one that puts them in the arenas. But none of that would make sense to her mother.

"Things are okay, Mom. It's just that now is when we've got to put in the time. If we don't put it in now, we'll never get a chance later."

"I understand, Barb. I do. More than you think. But you should also remember that there's more to life than work, no matter what your work is. Your family was here before you were a rock star, and we'll be here after you're not a rock star anymore."

"I know, Mom. I know."

"All I'm saying is, it would be nice to see your face again."

"I'd like to see you again too. And I will. But just...don't bug me about it."

"I'm not bugging you. Just—come home."

"Mom. You're bugging me about it."

"I'm sorry."

"You all right, Margaret?" Barb's father's voice filters to Barb through the phone.

"You want to talk to your sister or your dad?" her mother says into the phone.

Barb detects the sadness in her mother's voice, but she pushes aside the guilt, and says, "Nah, I'd better go. I've got to get ready for tomorrow. Tell them hello. And that I'll see them soon."

"I hope that's true," she murmurs, and Barb swears she hears her father say, "This is what happens when they live long enough to grow up."

CHAPTER EIGHTEEN

The figures aren't adding up. There's a mistake. The taxes for Deener Insurance aren't working out the way they should. They owe way too much, according to John's penciled scribbles. He rubs his eyes. He wasn't supposed to be working at his father's insurance company with a wife and two little girls. At thirty-six, he was supposed to have a dozen albums and be on tour.

John studied the numbers. When his father was alive, he always leaned over the books with a serious look on his round face and made the numbers dance under his fingers, smooth as couples in a waltz. John remembers the way his father wrote the numbers, neat and precise, every one reproduced exactly the same, every time.

John's numbers are a raging mob. Unruly and poorly dressed and refusing to add up. The first year he did taxes after his father died, they behaved themselves. Now they are feeling punchy and independent.

"How's it going?" Shirley asks.

"I may set a record here," John says.

"Yeah?" Shirley continues to clean up the coffee cups and soda cups that accumulated in the office.

"Yeah. Land-speed record for running a business into the ground."

"Oh," Shirley says. "I'm sure someone has done it faster."

"Thanks."

She's a plump, older woman who wears a white sweater almost every day, a snowman with blonde hair. At least until it becomes too hot in the summer. She's old enough to retire but she's fiercely loyal and would tell John if he screwed up.

"You could get a professional to do the books, you know," Shirley says, clinking mugs as she waddles by.

"I know."

"But your father always did them himself, so you want to do them yourself."

"Yep. You know too much, Shirley."

"I'm going to head out soon. You need me to do anything?"

"Just the taxes, but other than that, no."

"Good night, then."

It's light out as she locks the front door. John checks his watch. He told Margaret he'd be home early. He'll have to be late.

A little while later, there's a clinking at the door. He looks up to see two smiling faces peering in from under the half-drawn curtain. Two little blonde angels, hands from an unseen adult resting on their shoulders. One of the hands taps the glass again, making the curtain clink against the wood. John smiles and stands up, then groans at how stiff he is.

John goes to the door and opens it with a giant smile.

"Hi," Margaret says. "I picked up these darling little creatures after school, and we went to get some supplies."

"And some ice cream," Barb chimes in.

"And some ice cream," Margaret says with a laugh. "But I have a few more things to do and wondered if you might be able to take the little darlings home."

She gives him a wink that the girls can't see. Margaret needs some time away to get Barb's birthday presents. John looks down at the little faces peering up at him. They aren't so far down as they used to be. The girls are growing fast.

"Oh, I don't know, I'm awfully busy." John makes a faux-stern expression.

"Pleeeeeeeease," the girls say, as if he might not take them home.

"But they'll be all jazzed up on ice cream." He smiles more broadly. "They'll misbehave, surely."

"We won't misbehaaaaaave!" they say. "We promise."

Their chorus is just a little bit off. Bet waits to hear what Barb is going to say, which makes the girls sound like they have a reverb effect.

"Well, maybe they won't be too much trouble." He tousles their blonde hair, Barb first, Bet next. "How do you girls want to go home?"

"Walk!"

"I won't be long," Margaret whispers in his ear, then kisses his cheek. "I'll keep the stuff in the trunk and we can bring it in tonight after they're asleep."

John nods. The whole birthday routine is slightly less complicated than Christmas. It's Barb's birthday but Bet must get at least one gift—even though her birthday is months away—so she doesn't feel left out. The whole batch must be hidden because the girls are as talented and dedicated as bloodhounds in seeking them out.

"Bye, girls." Margaret plants a kiss atop each of their heads. "You be good, now. You told your father you would. I'll see you afterwhile."

They step out onto the sidewalk and John locks up. He hates to leave the books out on the table but any burglar who made off with his tax failures would be doing him a big favor. Margaret waves as she heads for the Chevrolet parked two car lengths away.

"You sure you're not too tired to walk home?" he asks the girls.

"We're sure!" they chime in their call-and-response way.

They start walking down Front Street. Empty parking places spread out between the big square Lincolns and Chevrolets and Buicks, most of which are a bit rusty or at least dirty, and a few age-worn trucks. The pedestrian traffic on the sidewalks is light.

John says hello to Mrs. Conway, who runs the Christian bookshop, and she smiles and pats the girls on the head. The drugstore on the corner is open and the girls clamor for ice cream, but John reminds them that they've already had some and they don't want to have stomachaches. Jack Hargis leans out of the drugstore to say hello. They pass another man and John's brows knit together, his mood changes, and he clutches the girls a little closer.

"Evening, John," the tall man says, not breaking stride.

"Evening, Dickie."

The girls look up John, a small frown on each of their faces that tells him they sense something significant, but he keeps his frown only a beat or two longer, then smiles down at them. He releases their hands, and they run free.

"Touch this leaf first and you win," Barb shouts, and Bet races for the leaf. "Whoever reaches that fire hydrant first wins!" Barb shouts.

Bet tries to keep up. Barb has a run of victories, but she's the one making the rules. Bet doesn't care, she runs breathlessly along, hurling her tiny body full tilt into any activity, whooping with joy, despite losing.

John shoves his hands into his jacket pockets. One of his fingers pokes through the bottom and he absently scratches his hip. He should be working on his fifth or sixth album by now, maybe in New York or Los Angelas. Instead, he's walking down the nearly deserted main street just around dinnertime, his two daughters running themselves crazy, while he fingers a hole in his pocket.

He sucks in a nose full of air. It's crisp and clean. Summer is over and the smog and humidity is filtered out, but fall hasn't quite arrived, and the breeze is still warm. The Hickory Hills rise behind the squat red downtown buildings. They're virtually the only high spots in Percival and were colonized by the local gentry long ago. The trees on the hills rise over the downtown with green benevolence. A flock of black birds wheels around the trees, disappearing into the thicket only to reappear, swirling in a different direction.

He can't wait to see Margaret again. He even looks forward to tackling the taxes, just to show to his father's ghost he can. He sucks in another lungful of air and watches his daughters dart over benches and around parked cars, pursued by their own peals of laughter. They shine through the lengthening shadows like fireworks. He'll have to calm them soon, grab their hands and anchor them as they head out of downtown and walk along the roads where the traffic will pick up, but for now he lets them dash. He lets them dash and play for the kids that didn't stay with him and Margaret.

Margaret still sometimes thinks they're only on loan. She still sometimes cries out in her sleep and then wakes, clutching the sheet, until the horrors in her head fade. She used to get up and pad down the hallway to check on them, but now she just blinks a few times and presses her head back into the pillow.

John never had nightmares about the deaths of his children. He had a deep, abiding ache, something that couldn't be dispelled with tears or cursing or even resignation. He'd never felt such an abyss before, not even when admitting Percival was dead. That pain, so real at the time, was a pinprick compared with the deaths of his children. Margaret's pain and rage got him through. He helped her through this gray, grim world, and in doing so, he helped himself. And then the angels came.

"Okay, girls, you need to come back," he calls. "The cars are going a little too fast."

They dash back and each grab one of his hands.

"I win," Barb says, although Bet makes contact first. The rules have shifted.

"Let's see how fast we can walk," John says, and their little legs, clad in white stockings, flash in the gloom, fast as millipede legs.

"I'm winning," Barb says.

"No, I'm winning this time," Bet insists, clearly emboldened by his presence.

"You know, I think I'm winning," John says.

CHAPTER NINETEEN

"Hey."

Barb jumps. Leaning in the doorway of the recording studio like he owns the place is a younger, better-looking Woody Harrelson, a tall, lean man with blond hair that just touches his muscular shoulders.

"Hey. Can I help you with something?" she asks.

"I heard you were out a bass player for a little while. I can help out if you need it."

"Oh."

Pod isn't the only band recording at Bear Paw Studio, and word has gotten around that David is sick. David swears between bouts of throwing up at the hotel that he's sick and not just hungover. Crash frowns upon excessive substance abuse during recording sessions. He also doesn't tolerate the use of session musicians, for any reason, even for a ticking expense clock.

"Sorry. We don't need anything tonight."

The early evening pink light gleams off a window down the hall. The members of Pod are musical vampires, sleeping all day and recording all night. David's stomach bug stalled their plans, but Barb came in to work on a couple of guitar parts.

The light makes the man appear as bright and sharp as a model in a cigarette ad.

"I'm sorry, I do know some manners." He sticks out a sizable hand. "Jack Viall. I'm with The Furians. We're recording here, too, but we're having some personality conflicts, so I don't think we're doing anything for the next couple of nights."

Barb laughs.

"So, you know about personality conflicts?" Jack says.

"Oh, no, of course not," Barb says.

"So, you're not the one *causing* the conflicts, I guess. Why are you looking at me that way?"

"You just don't look like the type to give yourself a punk name."

"A punk name?"

"Jack Vile. That's a cool name. I would figure with a name like that you would have pink hair or something. Or like a nose ring, at least."

"Ah, *mon cherie*. You are mistaking the name. It's spelled V-I-A-L-L. You know, like a laboratory vial, only with an extra L."

"Ah, jeez." Barb covers her face.

"No, no, you're right. Maybe I should change it. We haven't been in town long. You know a good place to get my hair done?"

"Quit it."

"So. No chance of sitting in with the famous band Pod?"

"No. And that reminds me. You have manners, but I apparently don't. I'm Barb Deener."

Although they already shook hands, she sticks hers out anyway, and he takes it, giving it a couple of quick pumps, then holding it for a pulse or two longer than necessary.

"Oh, I know who you are. You're the legendary Barb Deener, the best-looking guitarist on the planet."

It's a total cheeseball line, but it works. She's read that sort of thing in music magazines, but it's much more effective spoken, especially from his lips.

"If there is any blood in my head, I'm sure I'm blushing," she says. "I should be, anyway. Nobody's ever said that to me before."

"I speak only the truth. So, are you recording tonight?"

"Pod isn't, but I thought I might work on something. Gotta get fancier for the third album, you know?"

"I wouldn't know. But would you consider working on it after dinner? I know a great little place just down the road. It's got some sort of royalty in the name—Burger King, I think it is."

"Ooh, a big spender. I'm not sure how I could resist. Except I ate breakfast just a little while ago."

His smile doesn't falter at the faint rejection but picks up intensity. "And may I ask what breakfast consisted of?"

"Um, you know those plastic packets of little white doughnuts?"

"I am familiar with those."

"I had about half a packet of those. I would have had the whole packet, but I ate the others last night. And three cigarettes. And a sixteen-ounce cup of coffee."

He smiles and nods, clearly familiar with the road food of the modern rock group. But his shirt clings close to his body, he appears to be in great shape.

"I would humbly suggest that perhaps this breakfast would leave room for a semi-nutritious lunch. To which, I would be happy to treat you."

"The Furians must be doing well indeed."

"Not really. If we were doing well, I'd offer to take you to an expensive place like Shoney's."

Pod's second album has done well, better than the first, taking England by storm. It's sold more in pounds than in dollars, which is all right with her. She could afford to take Jack

Viall to lunch at Shoney's or even Red Lobster, but he's asking her out on a date, and she hasn't been on a date in a very long time.

THE CEILING OF HER CONDO HAS A WEIRD MINIATURE STALACTITE LIKE THE ceilings of her old house in Percival. The bumps twinkle when they catch the light a certain way. The streetlights and the passing cars put on a minor light show for her, making the little white stalactites shine like stars.

Barb is on her back. It's her first night in her new condo and Jack is making love to her, plunging in and out in his steady, dependable style. The only piece of furniture is the bed, so they're testing it out.

Jack finishes and rolls over next to her.

"So, what do you think of this place?" Barb asks.

She didn't come, but it doesn't bother her. She's too keyed up from buying the condo. She spent the morning signing documents and handing over a sizable chunk of savings. It felt good. Jack makes her feel normal. This makes her feel adult.

"I like it. It has potential. It overlooks a bar."

The condo is tiny, but it's in University City, which she was assured is the coolest part of town. All the university staples are nearby, coffee, beer, and doughnuts. The building is old enough to be interesting but renovated enough to be livable. And, as Jack said, there is a bar right across the street.

"It seemed like a good location. You know? Our bands swing back and forth through here all the time, right in the middle of the country. Whenever you're in town, or even near town, I want you to stay here. Okay?"

He smiles, his face half-hidden in a cloud of pillow. "Barb Deener, are you asking me to move in with you?"

She stretches, scratching his leg with her ragged toenails, making him yelp.

"Given that neither of us will be here much, I guess I am. What do you think of that?"

He stretches across the sheet and kisses her, a quick peck followed by a long gulp. "I think it's a fine idea. If I come in town and you're not here, I'll just be waiting for you in that bar over there."

"I was sort of thinking I might give you a key."

"I'll take it. I would almost like my idea better."

"You know, my mother warned me not to date 'rock people,' as she calls them."

He lifts his brows. "Did she now? I'm glad you disobeyed."

"It's not like I had a lot of choice. I spend my days with rock musicians, rock promotors, rock journalists, rock fans. Fellow musicians. Like you. I barely know anyone without the word 'rock' in their title."

Jack laughs, which makes the bed shake.

"I mean, if I were a banker, I don't think she'd ask me to not date 'bank people.' Or a lawyer, not to date 'law people.'"

Jack rolls over and kisses her on the forehead. "Your mother is prejudiced against rock and roll."

"Yeah. But anyway, anytime we both play here, we can stay here."

"I wish we played the same cities at the same time more often," Jack says. "Or even the same clubs. We aren't quite on Pod's level."

She gives him a hug. "Ah, you'll get there. The Furians are great."

She sinks her head into the pillow and looks at the twinkling on the ceiling. *I own property, and my boyfriend is moving in, sort of.* Most of her old friends from Percival have long been married and settled down, with children, in houses whose kitchens are as large as her new home. They would laugh at her faltering baby steps into normality.

Her mother is excited that Barb bought a place relatively close by. Although she obtains information about the world of popular music through various television shows, her mother persists in imagining her eldest daughter can traipse through that world without sullying her lily-white Christian soul.

So, she could never know about Jack moving in—though she would be happy to know her eldest daughter was considering monogamy. At least in St. Louis.

CHAPTER TWENTY

The rising sun spills into the kitchen as Margaret shambles through the door.

"Please close the door. It's so bright," her mother says. She continues peeling potatoes. "You look tired, dear. How was work?"

"Ugh," Margaret grunts. "They told Susan that she's getting laid off, so she's barely doing any work. There's a backlog of things to sew and cut, and not enough people to do it."

Her mother puts down the potatoes and takes her hands.

Margaret winces. "They hurt," she says. "They feel like crab claws."

"Oh, my baby. You're only eighteen and your hands hurt. I'm sorry you have to work. Breakfast is ready. Not much, but a little something."

"Thanks. I am a bit hungry. Let me go change."

Margaret walks down a short hallway to her room. 4515 Exeter Street in Jupiter, Missouri, is a small house on a small street in a small town with big men.

She goes to her tiny room, clenching and unclenching her

fingers to stretch out the stiffness. The radio plays softly in the living room, sharing news from the outside world. Margaret graduated high school in the spring and has been working at the textile plant ever since, almost not a part of the outside world.

A door slams at the front of the house. Her father is home. Edward Black is one of those big men in a small town. The small house shakes when he enters. He complains the truck gave him trouble on the way home and delayed him by half a goddamn hour.

Margaret changes her clothes. She dreads breakfast, but she's hungry. He won't wait on her to eat, she knows. She walks to the front of the house. She can smell him before she sees him. Her father hasn't changed clothes. He stinks of the mill and of anger and stabs at his eggs as if they are alive and trying to escape him. He's big but not tall, shaped like a cask, and bald. If God ever did get around to creating an object he couldn't lift, the result would look a great deal like Edward Black.

"How was work?" he asks Margaret.

She stares at her plate while she eats. "Fine."

"That's a good job. Don't go messing that up."

"I won't."

"You hear me?" he demands.

"I won't."

"You don't want to be like me, all broken down. My back feels like I got a metal pole in it. My ribs ache. My feet ache. I probably got cancer." Ed Black believes the world, down to microscopic organisms, is out to get him.

Frances Black looks at her plate, too, although she keeps an eye on her husband's as well, to make sure it stays full, and she touches his hand now and then to indicate her concern for his health. Ed is the only one who looks around during meals. He can be loving and kind, but the instances are so rare, they're like breaks of sun in rainstorms, nothing you can plan for or count on.

"You need to go see your Aunt Betty," her father says. "She's been in the hospital for a week, and you haven't gone to see her."

Aunt Betty is a female version of her younger brother. She's a bitter old crab. She has pneumonia. Sheer bile will keep her alive, probably beyond Margaret herself.

"I'll go before the end of the week. These are good eggs, Mom," she says, trying to change the subject.

"Go today," her father says. "You're home at a good hour. You won't go to sleep for a while. You don't have a broken back, like me. Go see her right after breakfast."

"But it's about to rain."

"Go see your aunt," he says, four blunt words that will tolerate no debate.

She'll have to take his rotten truck, the one he just complained about breaking down. The truck is like a lazy dog. It stops working whenever it can, particularly when the weather is bad.

Half an hour later, her fingers ache as she fights the wheel, which seizes every dip in the road as a chance to run off in a ditch. She fears she'll have forearms like Popeye from driving the thing.

Pitch County Hospital serves as a regional medical building. Several doctors have offices under the roof of the square, two-story building, built by the WPA and unnecessarily ornate. There aren't enough patients to fill the hospital. The rugged mountain people of Pitch County are either healthy or dead.

Margaret waits in the outer reception room, which is festooned with columns and eagles, until it's time for visitation. A few others are there. One is a young man, maybe a little older than herself. He's tall, fresh-faced, and good looking, with a wave of blonde hair suspended above his smooth forehead. She studies him more than she should since he's with a young woman. The woman is tall, pretty, and thin. Her wrists and ankles are crossed as if bound. Straight brown hair hangs over a gloomy expression.

The man talks to her in quiet, rapid bursts. He's angry.

Margaret's interest in him lessens then, like a candle blown out. Some men, like her father, have nothing and want something. Some, like the owner of the textile plant, Mr. Herring, have it all and want more.

"John!" the woman exclaims in a stage whisper.

He looks around, and Margaret looks away.

Aunt Betty doesn't last long into Margaret's visit. The older woman is groggy and falls asleep shortly into the visit, withdrawing into the sheets. Margaret seizes the opportunity to cut the visit short. She runs back to the truck through the rain, eager to go home and rest.

She gets five minutes down the road when the truck jerks, bucks, and limps to the side of the rutted road like a wounded deer, where it lies still. She turns the key, and the truck grinds, but the engine won't start. She rests her head on the cold metal steering wheel. The rain offers soothing patters on the windshield. A honk wakes her, and she jerks her head up.

A man is getting out of a car pulled off the road right behind her, his jacket pulled over his head. He runs to the truck and knocks on the window. "What seems to be the trouble?"

Margaret opens her mouth to speak but notices he's the guy from the hospital, and her tongue stops working. *John.*

"Hang on," he says. "I'll get in where it's dry if you don't mind." He runs to the passenger side and hops in, dripping on the seat. Her father won't like that.

"What seems to be the trouble?" he says again.

He lowers his jacket. His hair is messed up. Margaret finds it attractive.

"The truck won't start."

"I see. This will require a look under the hood, I think."

"You were at the hospital. I saw you."

"That's right. You were there, weren't you? I was—a little distracted."

"Is your wife okay up there?"

"My wife?" He stares at Margaret for a beat, then smiles. "Oh. She's my sister. She'll be okay."

Margaret remembers how angry he was. But maybe it's okay to be angry at your sister. She doesn't have a sister, so she isn't sure, but they would probably fight now and then if she had one.

"Are you from around here? I don't think I've seen you before," Margaret says.

"No, we're from Percival."

"Percival? What are you doing going to a hospital down here?"

"Just passing through. Pat—my sister—wasn't feeling well, and we saw the building, so we stopped there. Speaking of Pat, she's probably getting cold, so we better get on the road and get you on the road. Can you pop the hood so I can look at your engine?"

He gets out of the car into the rain and hurries around to the front of the car and pops the hood. H peers under the truck's curved hood, jiggles something, then runs back to the shelter of the truck. "You've got a crack in your alternator case, and when it gets wet your engine dies. It has to either be replaced or dry out before it'll work again."

"What does that mean?" Margaret says, her hopes of getting to sleep fading fast.

"It means, we give you a ride home."

Patricia Deener smiles when Margaret gets into the back seat of their car and introduces herself, but soon they sit in silence again. John Deener is quiet too. He looks back at Margaret enough that she worries he's not watching the road.

They get to the little white house on Exeter. Margaret is exhausted but doesn't want to leave the car. She sees only the tired, slouching women at work, people at church, tired but proud in their stiff good clothes, and her father and mother. John and

Pat, even in their ill mood, are young and fresh by comparison. She waits a beat or two too long.

"Let me walk you to the door. I'll cover you with my coat."

"Are you sure? It's raining pretty hard."

"I'm sure. My coat's already wet."

They get out and John starts out running to the house, holding his coat overhead like a makeshift umbrella, but Margaret slows him down.

"I'd like to see you again," she says, voice trembling.

Margaret isn't sure about John. He was angry before, he's in a dark mood now, but he's lifting himself out of it. And he is *new*, and that is enough.

"Uh—okay," he says. Not the most romantic response. He adds, "I'd like that, too. Could I have your phone number?"

"We don't have a phone."

"No?"

"No."

She looks for a sign of pity in his eyes but sees none. "You could write me a letter," she ventures.

"I'm not much of a writer."

"But you could."

"Yes."

She doesn't want to bring him into the house and expose him to her family for something to write with. She tells him the address three times, and he swears he'll remember. The water soaks through his coat and drops to his hair. He gives her a crooked smile and runs back to the car.

Pat yells at John as they drive away, but Margaret can't make out what is said. A twinge of shame from the need to ask a boy out was overshadowed by a soft ember of pride that she actually did it.

CHAPTER TWENTY-ONE

"Did you sleep okay, dear?" Bet's mother says.

"I did, Mom. Thanks."

"What would you like for breakfast?"

"I'm not hungry."

Her mother sits on the edge of the bed and presses a palm to her forehead. "You need to eat, Bet. And to take your vitamins. Your body is weak. I don't want you getting sick."

Her sheets are pulled up to her neck. It's nearly ten o'clock in the morning on a Wednesday.

"Don't you have to work today?" Bet asks.

"I'm taking some time off," her mother says, like she wants to take time off.

"Thanks, Mom. I'm so sorry."

Her mother fishes around under the covers for Bet's hand and grasps it. Bet's stomach turns, and writhes like a bag of snakes.

"Don't be sorry, dear. Don't ever be sorry. Did you sleep okay?"

Her nightmares alternated with bouts of nausea, but she nods. Her hair rustles against the pillow.

"Sleep a little longer. I'll get breakfast going. How about pancakes?"

Maybe layers of pancakes will soothe the snakes.

"Okay. Thanks, Mom."

She closes her eyes, but she can't sleep. Her old Barbies and stuffed animals are put away. Her schoolbooks, in excellent shape, line the shelves on the far wall. Her graduation photo hangs above the dresser.

Almost everything she has ever owned is in the room. She's lived much of her life in the same place, and the evidence is piled up like geologic strata in an old lakebed. Her father is on the phone down the hall. He took work off too.

"They're ready." Her mother steps into the room, smiles, then rests her hand on the covered lump that is Bet's knee. "Don't bother getting dressed. Just eat in your pajamas. it's just your father and me here. Brother Jackson would like to talk to you in the next day or two if you don't mind. I think it would be really good if you would talk to him."

Brother Jackson preaches at Grace Tabernacle Baptist and has for Bet's whole life. For them, it's not gossip talking to their church leadership, it's their form of therapy, as natural and private as a prayer. Part of her wants to. Part of her wants to hear that she's not bad for trying to end her life. Brother Jackson is a kind and gentle man and always knows what to say.

"Mom?"

"Yes?"

"Don't tell Barb."

"Oh, honey."

"I'm serious. I don't want you to tell Barb."

"But we should. She's your *sister*. She can help."

"Mother, I know I can't ask anything of you right now, but I do ask this one thing. Don't tell Barb."

Sorrow and anger flash across her mother's face, vying for control. It's a lot to ask.

"I'll tell her myself when I feel it's right."

Her mother releases a sigh. "All right, dear. That might be the best way."

"Please promise me you won't tell her."

Her mother won't break a promise. Her word is stronger than any glue. It could hold the universe together.

"I won't tell her, Bet."

"Thank you."

"Now, come on and eat. And then I want you to rest some more. Your Aunt Pat may come over tomorrow. You haven't seen her in a while. But we got some movies for tonight. We're going to turn off the phone, and curl up on the couch, and just watch some movies together, just the three of us."

Bet would like nothing else more in all the world.

CHAPTER TWENTY-TWO

"Mom, I can't come home right now," Barb says into the phone.

"Why not?" her mother asks.

"Why not? We're on tour. We're touring behind the second album. We have to do that, it's in the contract. What's the matter? Are you all right?"

"Yes, I'm fine."

You are? And Dad?

"He's fine."

"So, what's the problem? Bet's okay, right?"

Her mother heaves a sigh.

"All right. Look, Mom, I've got to go. I'll call you soon."

"Okay, okay," her mother says in that resigned voice that's like a knife to her heart. "What's all that noise? Are you outside?"

"Yes, I'm at a pay phone. That's traffic."

"Well, I love you," she says. "I hope you know that."

"Love you too. Hi to Dad and Bet."

Barb slams down the phone. "Jesus!"

Crash leans against the phone booth, a model of impatience. "We're late already. Let's go."

"We're always late, Crash. We're a rock band, we're supposed to be late."

Crash stomps toward the gassed and idling bus. Barb isn't moving. Instead, she lights a cigarette. She sucks in the smoke, her third since she started talking to her mother.

MARGARET HANGS UP THE PHONE. HER FACE COLLAPSED INTO A FROWN, as it often is when she talks to Barb these days. John watches her over the top of the Percival Junction.

"Not coming home, I guess, huh?"

"No. She's on tour, she says."

"Well, she probably is. That's how you sell albums. Selling albums is how you make money. If she's going to be stupid and drop out of school, she needs to at least make some money."

Margaret knows he *is* proud that Barb has made enough to buy her own condo, even if he doesn't admit it.

"But she needs to know about Bet. I know she could help," Margaret says.

"Then tell her."

"I promised Bet I wouldn't." She plays with the phone cord, her fingers knitting and flexing like a bug trapped in a spiderweb.

"That's a promise I don't believe you should keep. It isn't Bet's place to try to kill herself and leave herself there for her roommate to find her, then tell us what we can do about it."

"You're still mad, aren't you, John?"

He snaps the paper down on the table. Margaret jumps, dropping the cord. "Of course, I'm still angry! She tries to kill herself for no reason, and she won't let us in her head to figure out why. Barb could get in her head, but Bet won't let you tell her. I think it's a stupid to promise, and stupid to keep trying to bring Barb home without telling her why."

Margaret's face heats. "Don't you tell me what's stupid. Bet said she would tell Barb when she's ready, and we have to respect that. But she won't tell her if Barb's not here." Her trembling voice is rising, angry, and Bet could hear.

"Honey, I—"

"Do you think this doesn't make me angry, John Deener? Our daughter put her eternal soul in jeopardy. I know you don't believe that, but that's what she's done. She could have lost everything. And that scares the hell out of me." Tears well up and break the bonds of her lashes, running down her cheeks. Her chin quivers.

"Honey, I'm sorry." He shoves the paper aside, stands, and hugs her, entangling them in the cord. "This isn't easy for any of us. You keep your promise. We'll keep asking Barb to come home. Maybe she can find some time."

But he knows better. Barb can't return home...or, more accurately, return to Percival. That's how Barb saw things. And he couldn't half-blame her. Margaret had made his staying tolerable. A child shouldn't return home for a parent. Not really.

CHAPTER TWENTY-THREE

"We don't have to go to a movie tonight, John. It's okay, I don't mind." Margaret stands with John under the eaves of her parents' house, every cell in her body crying out for them to leave. She took a solid hour and a half to get ready for their date, mostly because her clothes are old and need a lot of care.

John looks over her shoulder, clearly lost in his own world of misery and disappointment. Margaret wants to leave before her father wakes up and wants to talk to John in a boozy harangue that could go on for hours. John experienced one such lecture, which he endured with good grace.

"No, let's—let's go," he says, coming out of a trance.

He holds out his hand, and she takes it, and that's enough. The callouses where his fingertips have pressed the guitar strings a thousand times scrape against her skin as he curls his hand around hers.

John's walks her to his car and shuts the door after she scoots onto the bench seat, but his spirit is off winging its way through the universe.

"Maybe—maybe we should just eat," she says when he slides in next to her.

"No, the movie's fine. Unless you're really hungry."

"Not really. I mean—not really."

It takes an hour to get from Jupiter to Percival and another ten minutes to reach the theater. She can tell it takes all John's energy just to keep the car on the road. Margaret keeps a running commentary, pointing out interesting things or people as they pass, which takes some doing as there is not much to see. By the time they arrive at the theater she's as listless as he is.

He buys her ticket and popcorn, and they search for seats in near silence like a couple married for thirty years, not two kids on their fourth date.

The movie is loud, stupid, and keeps going out of focus. Margaret sneaks a look at John. The images reflect off his eyes. He laughs when everybody else laughs, not because he sees anything funny. She watches the movie, so few things are funny, but it's like eating garlic next to a vampire. He's not enjoying it.

His eyes open wide when she stands up and pulls him along midway through the film. He offers no resistance, no sputtering declamations to finish the movie. He follows her up the aisle, his rough fingers in hers, the way they entered.

"You didn't like it?" he says when they're outside.

The cars trundle and sputter by, low voices of people talking and dogs barking filled the downtown night air. Margaret walks him to a bench across the street.

"I want you to tell me what's wrong."

"Nothing is—it's that obvious, is it?" John responds, puzzled.

"John. It's obvious."

"I'm sorry. I guess I'm not very much fun tonight."

Margaret takes his hand and tries to look into his eyes, but he stares fixedly at the sidewalk. She doesn't say anything, just holds his hand and waits.

"It's just stuff at work," he says after forever is half over. He stands up, his hand slips from hers. "Listen, it's not really a good night for me. Maybe I better just get you home. Unless you— unless you'd like something to eat first."

"No, that will be fine. I had a big lunch." She hadn't had lunch at all, expecting dinner, but her appetite is gone.

"Okay. I'm sorry. Let's go."

He leads her to the white Buick. The rust creeps up from under its bulbous wheel wells like a heavy woman with muddy skirts.

Margaret settles herself in the seat, a little farther away from John than on the ride over. He cranks the car and pulls into the sparse traffic. Percival is rolling up the sidewalks for the night and now it's back to Jupiter, which will be snoring under covers. She looks out the window and sighs. She's trapped. Things will never get better.

"It's just—" he begins

"What?"

"I'm sorry," John said. "Just talking to myself." He drives on, faster. "If they only knew."

"What?"

"If they only knew what really happened. They think we're just not professional, but it's not like that...that stupid son of a bitch, Dickie. Couldn't keep his mind on it—"

"John, you're driving a little too fast."

"Am I? I guess I am. I'm sorry. I'm not really in a hurry to get you home." He slows the car.

"John, I know something's wrong. You can tell me about it. Honest."

He looks across the seat to her, a good arm's length away. His face changes in the yellow glow from the streetlights. The passing gold sweeping across his face makes him angelic, but then the darkness reclaims him.

"Did—did you hear what happened at Marcia Tilden's party?"

She frowns. "Whose party?"

He whips the Buick to the side of the road so fast she slides across the seat toward him. Before she knows what is happening, he is upon her. At first she thinks he is going to rape her. Then a warm, wet cheek presses on her shoulder. His fingers dig into her back.

He hugs her and sobs. "It's all over," he says, half incoherent. "My band is over. Everybody knows. I'm ruined in this town. If I want to start another band, I'll have to move away."

Astonished, she hugs him back, not quite as forcefully. His sobs subside into ragged breathing after a minute. A couple of cars pass. Margaret is afraid the police will come and have a misunderstanding, and her father will find out. She'll be locked up like a nun if that happens. But it doesn't matter. John is here, and he needs her. He tells her the story.

For her, it means John is unstable, vicious, violent. A faint thrill runs through her, although she would never admit it. John is no longer a mild-looking, normal young man. Underneath his cheap plaid jackets is the whiff of something dangerous and wild, primitive and uncharted. For the first time in her life, Margaret understands what must have attracted her mother to her father. Ed Black must have been like this once, before the brute drove everything else out and took over. Maybe she needs one unstable, vicious, violent man to help her get away from another, and then she can keep the beast at bay.

"I'm sure you had a good reason," she says. "He had it coming."

"He did," John agrees into her shoulder.

"Can't you—are you sure you can't have another band?"

"Would *you* work with me? Always afraid I might hit you in the head with a guitar?"

"You could always stand up front."

He laughs and she laughs with him, a momentary break in the tension.

"I suppose I could. But no, it's over. The one thing I've wanted to do in my life is over. Even if I moved to St. Louis, they've probably heard of this by now. No one will have me."

Encouraging him means he'd move to St. Louis. Margaret wants this strange, sobbing boy to stay in Percival, near her. It is the only thing she's ever really wanted, aside from being away from her father.

"It's just a job." She rests her chin on his blond head.

"A job?" he says. His head jerks a little but not enough to dislodge her chin. "It's not a job. It's a dream. It's a calling."

A couple more cars whizz past.

"But if it stopped being a dream, it would be a job. You'd end up playing the same songs over and over and you'd get tired of it. Just like anything else."

A moment passes in silence.

"I can't imagine ever growing tired of it."

"But this is better, don't you see? Now you'll never be tired of it. You don't get tired of dreams. They can never be bad for you."

"That doesn't make sense."

"It does. If you make this dream a reality, you have to find another dream. This way, you have the same dream you love."

"You aren't a creative person, are you, Margaret?"

She's hurt. She moves her chin and pushes away. "I am," she says, although no proof of that statement comes to mind. "I am."

"I don't mean to hurt you," he says. He straightens up and wipes away the evidence of his tears. "It's just that some people are happy to have a job and do it well. Other people want to express themselves."

"No one's stopping you from expressing yourself," she says a little coldly.

"But I want to get *paid* for it. I want to do it for a living. And you're saying I shouldn't even try, that I should just give up."

"I am *not* saying that," she says. "I said you could go on, you're the one who said you couldn't. I'm just saying it's not the end of the world if your band doesn't go anywhere. You're still the same person you were in the band. You still have your family and friends. You haven't lost anything."

"Just my dream. That's all."

She sighs. The conversation is choking itself. "Just take me home, John."

He jangles the keys in the ignition but doesn't crank the car. "I'm sorry to waste your time with this, Margaret."

"You haven't wasted my time."

He smiles. "Yes, I have. But you're right. I'm still me. Maybe I can make something happen."

"That's right," she says, with a chilly edge, tired of trying to pep him up.

"Or maybe I will just work for my dad like he wants and run the insurance business until I retire. And never leave Percival. Just do a job and come home."

"Would that be so bad?"

He reaches over and puts his arm around her shoulder. He pulls her closer. Her dress tightens around her hips as she moves across the seat. She resists, at first. He leans in and gives her a kiss. His lips wander around hers, then mount quick expeditions across her face and eyelids.

"Maybe that won't be so bad," he says between gulped breaths.

CHAPTER TWENTY-FOUR

"Ding dong," Aunt Pat says through the open kitchen doorway, carrying a turkey-sized pot with a turkey-sized lump of foil over it.

Bet, her hands lost in oven mitts, opens the door.

"Oh, Pat," her mother says. "I hope you didn't bring a turkey. You know I cook one every Christmas."

"I know you're cooking one. But I also know there are a lot of people coming. I thought you could use a little help."

Pat is almost everything her brother isn't. He is thin, and angular, with prison-camp hair and pale eyes. She is tall, too, but also round, plump, not a sharp edge on her, a pile of hair over dark eyes.

"Well, I guess I could," Bet's mother says. "But we have ham and casserole too."

"And pie, I hope," says Pat.

The screen door is set open on its latch. Bet manages to turn the doorknob with one oven mitt and then props the door with her foot. Pat uses her sizable rump to push the door open the rest of the way.

Pat is like a Christmas tree in her red sweater with green sleeves, one of many garish Christmas sweaters. She didn't wear the one with bells on the sleeves, and for that Bet is grateful.

"Whoo, you've been cooking up a storm in here. I'm hot already. And it's right chilly outside, Pat says."

"Hey, Aunt Pat."

"Hey, Bet. I'll hug your neck, but I've got to put this turkey down first."

The stove is covered with a sculptural arrangement of pans, lids, and wads of foil, but Bet finds room for the bird.

"It's not a very big one," Pat says, clearly worried Bet's mother is upset an entree has arrived uninvited. "But you can always use a little extra."

"You'll just have to come over for turkey leftovers, turkey soup, turkey sandwiches, and any other turkey products we'll be eating all next week," she says, smiling.

Bet detects the genuine irritation lurking behind the smile. As far as Bet can tell, her mother is the only person in the world who doesn't really care for Pat Deener.

Her mother has had her head in the oven half the day, keeping an eye on the little red bulb that's supposed to pop out from her twenty-five-pound bird, but she looks as crisp and fresh as the salad cooling in the fridge. She isn't all that upset about the arrival of another turkey. She's torn. Barb is playing some special concert and couldn't come home. But although she hasn't said anything about the suicide attempt, now months in the past, Bet knows her mother is thankful she's home. Her mother keeps Bet busy in the kitchen, although she needs no help. She just wants to keep her around. While she's around.

The family arrives not long after the spare bird. They're her father's family and they come in clumps of threes and fours, hands full with bowls of stuffing and salads, ending conversations and arguments that began in the car so they can say hello. Her father's younger brother Ted, his older brother Reggie, their families and grandmother Helen, edging eighty years old but with nearly as much energy as the kids. As tall as her offspring, the curls helmet-tight on her head. She drives herself over in a bright yellow Chrysler, three decades old, with fewer miles on the clock than any other car on the street.

Bet's mother has no sisters or brothers, no one to come joke about the past. Her mother and father are dead. She talks of her mother, Frances, now and then, but never speaks of her father, even when prodded. He's a black hole, a void. A lack of family at holiday gatherings has never bothered Margaret. She flits through the small tiffs and triumphs that animate her husband's family, often intervening when he will not. She remembers more about the Deener family than he does.

Christmas dinner is consumed in a whirl of activity, with comments mostly limited to the food or the children at the kids' table. The table is a purgatory, although Baptists do not believe in such a thing. Bet herself graduated from there just two years before and sometimes wishes she could return.

"Where is that lovely Barb?" Helen asks.

"She's working," Bet's father says. "We need her to keep making that rock star money."

Helen chuckles, not quite getting the joke. Bet's mother's mouth is a thin, straight line.

Things loosen up after everyone is full and complains that they ate too much. Her father and his brothers play five-card draw in front of the TV. Helen, Bet's mom, and Pat technically don't approve of gambling, so the men bet under the table and keep their money in their pockets until it's time to pay up.

Everyone else wanders around getting coffee, spare slices of pie, and commenting on the house or looking for Bobby Jr.'s tie.

"So, Barb's in a band, huh?" Bobby Sr. asks.

"Yes," Bet's father replies.

"A couple of records out and everything."

"Yes. They're good."

"I didn't know Barb could sing."

Her father signals he wants two cards. "She sings some. She mostly plays guitar."

Bobby Sr. deals two off the top of the deck. "I didn't know she could play guitar either. Can you play guitar?"

Her father shakes his head. "Nah."

Bet borrowed a friend's guitar, and chord book after Pod's first album came out. Barb could do it, how hard could it be? The strings cut into her fingers, and the chords were too hard like she was playing Twister with her fingers. She practiced until she could play a lurching version of "Wild Thing" and then gave the guitar back.

"They're doing pretty well?" Bobby Sr. asks. "Could I find their stuff at Wal-Mart?"

"I don't think so," Bet says. "You can get them at Record Bar, though."

"Maybe I'll try to swing by there on the way home." Bobby Sr. and Sandra live out in the boonies. If something can't be found at Wal-Mart, they usually do without. "Although, maybe not," he says. "It's Christmas day."

Reggie looks up from the card game. He's ahead and doesn't stare at his cards as fervently as his brothers.

"Hey, Bet. Why don't you play one of those Pad records? Do you have 'em here?"

"Pod. Yeah, Mother's got them. Are you sure you want to hear it?"

"Yeah," Bobby Sr. says.

"I vote for it too," Jack says, walking up with a paper plate of pie. "Maybe it will drown out those kids for a while."

The rug rats are in the back room, shrieking over their

Christmas presents, playing as much with the wrappings as the gifts.

"All right." Bet turns down the TV, which prompts a groan from her father and Ted.

"Sorry, guys, we have a vote for some music.," she says.

"Then don't put on Barb's stuff," Ted says. "Just kidding."

The record player perches atop the stereo stack to the right of the television. Two smallish speakers lurk behind the cabinet. Bet is the only one who plays anything on it, although her father has some old stuff from the Fifties and Sixties and her mother has some inspirational music, choirs, and country gospel. She pulls out the first Pod album and slides the record out. She hands the sleeve to Jack, who looks at it with his eyebrows raised.

"Doesn't look like your Alabama albums, does it, Jack?" Bobby Sr. asks.

"No, it doesn't."

The needle pops as it settles in the groove. Barb's voice floats out of the speakers.

"I missed you. I missed your airrrrrrrr."

Then the music kicks in, first the bass, then the drums, then the guitar. Jack bobs his head to the beat. The men look around with vacant expressions as they listen.

"She's got a good voice," he says.

"It's a little harsher sounding than I expected," Bobby says. "The song, I mean. Is she singing about being an inflatable doll?"

"What are you teaching these girls, John?" Reggie jokes.

"She certainly cusses less than you did," Ted says to Bet's father.

"Oh, shut up," he replies.

Bet frowns, not getting the joke. The song ends, and another one comes on, one that starts fast and gets faster. Barb is all guitar on this one, banging out shards of sound to accompany Crash's shouts.

Helen enters the room. "What is that devil music?"

"It's Barb's band," Reggie says. "You were asking where she was. She's with us, in spirit."

Helen stands still, listening. She shakes her head. "I'm sorry, John, but that racket is horrible. It's all been downhill since Nat King Cole died."

THE LIGHTS REFLECT RED AND GREEN ON BARB'S CONDO LIVING ROOM window. She has no decorations at all. The lights emanate from the closed bar across the street.

Barb shifts beneath the blankets on the couch and turns up the TV volume on "It's A Wonderful Life" to drown out the silence, then takes a sip from her margarita. She winces. Too much tequila and not enough triple sec. She would prefer to be almost anywhere other than alone, drinking her own concoctions. Her stubbornness has left her stranded on Christmas.

She told her parents that Pod has a lucrative Christmas show in northern California the label won't let them cancel. There's no way she'll make it home for Christmas in time. She's in Missouri, like all the members of Pod. Even Crash is home with his folks. He probably went to bed early to wait for Santa.

Jack is home with his family too. He invited her to come along but she didn't want to go to Illinois. She talked to him earlier, turning up the volume on the TV and pretending she was at home. She didn't want him calling her actual house only to discover she's not there and give the game away to her parents.

She called her parents to wish them a merry Christmas earlier in the day, before she started on the margaritas and self-pity. She selected a different show to convey the sounds of northern California. Her mother sounded happy to hear from her, but a little irritated too. Everybody was coming over. She wished Barb could be there. Barb wishes she could be there, too, but she doesn't want to get into whatever drama her mother is concocting.

Christmastime in Percival is always the same. The snowflake wreaths will be hung across Front Street, and Santa and Frosty the Snowman peek from most of the storefronts, even some of the abandoned ones. The houses of Hickory Hills will sport a profusion of reindeer, snowmen, fat Santas, and plump baby Jesuses, all lit from within, and people will drive through the streets to see them. The Percival Mall will hang its gang of golden cherubs, so aged, that many are speckled with white where the gold paint has flaked off, suggesting the outbreak of a skin rash in Heaven.

Flaking gold reminds her of her favorite Christmas tree ornament, a golden plastic reindeer frozen forever in the act of flying, hoofs proudly cleaving the air. She knows it's Rudolph, even though it has a golden nose. Her mother will hang it on the tree even though she is not home.

She burrows deeper into the blankets. Snow taps against the windows. It isn't a white Christmas. The snowflakes are conducting suicide missions against the wet pavement. It's too warm for them to pile up, so they convert into gray slush as they hit the ground. Gray, like her mood. This is the worst holiday of her life. She raises her glass and takes a long sip, then raises a silent toast to everyone in the world, everyone she has lied to and misses.

"Merry fucking Christmas."

CHAPTER TWENTY-FIVE

After dinner, and after Ted, Reggie, and all the other relatives have gone home, Bet's mother kicks everyone out of the kitchen to clean up. Bet is happy to cede the task. Pat puts up a token defense, but Bet's mother will not be moved.

"Bet, why don't we take a little walk?" Pat says.

It's getting dark, so Bet pulls on a heavy coat. They walk through the neighborhood, blinking against the feeble snow flurries, breathing in the bracing, astringent smell of burning wood. The evening is quiet. Few cars, no planes drone overhead. The occasional laughter bursts from inside houses, but it fades, pressed down by the silence.

"Why did you do it, Elizabeth?" Pat asks.

Pat looks at Bet, but Bet doesn't look back.

"It's complicated. You wouldn't understand."

"You'd be surprised about what I would understand."

Aunt Pat's pillowy face accents her sharp, blue eyes. Bet hasn't ascribed much to her aunt except jollity. Pat is the least complicated relative she knows, but it occurs to her that maybe she doesn't know Pat that well.

"The thing is, there's really not that much to tell," Bet says. "I was drinking. A lot. And I had the pills. And I just started taking them together."

"But you knew what that could do. You must have had some thought driving you that way. Elizabeth, do you get depressed?"

"Sure, I get depressed. Everybody gets depressed."

"You know what I mean. Real depression."

Bet's so content and stuffed with food that it's hard to imagine feeling any other way. "I don't think so. Really."

And she's sure that is the truth. It was a frustrating Monday that day. Nothing had gone right at work. Bet sells nothing, has two shoplifters get away, and comes up seventeen dollars short. After work, she goes to Yale's with Erica. It's early, but the bar is packed, and they're lucky to get lousy stools near the waitress station. The bartender spills half the first beer on Bet's legs.

And then Stan Swinea walked into the bar.

He waves to friends in the back. Pudge fills in the harsh contours of his face, and his hair is shorter, more stylish, but his eyes are the same.

He stops when he sees Bet. "Oh," he says. "Bet. How are you doing?"

They exchange a quick hug.

"Great, Stan, just great."

The awkwardness settles around them like smoke.

"This is Erica. Erica, this is Stan."

"Nice to meet you," Erica and Stan say simultaneously.

Stan looks around, at the floor, at Bet, at Erica, at everything, at nothing.

"So, what have you been up to?" he asks.

"Not much," Bet says. "You?"

"Not much. I moved away for a while."

"You did? To where?"

"St. Louis," he says.

"Oh, okay."

"But I'm back now."

"Doing what?" Bet asks.

"Just working."

"Where?"

"Nothing exciting. Just K-Mart. You?"

She shrugs. "Just at the mall."

"Oh."

"Would you—would you like a drink?"

He appears to consider it for a nanosecond. "I'd like to, but I'm supposed to meet some friends. Back there. Listen, it's been great to see you."

"You too, Stan. You take care."

"Okay. Hey—how's Barb?"

Stan barely knows Barb. The whole time they dated, which wasn't long, he never said a word about her sister.

"She's fine."

"She's in a band?" he asks, but she can tell he knows she does.

Bet nods. "Yep."

"Pod, right?"

"Right."

"My wife has her album. She likes them a lot."

"Wife?"

"Yeah, Megan. She's great. My daughter Rachel even likes it and she's only two."

Bet lifts a brow. "She's two, and she listens to Pod?"

"Yeah. I know she probably shouldn't, but I didn't hear any cussing on it, so I figured it was okay. She just likes to bounce around to it. You know how kids are. Anyway, do you think I could get an autographed copy of their album? Megan would die."

"They have two now, you know."

"They do? Wow, I didn't know. If I could get an autographed

copy of the new one, that would be even better. Since we have the first one already."

"I don't know when I could do it."

"That's no problem. Just whenever. Um, here, let me write down my address for you." He pulls a pen from inside his jacket pocket and writes the number down on a napkin sitting on the table number. "I'll pay for it, of course. Just uh, just let me know."

"Okay. Thanks."

They hug again, even quicker this time.

"Great seeing you," he says, and walks away.

"Who was that?" Erica asks. "Old boyfriend of Barb's?"

"No. Mine."

"Yours?"

Bet is a whole different person than the one that slept with Stan Swinea. She remembers him fondly but not deeply.

"He sounded much more interested in Barb," Erica says.

"The burden of a semi-famous sister, I guess."

Bet and Erica focus on drinking beer and complaining about work. Bet envies Erica's job, but for Erica, the ability to play whatever records she likes doesn't make up for the tedium. Stan pops up in Bet's periphery a few times, but she feels nothing.

In the parking lot, Bet's Camaro won't start. It whirrs and clanks but won't awaken. Bet sits with the door open and turns the key again. Then again, urging the engine to spring to life. It declines. She paid twenty-three hundred dollars for the car and already has had to drop another five hundred on it. The car's blue body is beautiful, but its guts are rotten and getting worse. Bet slams the door and chases after Erica before she pulls out of the parking lot.

Erica drops Bet home twenty minutes later, and Bet eats a cold KFC chicken leg left over from the day before. She washes it down with a warm beer.

She puts in a load of laundry. Ten minutes into the cycle, her neighbor from downstairs bangs on his ceiling with a broom handle. The thin apartment walls and floors mean he can hear the washer droning and shaking. Bet sighs, but there's nothing she can do, she's been at work all day.

Bet pads over to the bed and roots underneath it until her fingers hit glass and pulls out her prize, her hidden bottle of whiskey. She's too tired to watch television. She leans against the wall and slides down to the floor, sipping from the bottle and watching the washing machine rattle.

Numbness steals over her. The future stretches before her, a flat gray horizon, nothing in sight. She doesn't have the energy or will to go forward. Or backward. Or anywhere. Like the motor in her blue Camaro, her engine stopped working. She swigs from the bottle and decides she'll swallow the sleeping pills in her bathroom cabinet. There's no internal debate about this. She just opens the bottle. She shakes a pill into her hand, and another, and another, swallowing them one by one, her eyes unfocused but pointed at the washer, which shakes and thrashes as if it wants to stop her.

Bet breathes deep of the night air and doesn't have to look at Pat to know her aunt's eyes are boring into her. "I think part of it was that I was so tired that night, and I'd had a lot to drink," Bet says. "I don't know if dad told you that."

"He did," Pat says.

"It wasn't really depression, I don't think. I just didn't feel like going on. There wasn't any strong feeling behind it. In fact, there was *no* feeling behind it, if that makes any sense."

"It does," Pat says.

"I'm beginning to think there's a story you're not telling me, Aunt Pat."

Pat smiles. When she smiles, her lips disappear into her

chubby face, and her cheeks protrude like inflating balloons. "Oh, no."

The rest of that night is a blur. She tried to walk down the hall and fell. Lisa came home and stared at her in horror before sitting Bet up. Bet threw up at some point, vomit caustic enough to warrant replacing the carpet. There was a red light glowing before her eyes. Her Baptist training kicked in, and she was sure she was in Hell and about to appear before the horned one himself.

"Your mother said that you won't tell Barb about—it." Pat's voice pulls her from the memory.

"I will tell her, just not yet."

"But she could help you, Elizabeth." Pat tilts her head and stares hard at Bet as if this will help steer the message around Bet's defenses.

"Not yet," Bet says, a little more harshly than intended.

Pat's chubby cheeks bunch up in reproof. "I swear I don't understand you girls. You look like twins but act like enemies half the time."

"No, we don't."

"Well, you act like strangers sometimes."

"I don't think so. We just act like sisters."

Pat shakes her head.

"It just hurts me to watch you sometimes. I love you like you're my own children, but—I don't know. Barb with this band, and quitting school and about giving her father a heart attack, and you—"

"Me trying to kill myself."

"Well, yes. If you two knew how much you were wanted, you wouldn't do anything to upset your parents."

"Do you ever regret not getting married and having children, Aunt Pat?"

"Oh, sometimes, I guess. You always wonder about the road

you didn't go down. But I don't let it worry me too much. Like I said, I've always had you and Barb to help look after."

"Aunt Pat, you don't get along too well with Mother, do you?"

The question comes out of the blue, and Pat's face hardens. "We get along all right."

"No, I've seen you two. There's some tension there. I think it's always been there."

Pat shrugs. "Maybe. We're just two different people, I guess."

CHAPTER TWENTY-SIX

"Pat, for a single girl who lives alone, you sure have a lot of stuff," Margaret says.

Margaret puts Pat's green dishes in a tattered box from her last move. Pat's shirt is raised at the navel and tied in a knot, sweat glistening off her in the heat. A little risqué, even for 1967, in Margaret's opinion. She's slim, sleek, and sporty. Margaret's ripped-up sweatshirt doesn't cover her lower arms like she wants, despite the warmth of the kitchen.

"A girl *needs* her stuff," Pat responds with a laugh.

"Not that much stuff," John says. "Either get less stuff or quit moving."

He leans against the kitchen counter, drinking a bottle of Coke. He'll carry the boxes of dishes to the truck but is not entrusted with the delicate task of putting the dishes away. John has broken a glass or two at home. To John, glass should be stronger.

Pat is tall, and not particularly pretty. She moves through life with sharklike assurance. She's accomplished things Margaret can't imagine. She left home without being married, for no good reason. She states her political opinions in arguments. She drinks beer occasionally. She even smokes now and then, although she tries to hide it.

Margaret has no interest in drinking or smoking and thinks less of Pat for doing it, but she would be the first to admit she would have liked to have left the house of Edward Black a lot sooner. She left it in the traditional way, on the arm of John Deener.

Pat wipes down a counter and spills some cleaner on her hands. "Do you have the box with my towels?" Pat asks.

"Oh, gimme a break," John says. "They're already in the truck. I told you I was taking them out a long time ago. I used them to keep the bed rails from scratching the truck bed."

They borrowed Reggie's truck but didn't get Reggie. Reggie didn't let the truck go without spending some time discussing the high quality of its paint until even the family German Shepherd got the hint.

"Well, I really do need a towel. I don't want to borrow one from Mrs. Fadiman and get her back in here nosing around."

With a snort of disgust, John heads for the truck. Margaret walks into the small living room to take a break. Several cardboard tubes are in the middle of the floor. Pat rolled posters and prints of paintings into them and left them in the center so John could move the furniture away from the walls. There was a poster of an art exhibit from St. Louis. Pat went to it years before and talked about it ever since.

Boxes line the far wall. Margaret kicks a couple. They aren't too heavy and slide a bit. She walks to the window. John roots around in a box in the bed of the truck. He pulls out a towel and puts it on his head. He mutters all the way back to the apartment.

"Pat?" Margaret calls. "I'm going to take a couple of these boxes down to the truck."

"What?" Pat sticks her head in the door.

"I'm going to take a couple of these boxes to the truck."

"Oh, okay. I think I'll go see if John found a towel yet. I could knit one by the time he brings it back. Those boxes on the left are the lightest."

Margaret walks to the boxes on the left for some exploratory kicks. They are lighter, no doubt. For some reason, which she will never understand but will often think about, she walks to the boxes on the right. She picks one near the end and hunches down. Years of work at the textile plant hauling boxes full of bolts of cloth across a wide factory floor gave her uncommon upper body strength for a woman, and her muscles retain the memory.

She heads back across the floor. She steps on a cardboard cylinder and tries to step off of it but it rolls under her foot. She staggers back and the box goes up in the air. It drops and practically explodes, spreading papers across the floor.

"Oh, shit," she says. She is too aghast to be upset with her own language.

Margaret frantically corrals them and tries to stuff them back into the cardboard. One side of the box is split, but she can blame that on the truck. There are old bills, scraps of envelopes with notes scribbled on them, postcards from exotic locations like San Francisco and London, sent to Pat by friends. Most of the papers are folded and creased down the middle. One opens as she hustles it toward the box. It's a letter, written in a neat hand in blue ink. She almost has it in the box when a word jumps off the page.

Procedure. As in, *I wanted to see how you are doing after the procedure.*

Another word catches her eye. *Bleeding.* As in, *there was quite a bit of bleeding, as you know. But all in all, I think things went well.*

Despite her best instincts, Margaret reads the letter. It's written in a light code, so a casual reader might miss its point. Margaret thinks she understands it very well. The blood in her head thumps with each pulse of her heart. If Pat walked into the room, Margaret wouldn't hear her over the roar.

Call me if you become concerned about your future prospects. I don't foresee any long-term health risks or issue problems.

Sue.

The letter is old, it predates her own marriage. It predates her failed attempts to bring a child into this world and keep it alive. It puts Pat in a completely new light.

Footsteps shuffle toward the apartment. Margaret knows she should shove the letter into the box, carry the whole thing down to the truck, and pretend she never saw it. But she can't move. Her breath comes in shallow, quick bursts.

"I got a towe—"

Margaret jerks her head up to meet Pat's eyes. "How could you?" Margaret nearly shouts, uncertain and trembling.

Pat's eyes narrow. "What are you doing? That's private."

Margaret's eyes are misting, and her vision blurs from the tears and anger. "Killing a baby is not private, Pat. It is not."

Pat knots the towel in her hands. The towel is black, the color of death, Margaret notes. It is an absurd detail to absorb, but the whole scene burns itself in her mind. Pat, knotted shirt, sweaty hair, and barefoot in her bare living room as she strangles a black towel. Pat's eyes are afire with anger and fear, her jaw working as if she is eating a tough piece of bacon.

Margaret imagines babies, plump and pink, legs awiggle, semicircle mouths issuing gurgles and laughs. Then her own dead babies, touched only for a moment with the divine spark, now cold and unmoving, forever asleep. She would gladly take a baby, any baby in the world. Pat had a baby but gave it back to its creator. One of the many requirements for Hell.

"How could you, Pat? You know how hard John and I have been trying and you've been so supportive and...this." She shakes the paper, then stares at it. It is a snake in her hand. Margaret shoves the letter into the box.

Pat's words catch in her mouth as she cries. "You don't know, do you? He wouldn't have told you."

"Who wouldn't have told me?" Of course. Pat's brother would know. Her husband *would* know and *wouldn't* tell her. She is a confirmed Christian and he only darkens the door of Grace Tabernacle Baptist at Christmas and Easter if he can help it.

"It was—it was around when we first met you. Didn't you ever wonder why we were at the doctor's all the way down in Pitch County when we're from here?"

Margaret reminisced on the night from time to time, how her visit to wretched Aunt Betty changed her life. It was such a sweet story, how a boy helping his sister led to true love for a woman who desperately needed it. Now the fairy tale is tainted. While she was preparing to be happy, a human life was brutally snuffed out. Her happiness came at the sacrifice of human life. The thought forces tears from the sides of her eyes.

"Why all the standing around?" John says. He stands in the doorway, munching a green apple. "Lots of space in the truck. We better get moving, it's starting to cloud up."

He frowns. "What's going on, you two?"

"All this time, and you never told me," Margaret says. "Just going on letting me be happy and stupid. All this time."

"What in the hell are you talking about?" John asks.

"My abortion," Pat says. "She was snooping in my box and found a letter about it."

"I was not snooping."

"A sealed box is opened, and a private letter is read," Pat says. "I call that snooping."

"I nearly fell," Margaret says, irritated. "It came open. Anyway, it doesn't matter how I found out. What matters is that some people try so hard to have children and you could have had one and just threw it away. And you"—she points at John with a waving finger—"you knew about it and didn't tell me. Aren't we married? Aren't we supposed to not have any secrets?"

"It's not your secret, it's mine," Pat says. "Although, I suppose it won't be just mine much longer. I guess you'll rush off to church and tell everyone who will listen."

"I will not—"

"Margaret, you don't understand." John steps between them. "Jesus, it was a long time ago."

"Don't you take the name of the Lord in vain," Margaret snaps.

"It was a long time ago," he repeats. "You don't know the circumstances."

"And she didn't ask the circumstances," Pat says. "She doesn't care. She lives only to condemn anyone who doesn't agree with her narrow little view of the world."

"Now, that's not fair, either," John says.

Margaret's circulation is getting cut off. She swivels to her feet and kicks the box toward Pat.

"I'm not going to tell anyone. I'm not the one you have to answer to. John, take me home. I can't stand to stay here anymore."

"I can't do that. The truck's half loaded up. We're here to move Pat and that's what we're going to do."

"Then I'll walk home."

"No, you're not going to walk home either." His voice is clipped and firm. "It's miles and it's probably going to rain. You just shut up, the both of you, and let's get this done. Then you can fight it out some other time."

Margaret glares at Pat through her tears and Pat glares right back through hers. John bites into his apple with more force than is really necessary.

"Tell her," Pat says. "I want her to know."

"*You* tell me."

"I made a mistake. He dumped me when he found out. You may think you know what I should have done in that situation, but you don't. You don't know until it's you and you've been there."

"With who?"

"A boy named Dickie," John says. "You don't know him and you won't know him. He was in my band."

"He's the guy John hit in the head with his guitar," Pat says, a trace of admiration and gratitude in her voice. "Halfway killed him."

There was something missing from the story of the demise of Percival, the band. The John Margaret knows is not violent or prone to hitting people with musical instruments. She always suspected there was some seed to the violence, but he always talked around it. Over time, the story had faded, become covered with the dust of other memories, and she stopped trying to sort it all out. Now it's clear, sharp, and recognizable.

"What happened to this boy?"

"He's still around, unfortunately. I see him from time to time. He crosses the street when he sees me," John says, a faint, grim smile on his face.

"So, there's your story," Pat says. "Not that you asked. Weren't you always wondering why I left home?"

"Your parents know? Helen knows? Archie knows?"

Pat nods slowly.

"Helen knows. Archie knows. They always used to bug me. Get married. Give us grandchildren, look at Ted and Reggie. We want grandchildren from you too. And then this."

Margaret can't imagine what her father would have done in a similar situation. He would have killed her. He would have beaten her to death right there.

"Where did you have it done? Not in Pitch County."

"No, not in Pitch County. There are places. I guess you good little girls don't know about them. There were some minor complications. I went back home. Mom and Dad said they loved me and supported me, but I could tell what they were thinking every time they looked at me. I decided to move out. They didn't stop me. Didn't argue against it at all."

Margaret just stares at her, the anger lessening. But as hard as things were for Pat, they were harder for her baby, who never even got a chance.

"Mom and Dad looked into some sort of legal action against Dickie," Pat continues. "They decided not to do it. It's a small town, people would talk. They might not know about the abortion, but they would always wonder. They dropped it, and I agreed not to pursue it alone. What would people say, you know? What would people say."

"Did you—ever think about adoption?" Margaret would adopt. Her womb has already proved an unfruitful place for three children, she's not sure another organ, her heart, can take another failure.

"I did. I did. I really did, Margaret. But Dickie was a bastard and the thought of having a child of that man growing inside me for nine months was more than I could stand. Margaret, you can't know what that was like. I hope you never do. You shouldn't think I enjoyed any of this. Don't you think that for even one second. I don't enjoy it to this day. I haven't had a serious relationship with a man since that day. I'll probably never get married. I doubt I'll ever have children." She steps across the floor, edges John out of the way, and sticks a stiff index finger under Margaret's nose.

Margaret flinches, as does John.

"Don't you think I have enjoyed any of this for even one second." Pat's eyes burn into Margaret's.

Margaret believes her, she has no choice but to believe those eyes. But it's not powerful enough to dislodge her faith. Nothing on Earth is that powerful. "I don't doubt that, Pat. That doesn't mean it's right."

On the drive home, Margaret rests her head against the window. Rain streaks down, blurring the landscape into swaths of white and green and blue. Pat's lips were quivering when they left, and Margaret has no doubt that her sister-in-law is doubled over in an empty room right now, crying. Crying for her bad choices. Crying because she is alone. Margaret isn't sure that she doesn't deserve it.

CHAPTER TWENTY-SEVEN

Margaret works the crossword in the Percival Junction that takes up a quarter of the page. Margaret finds the puzzle harder than usual. The words are easy once she sees them written down, but her brain won't get in gear.

John rests his hand on her shoulder and she taps it absently with her left hand. Her right hand clutches a pencil, waiting to strike. A five-letter word for "kitchen gizmo." *Spoon? Hardly a gizmo, and there's no S.* The word just won't come.

"You want to go out?" he asks.

"Go out?"

"You know, out. To a movie and dinner, maybe. Bet's gone, she won't be back until who knows when. There's nothing to do around here, we might as well go out."

"Well, that's certainly a romantic way to put it."

She puts the pencil down. *Gizmo has five letters.* She'll never finish this one, and she used to tease people who couldn't do the Junction crossword.

John squeezes her shoulder. "I'm sorry. My dear, I would love to have a date with you this evening. I shall take you to only the very finest cinematic experience, and to the most delectable restaurant in town."

She stands and gives him a peck on the cheek.

"The Ponderosa and the Tri-Plex. It just doesn't get any better than that," she says.

"Well, we could leave Bet a note and head into St. Louis for the weekend."

Margaret looks at John to see if he's serious, hands on her hips and a smile playing at the corners of her mouth. A little chill runs up her spine and wipes the hints of the smile away. *Bet. What Bet almost did.* The chill has never gone away and she doubts it ever will. Bet is fragile, much more fragile than her sister. Barb is a bull in a china shop, Bet is the china.

"I think St. Louis will have to wait. I'm supposed to help clean up the basement at the church tomorrow. They want to expand the nursery and put it down there."

"Lots of kids around these days. What is Brother Jackson talking about in those sermons, anyway?"

He gives her a playful swat on the rear, and she responds with one to his shoulder.

"You might know if you went like you should. I don't suppose you'd like to help us tomorrow?"

"I'd love to, but I suspect the grass might grow a little bit overnight and I'll need to cut it. So, how about our date?"

"The Ponderosa and Tri-Plex sound like all a girl could wish for. No doubt a very fine love story is playing there now, one based on good wholesome values and devoid of car chases and explosions."

A smile flickers on John's face. "No doubt."

"I'll get dressed."

She takes her time as she figures out what to wear. The Ponderosa isn't fancy, but she wants to look nice. She sorts through her dresses, all church dresses, not out-to-dinner dresses.

John puts on khakis and a blue shirt she pressed the day before and he's ready. He reads the paper while he waits, checking the movie times. "We need to go if we want to make a movie. They all start around seven."

"One minute!" She decides on slacks instead of a dress and finds her nice orange top. She has trouble getting it on. Her arms don't want to navigate the sleeves. The buttons boycott their holes. By the time she gets the top on, she's exhausted. She needs a little rest and lies down on the bed.

"Honey, we really do need to go," John says after fifteen minutes go by, the light tone gone from his voice. He's getting irritated now.

He stomps up the steps, muttering. She can't make herself move.

"We might as well forget about the movie now—honey, what's wrong?"

Tears flow from the edges of her eyes to the white bed sheet. He hovers over her, face white and concerned.

"I'm not feeling well."

THE DOCTOR IS YOUNG. *TOO YOUNG*, JOHN THINKS. *HOW COULD HE BE A doctor? He's probably not done with medical school.* John wants the best doctors, doctors who have been around and seen things, had experiences, and success in curing diseases of all kinds. Especially cancer. He wants doctors who laugh at cancer. Doctors that remember curing a patient decades ago.

Or maybe a young doctor *is* the way to go. They're young, they're not hidebound, they're up on the latest treatments. They read obscure journals all the time and remember references they read months ago. They remember that and they're willing to give it a try when nothing else works.

"Mr. Deener?"

"Yes?"

"I'm sorry," the doctor says, a quizzical smile on his thin lips. "I thought I was losing you for a moment there. This is very hard to take, I know."

He can't know. No doubt they taught him how to deliver bad news in school, probably had people sit down and act it out with him. It's not unlike selling life insurance, really. You're having to sit with people and talk about a time when they won't be around anymore, when their family will miss them and need their financial help from beyond the grave.

John knows the tricks of such discussions. *Keep your voice calm and level, your eyes and voice steady. Eye contact.* Presentation means so much at such times. The presentation must be good or the words won't get through.

This *kid* doctor has all the right mannerisms. He carries a clipboard, which looks official. He is serious but not downbeat. He's not bringing bad news that will end John's life, his dreams, he is merely discussing some upcoming challenges. Difficulties, really.

"I've spoken to your wife. She wanted me to speak to you alone. But you both will need to talk this over at home, and I have a number of someone who can help you with counseling. I also have some material you should read."

He hands John several crisp pamphlets. John looks at them but sees only letters. His brain refuses to read the words.

"How long—how long does she have?"

The doctor smiles, a gentle, understated smile to show that he is not amused, he is encouraged, uplifted.

"Really, you shouldn't worry about that. It could be quite a long time. We have mapped out an aggressive course of treatment and your wife seems up to it, she's ready to fight. The best thing now, the very best thing you can do, is keep your spirits up. Be positive."

"What's the first thing we should do?"

"We need you both back here to talk about the treatment, and I cannot urge counseling strongly enough. I don't know if your plan covers it but it's worth it even if it doesn't, if you can afford it. It will really help you a lot. I also urge you to turn to your faith."

John's willing to do whatever it will take to make Margaret well, even if it means going down on one knee before a God he's not even sure exists.

"That won't be a problem for my wife," John says with a small smile of his own.

The doctor nods and smiles that encouraging smile. "She's a woman of strong faith, I could tell that even in the little time I've known her. That's good. She can go deeper into that. Support her in that, it will be a big help."

"I couldn't drive her away from it if I tried," John says.

He's more afraid that Margaret will go deeper into her faith, disappear into it, and leave him outside in the rational cold, alone.

"That's good, I'll say it again. Listen, I know I sound like a Pollyanna, but you really should keep a positive attitude. This is not a death sentence. This is a challenge. A lot of people beat it. I'm not giving any guarantees, but I'm telling you it can be done, and you should try."

The young doctor's eyes are blue, intense, and unblinking.

He believes it, John thinks, *and so will I.*

"I'll try. I promise, I will try."

"Good. Margaret is waiting to see you. Are you ready to see her now?"

John's knees pop when he stands up, reminding him of how old he's getting. He can't think about that, he must be strong.

"Yes, I am. Yes."

CHAPTER TWENTY-EIGHT

"What do you think about 'How Green is My Valley?'" Bet looks through the meager Deener VHS collection on the shelf in the living room.

"That's my favorite movie," her mother says, her thin faced etched into a smile.

"Roddy McDowell," Bet reads. "Wasn't he in 'Planet of the Apes?'"

Her mother laughs.

"I think he was. He's much cuter in this one."

Bet puts the video in the machine, hits play, and sits on the chair near the couch where her mother lies. They don't make it very far into the movie before her mother announces she needs to go to bed. She wraps herself in a blanket from the couch and makes her way up the stairs, refusing Bet's offer of help.

An hour later, there's rustling upstairs. Bet mutes the television. She listens closely. Her mother rolls over and snuffles in her sleep. Bet insisted she leave the door open. Bet sighs, unable to handle another vomiting jag. She listens a bit longer. Hearing nothing, she's glad her mother is still asleep. She shuts off the movie, not wanting to finish it without her mother opting to mindlessly surf channels.

Bet's father is away at an insurance conference in Kansas City. Her mother urged him to get away for a little while.

"How are you feeling?" he asked her mother, over and over, until she laughed and pushed his concern away.

"My gosh," she said. "I'm feeling better every day. Go to your conference. I'll be here, better than ever, when you get back."

Now Bet wishes her father was here. She stays within earshot of her mother's room and comes across an episode of "Law and Order" she's already seen twice. She needs reassurance the world works as it should be and watches the show as if she has never seen it before. She unmutes the TV.

Barb is on a world tour with Pod, promoting their second album and unaware of her mother's illness. They call it a world tour even though they're only playing in the U.S. and Canada. Her mother sleeps extra so she'll sound perky when she talks to Barb. A framed picture of Pod from an obscure music magazine hangs in the hallway just outside her mother's room, although she laments that Barb didn't smile in the photograph.

Bet doesn't talk to Barb much these days. Barb tells her stories about people she doesn't know. Bet tells her sister stories about people Barb knows but doesn't care about. It doesn't take them long to have a conversation.

Another rustling sound comes and Bet mutes the TV again. She misses some dialogue and huffs, Sam Watterson's face indicates it was a key plot point. Her mother has waves of nausea. She has waves of shame.

This isn't how it should be, she thinks. *My mother should live forever. I shouldn't have to see her die.*

A tidal wave of memory hits Bet. Those same words came from her mother's mouth through the closed door of her bedroom the year before. Bet awoke, groggy, the third day after her suicide attempt. Her body fended off Jack Daniel's, Sleep-EZ, whatever machine or chemicals they used to pump her stomach, Tylenol, and cold chicken.

Her mother cried to her father. "This isn't how it should be," she said, her voice too loud, out of control. "I shouldn't have to see my daughter die."

"She won't die," her father said in his reassuring insurance salesman's voice. "She won't die."

I should be on trial for making her mother say those words, Bet thinks.

"It is natural for a daughter to see her mother die," Sam Watterson would say to her, while she sweats it out in the witness box. "It's not natural the other way around. Is that not true, Ms. Deener?"

She would look at the jury with fear and hope in her eyes, but she would have to say it was true.

THE DIALOGUE FROM THE SHOW MAKES IT UP TO MARGARET'S EARS, EVEN though Bet has the TV turned low. She wishes Bet wouldn't watch those police things. They are so full of dead people, and someone Bet's age should embrace life. Margaret grips the wet sheets, taking her own advice. Her insides are on fire. Any food she takes in tries to leave her body as soon as possible and isn't particular about how it goes.

She knows what awaits her and knows it will be glorious, but she's afraid and doesn't want to die. Not yet. She wants to see Barb. Bet, her formerly wayward daughter, is now her rock, but she wants to see Barb, her first child that lived. She could summon Barb to her bedside. but she wants to get better first.

She has followed Bet's bad example and sworn her youngest daughter and husband to secrecy. She thinks back across all the years to the small dinner table in Jupiter, where her father spent day after day complaining about his ailments, drawing Margaret and her mother closer to him through a web of pain.

"My knees are giving out," he would say, and his wife would touch his hand to feel his agony.

"The back of my head hurts," he would say, and his wife would caress the stubble on his fat neck.

I won't be like my father, Margaret thinks. She won't use her illness to force Barb to return. Whatever problems they have they will work out on their own.

A bolt of pain shoots through her midsection and she groans softly through her teeth. She only hopes she has enough time.

CHAPTER TWENTY-NINE

"Hey, Aunt Pat." Barb gives her aunt a hug and rests her head on her well-padded shoulders.

Pat is in the kitchen baking, sweat bleeding through her shirt. Barb has been on a plane much of the day and is also moist, but neither mind.

"How are you?" Pat says in a near whisper.

"Fine," Barb says. Her lower lip trembles.

"Been a long time," Pat whispers.

Barb nods. When she pulls away, she blinks her eyes several times to clear them, and Pat does the same.

"She's in her room," Pat says. "Why don't you go on back?"

Barb turns to check on her father as he comes through the door with her bags.

"What've you got in these things? Amplifiers?"

She reaches to help him, but he shoos her away with a flick of his head.

"I'm just kidding, they're not bad. Go on back and see your mother. I'll put these in your room."

Barb straightens her hair as she walks through the house. It's been a long time, but it all looks the same, even the same Good Housekeeping and Reader's Digests in the magazine rack. She pads slowly up the stairs. The door is open just a crack and she hesitates before stepping through.

"Oh," her mother says when Barb steps inside.

Her mother is stretched out in bed, propped up on a pillow, with a trashy romance novel open next to her. A blue scarf winds around her head, tight enough to show there is no hair underneath it. A dogeared Bible and a half-full glass of water rest on her night table.

"Come here, let me see you." She strains to sit up.

"Don't," Barb says.

She sits on the side of the bed and melts into her mother. Barb knew this time would come, but she always figured it would be much later, maybe even when she is old and on death's door herself. Just two old gray-haired ladies ready to shuffle off this mortal coil together. They could pick on stooped, gray-haired Bet.

Barb is crying but her mother isn't. Her mother waits patiently for Barb to quit soaking the shoulder of her nightgown. She sniffles a few more times and sits up.

"You look—good."

Her mother smiles. "I do not. But thank you."

"No really, you do." Barb touches the scarf. She can feel her mother's skull just beneath. "This looks kind of punk rock, if you want to know the truth."

Barb smiles through her tears and her mother pats the scarf to keep it in place.

"That's certainly the look I was going for. I was hoping Crash would ask me to sing backup."

They smile at each other for a moment.

"Mom. I would have been here so much sooner if I had—"

"I know, dear, I know. I didn't want to tell you. I was hoping to get better news and then I could just share that with you."

"But I *want* you to tell me—"

"I know this is a hard time for you," her mother interrupts. "I was hoping it would be good news."

"But you were always calling me, wanting me to come home. Was that to find out this? If you had just said—"

She sinks back into the pillow. "No, I didn't want you to come home for this. I'm sorry about that. I was just worrying too much. Really, it wasn't about this. I was feeling a lot better then. I wouldn't have let you know anyway."

She grabs Barb's hand with thin fingers. The tendons push up against the skin like tiny suspension bridges. Her mother is a machine, a machine that is failing, falling apart.

"I wish I had *come*." Barb squeezes her mother's fingers. Her mother winces just a bit. "I would have come home, the band doesn't matter, none of that matters. I should have been here."

"It does matter, Barbara, it does. It's what makes you happy. That's really all I've ever wanted, was for you to do what makes you happy. It's not what I would have chosen, I guess. But— Do you remember when your grandfather died? Grandfather Ed?"

Barb remembers, but she only met him once and pictures him as a huge presence, a dark shadow or bear looming over her.

"When he died, I didn't take you to the funeral. I just went myself to make sure he was dead. That was my father." Small strands of tears leak from the corner of her eyes. "I can't believe I'm saying bad things about him at this point, but the reason I felt that way is because he never wanted me to do what I wanted to do. He never wanted me to be happy. He wanted to control me. I wanted to be better than that. I wanted to show you the right way, but then let you make up your own mind. You and Bet both."

"You did, Mama. You always did."

"I know." She gives a faint smile. "I know for a fact that your father was not crazy about your music. And definitely not about making it a career. But I knew how much it meant to you."

"Thank you, Mama."

"Just do what you like, but don't have any regrets. I don't know that I should be giving advice at this point, but that's what I would say."

"You can give advice."

"I know I just said you should do what you want but I think maybe you can take it too far. Tell me, Barb. You don't go to church at all anymore, do you?"

It is not the time for lies. "No, Mama, I don't."

"I didn't think so. And you still drink, don't you?"

"Yes, I do."

"You drink too much, don't you?"

"Well—yes."

"And you have sex with a lot of men?" her mother prods.

"No."

"No?"

"Not a lot. Some. A few, really. Just one, actually. I sort of have a boyfriend."

"A boyfriend? You should bring him around."

"I will. You might even like him. There aren't very many good ones out there. It's easier to find good beer than good men."

Her mother laughs. It's a relief to answer truthfully. Her mother receives the answers without anger. They're just two women talking.

"You just need to be careful," her mother says. "You know drinking can be dangerous. I can see it in your face, Barb, it's a little puffy. Your pretty face. So many calories in those drinks."

"I know."

"And the men, your boyfriend and all—just be careful."

"I will."

"And I would like you to think about church some. I know you enjoyed it when you were little. It's good for you, it takes your mind off things."

Barb nods. "I'll think about it."

"I hope so. You'll think about it more as you get older. I have a hope of Heaven and I want you to have the same hope. It puts everything in perspective. Even this." She sweeps a hand along her frail body under the sheets, like a game show hostess displaying an appliance.

"That would be nice," Barb says.

"So—how long are you here for?" she asks.

"I think a good while. We're taking some time off."

This isn't true. She is disrupting what is going well. Ben, David, even Crash, all have mothers who are still alive and, like her, they can't imagine anything different. They patted her on the back when she left, hugged her, found a few words to say, but they understood.

"That's good. You've been working a long time. But your music—it's going well still?"

They tour behind their second and best album and are preparing for the third. The critics still love them, copycat bands spring up in their wake. The music is going well, but it's not her music. It's Crash's music, she just helps make it. But as she looks down at the spindly form of her mother, this doesn't matter at all. There's nothing she could write that could capture her mother wasting away, her eyes slowly closing.

Is this how they will all remember her? Barb recalls her parent's wedding picture. Her mother doesn't keep the picture on a wall like most people do. The pictures are in a photo album gathering dust in her bedroom closet shelf.

CHAPTER THIRTY

Margaret watches from the landing upstairs of her parents' house as the minister who will be marrying her and John, Brother Gerard, or Jerry, as he likes to be called, greets newcomers at the door. He takes their coats, puts their white-wrapped gifts on the metal folding table, and guides them to the living room. Wooden folding chairs flank both sides of a makeshift aisle. Wreaths and runners of fake white flowers bloom along the windows and seem to sprout from the radiators.

She trembles with excitement. The place is as grand as any palace in England decorated for a royal wedding. Her mother stands next to her, sharing her excitement and radiating love and concern. Margaret scans the room for John Deener, the man of the hour. The man who grew up in this large, normal house. This house where the shades are not drawn at noon to keep out the light so the night-working vampires can sleep.

John is clad in a dark suit, white shirt, and black bowtie. His hair is slicked back. He chats with his father and Reggie. Reggie is outsized for his suit, a gawky kid in last year's clothes. Mr. Deener's suit fits but can't hide the round mound of his stomach. He is tapered on either end, with slim shoulders and thin legs.

If someone gave him a strong tug he would spin like a top, Margaret thinks.

John is calmer than she feels but, still, he wrings his hands. She's glad to see it. She isn't the only one scared.

"Margaret, come away from there, he'll see you," her mother whispers, as if John can hear her.

"So? He's going to see me every day for the rest of his life."

"But don't start yet. Come on, let's find Mrs. Deener and see where we're supposed to be."

John's mother is a fearsome-looking woman, and Margaret is somewhat afraid of her, but the happy occasion softens her edges. Or maybe she's dipped too much into the wine. There is no doubt that her father has. Margaret can't see her father, but she can hear him, back somewhere behind her soon-to-be husband, noisily braying about something to someone.

Margaret walks with her mother through the door, which leads to a small room with a door to the outside. The Deener household is like a maze intended to drain noise away from the quiet bedroom on the second floor.

They open the door and start down the concrete steps, careful not to mess up her white dress. It's the same white dress her mother wore for her wedding, with some updating Margaret did herself. Margaret hopes the work has driven away any taint the dress may carry. It led to something that never made her mother happy. She doesn't want the same fate.

Sharp edges of cars peek around the house. They have filled the driveway and sprawl onto the grass.

"Have you told him yet?" Frances asks.

Margaret stops in the middle of the stairway and looks out on the flat expanse of the Deener farm, which expands to the far horizon and beyond, possibly forever. She can understand why Archie Deener turned the farming over to his son and took up insurance; humans are mortal, and this acreage seems endless.

She looks back at her mother.

"Well?"

"I sort of mentioned it. In the car. I don't really think he understood. But I did mention it." Margaret leans against the wall of the house, strangely cool in the day's heat. "Mom, I don't want to do it if it's going to cause you trouble tonight. I can't enjoy my honeymoon if you're in danger."

Her mother smiles and flutters her hand as if brushing the suggestion away, but there's fear in her eyes. "Oh, I won't be in trouble, dear. He'll understand. He would probably rather not be bothered, really—I don't mean that in a bad way."

"No, you're right. But he's going to be home with you alone, and he'll be drunk. He's probably already drunk. And if he's going to be mad—why don't you stay with the Deeners tonight? Say you're tired. John's room will be open."

"Oh no, dear, I couldn't do that. I couldn't leave your father alone. You know how his health is. He'll be all right with it. And I will be all right, I promise you."

"No, I don't want to be worrying about this."

John rented a cabin on the shore of the Lake of the Ozarks for this auspicious night. The weather is perfect, the leaves are just starting to turn. She doesn't want to look in the lake's mirrorlike surface and wonder if her father has killed her mother in a drunken rage.

"Let's just forget it," Margaret continues. "I'll just do the usual thing."

"No." Her mother's voice has an unexpected snap. "You asked me to do this, and I accepted, and it will be done. And you're right, Margaret. You're right to want to do it this way. I—I feel so close to you, but sometimes I feel I've let you down. I haven't stood up to him the way I should." Her chin quivers and her eyes shine like dark gems under a film of tears.

Margaret grabs one rough hand and massages it. "Mom, that's not true. You did what you could, you always did. Sometimes I feel like I abandoned you. I went away to work, now I'm running off to get married."

"Oh, Margaret." The tears spill run down her face, shake on her still-twitching chin. "You've never abandoned me. You've made me so happy. You're independent, you're marrying a wonderful man."

"But I'm worried, Mom. What if he *does* get really angry and does something?"

Her mother could be as stubborn and unmoving as a tree stump, and she would never admit she made a mistake when she married Ed Black. She'll dance all around the subject but will never touch it, but Margaret knows the code she needs to get close to the truth.

"Margaret." She stares into Margaret's eyes, hard, strong, and unexpected, a rock underneath a stream. "Listen to me. We are going to do what you wanted to do. And nothing is going to happen to me."

Margaret believes her. Things won't be the same for Ed Black around the house. She hopes. She wonders if maybe she should have left sooner. "All right, Mom. I'm glad."

"I'm glad too."

"Oh, there you are." Mrs. Deener springs from around the corner of the house with a dainty walk, careful in the grass in her flat shoes. "I'm sorry, am I disturbing anything?"

"No, not at all," Margaret's mother says. "Just a little last-minute chat, you know."

"I do know. This is only the second of mine I've managed to

send off into married bliss. Both of them boys, so far. Someday I hope to see Pat walk down the aisle, and I'll have that chat with her. It's different for girls, you know."

"I guess so."

"Well, anyway, if you're ready, I think we can begin. Everyone's in place. We thought it would be very nice if you could walk down the stairway from the landing inside. Would that be all right? Should I go get your father?"

"That would be fine," Margaret says. "But don't get my father. My mother is going to walk me down the aisle. Or the landing, I mean."

Mrs. Deener gives them a curious look, then shrugs, relieved, no doubt, not to have Ed Black traipsing down her clean carpeted stairs.

The singing starts. There's no piano, no room for one. A singer from John's church, a tiny woman with a big voice, sings gospel songs that touch on the idea of marriage. Margaret focuses on staying upright, not tripping, and keeping a calm expression. It takes so much concentration to operate the machinery of her body that the songs seem to come from a great distance. She paces down the steps in perfect synchronization with her mother, who clasps her arm, firm but gentle. They reach the bottom of the steps, all eyes on them. There are around thirty people in attendance, virtually all from John's side, the Blacks don't have many friends.

Margaret can feel her father's eyes on her. He's positioned on the back row on the aisle, ready to escort her. She glances at him. He is stuffed into his old suit like a lumpy sausage and his face is sweaty and impassive, letting no emotion through, neither pride, nor anger, nor sadness, nor anything human. She gives him a quick smile and a nod, and his eyes soften, the corners wrinkling ever so faintly to indicate the possibility of a smile. She hopes so. She made the gesture only for her mother's sake.

John waits at the far end of the makeshift aisle, his hands still, but white-knuckled. A series of smiles flash through his efforts to keep an impassive, stoic face. She smiles, too, seeing only him. She walks away from one man and toward another, in pace with her mother. She is walking toward her new life and she is confident it will be happy and long and good.

CHAPTER THIRTY-ONE

Barb walks stiffly alongside Bet across the Thompson's Funeral Home parking lot. It's a beautiful day, crisp and clear. How can anyone be dead on a day like today?

Bet dressed up now and then to accompany her mother to church, but Barb can't remember the last time she wore such nice clothes. None of her old ones fit her and she had to go buy new ones. She tried on nearly every dress in the store that was anywhere near her size. Her new heels clack on the pavement.

Their mother lies waiting for them inside, her hands folded neatly across her stomach. The funeral home did a good job, their father told them this morning. She looks very lifelike.

She died at home in bed. There was no emergency dash to the hospital, no flashing lights, no breathless physicians, just one breath not followed by another sometime in the night. John woke Barb and Bet and told them, and they all came to look at her. The whole thing was so undramatic they just hugged until their father pulled away and said he had some phone calls to make. Barb and Bet were happy to let him do the adult work. They were little girls again, who missed their mother.

Thompson's Funeral Home is a squat brick building surrounded by a vast black parking lot. It has been there for longer than Barb and Bet have been alive. Strip malls and chain stores have sprouted up all over Percival like mushrooms, but nothing else grew so near the shadow of death. Almost everyone who dies in Percival goes there, except for the few non-Christians whose voyages to eternity don't require going through its tall, brown doors.

A man in a conservative and up-to-date gray suit opens one of those tall brown doors for Barb and Bet as they get near, Jared Thompson, youngest of the latest Thompson family members to run the place. His hair is slicked back, still thick but going white. He went to school with Barb and saw her perform with the Yellow Derringers in the gym. He owns both Pod albums, by far the most unusual music in his collection.

He utters a calm, "I'm so very sorry," and ushers them inside.

The interior is dark wood that absorbs the dull yellow light from a tasteful chandelier and several small tables.

"Just down this way." Jared points down at the pews. He keeps his post at the door, looking out a little slit like a medieval castle guard.

The main hall splits off in several directions. A black sign, waist high like the kind in a restaurant, indicates the Deener family is receiving guests just down the central hallway. Bet pushes the door marked "Deener" and they walk through.

Their father stands before the casket, looking down at the remains of his wife. It's such a private moment that Barb considers backing out, but he glances up and beckons them inside. The large room is decorated with just a couple of wreaths, one from Grace Tabernacle Baptist, one from the plywood sales office their mother managed. Fifty-two years, two wreaths, two daughters, one husband, that's all that's left for Margaret Deener. Their father lines up with one of them on each side of him and they look at their mother and cry. Their father squeezes them in a tight embrace, and they squeeze back.

"I can't believe she's gone," he whispers.

They can't believe it either.

The family comes and the gloom lifts. They enter, give solemn smiles, hug, look at Margaret and cry a bit. It's the same move for most of the people that come in. They then move to talk to John and Barb and Bet.

Grandmother Helen enters, steely as a battleship in her dark gray dress with matching hat. She hugs her son and looks at her daughter-in-law. "I have attended too many of these things," she says to Barb. "I don't know why other people keep getting called home, but not me. I'm beginning to think the good Lord doesn't want me."

Barb puts an arm around her, which is like hugging a tree. "It's because we want you here more, Grandmother."

Visitors filter in after half an hour. Little old ladies from Grace Tabernacle Baptist, smaller and more hunched than Barb remembers.

The years are pulling them down, but their eyes light up when they see Barb. "Oh, you are still so beautiful," they say, or "have you put on a little weight?" They say the same things to Bet, even though she still darkens the church door now and then.

"Still singing?" Mrs. Evers says to Bet, who quickly points her to Barb. Mrs. Evers doesn't keep up with Pod. "You girls always had such beautiful voices. I used to tell Margaret that all the time."

"I'm still singing," Barb says.

"I'll have to come hear you sometime," Mrs. Evers says.

Mrs. Evers' bright blue hair matches her bright blue eyes. Barb would like to see her in the front row at a Pod show.

The conversations quickly turn to the mundane—the weather, the new tires on the car, the new Arnold movie—

anything but life and death. It's a huge relief for Barb and she figures Bet feels the same. Now that their lives have changed forever, it's a pleasure to talk about things that don't matter.

Their mother's friends from the plywood office come through, as well as some total strangers. A few share reminiscences or funny stories, look down at her sadly and leave. Their father's office consists of only himself and Shirley, his secretary and his father's secretary before him. She's old enough to be his mother and takes on the role as she stands beside him, stroking his arm like he is an orphaned child.

The members of Pod are there, ill at ease, like criminals trying to avoid detection. Barb gives each a big hug and thanks them, which makes them even more uncomfortable. David and Ben pay respects to her mother, then retreat to a far corner, nodding at the little old ladies and talking to each other. Pavel, at home in a black suit, stands with her for nearly a minute, then shakes hands with her father.

A storm has caused airline delays out of Detroit, stranding the Furians in Minnesota, so Jack Viall couldn't get a plane out. He did call the night before, and he comforted Barb as best he could. He even sniffled a little. Maybe he couldn't summon his own emotions and had to mimic hers.

Brother Jackson stands stiffly at the podium. He tells stories of how he first met Margaret, years ago, and how she loved the Lord.

"She loved her church," he said, and gray heads in the audience nod. "She loved her family."

Bet feels the tears on her cheeks and lets them flow. She didn't quite realize, until she hears it from Brother Jackson's mouth, what an achievement her mother's life was.

The weather is still bright and beautiful when they stand next to the grave and her mother is lowered. Bet wears her sunglasses to hide her red, puffy eyes. Barb stands next to her, beautiful in one of her new dresses, also with her sunglasses clamped firmly on her nose. Brother Jackson makes another small speech, and the silver casket carrying her mother disappears.

Their father's hands are crossed at his waist. His knuckles whiten as the casket is lowered out of sight. Bet hides behind her sunglasses and watches the whole thing like it's a movie. She's glad she is a Baptist. She is just expected to stand there and be sad, and she can do that very well.

Once the casket is gone, the service is over, people drift away, giving Bet and Barb somber smiles, waves, or pats on the back. Their father hugs them again. Brother Jackson gives Barb a hug and a few words of encouragement, then gives Bet a longer hug. She spent several hours talking with him after her suicide attempt and she's still grateful for his advice.

Barb's Pod mates stand in the parking lot by their rental Mercury Sable, looking fixedly at her, ready to go.

"We'd like to come over," Ben calls, "but we don't know where you live."

"Follow us," Bet calls back.

She slides behind the steering wheel of her Toyota, the foul Camaro's replacement. She's grateful for the leather seats when she's wearing a dress. Barb plops onto the passenger seat and wiggles like she's trying to slide out of her dress.

"Can you turn the AC on?" she asks. "I know it's a nice day, but I'm hot. I'm not used to wearing this suit of armor."

The air conditioning barely worked in the Camaro, but it's a loyal friend in the Toyota. Bet turns it on, and a cool rush blows against her skin.

"How are you doing?" Bet asks.

"All right, I guess," Barb says listlessly. "It's just so goddamn depressing."

"It was nice of Crash and those guys to come."

Barb grunts. "Yeah. I didn't think they would. I'm glad they did. It made me feel better."

"They don't look like what I would expect," Bet says. "They look normal."

Barb just nods, then rests her head against the window. She makes a little gurgling sound and Bet looks over at her. *Is she crying?* Bet can't tell. Until last night, she hadn't seen her sister cry in years.

"Barb, are you okay?"

Barb just looks out the window. Bet starts the car and heads out onto the road.

"I feel bad," Barb says after a while.

"Me too," Bet says.

"No, I mean, I'm afraid that my memories of mom will be of her when she was sick. So thin and all. I can't stand it, but I can't get that picture out of my head."

"But you didn't see her decline," Bet says. "You saw her healthy, and then you came back and she was sick. I think it's worse to see her change."

Bet looks into the rearview mirror, making sure the white Sable is still on their tail. She can feel Barb's eyes burning into the side of her face, hotter than the sun.

"How long had she been going down?" Barb asks, her voice shaky. "I would have come home if someone had told me."

"Mom didn't want to tell you. She told us not to. She wanted to get well and then have you come home."

Barb looks out the window again and thumps her head softly against it. "But that doesn't make sense. She used to call me all the time, around Christmas and even before that, wanting me to come home. And she wouldn't say why. And then she doesn't want me to know?"

"Well—that wasn't about this." Bet holds Barb's gaze as long as she can without getting into a wreck.

"What was it about, then?"

Bet takes a deep breath and exhales. "Last fall—I tried to kill myself."

There is an overwhelming silence. Then Barb shrieks, "What?"

"You heard me."

"How? And why?"

Bet releases a long sigh and gives an exaggerated shrug. "It was just stupid. I was just drunk one night and depressed. I had some pills. I took them and just kept drinking. I meant to do it and I didn't mean to do it. My roommate, Lisa, found me. You remember Lisa? That's why I moved back home."

"Fuck," Barb says. "Ah, fuck. I should have known—"

"And mom wanted to tell you, but I made her promise she wouldn't. I didn't want you to know, Barb, I was ashamed—"

"If I had just fucking paid attention to what she was trying to tell me—"

"I just didn't want her to—"

"You tried to kill yourself? How close did you get?"

"Too close. I had to go to the hospital."

"What were you thinking? I mean, what the fuck were you thinking? Are you depressed or something? Like clinically depressed?"

Bet shakes her head. "I can't really describe it. It's gone now. I'm so glad it didn't work. I want to live, I really do. Don't worry about me, Barb. Barb?"

Barb's face is slick with tears, flowing under her sunglasses.

"Barb? What?"

"I'm just thinking—all that time I wasted. Mom was alive, and fine, and I wasn't coming home because I was mad at her because she was bugging the crap out of me. I could have seen her when she was still well."

"I'm sorry."

"I could have seen her when she was well. I could have seen her well."

"I'm sorry, Barb, I—she didn't—"

"Fuck. I would have come home, Bet."

"I know you would, but—"

"I would have come home if you had just told me. And I could have seen mom. Goddamn it, Bet."

"I'm *sorry.*"

"Stop this car. Stop this fucking car!"

"What? We're in the middle of the road."

"Stop the car!" Barb shouts.

A truck honks as Bet pulls to the side of the road. The gravel crunches under the wheels and the brakes give a slight squeal as the car stops.

"Barb, we can talk at home."

"Fuck it. I'm not riding home with you."

"Barb!"

Barb slides out of the seat and slams the door so hard the car shakes. "I'll see you later," she practically snarls.

Barb staggers across the gravel to the front of the car and beyond in her high heels. Bet throws her door open and leans out.

"Barb! We are three miles from home!"

"Look behind you," Barb says.

The Pod Sable sits behind the Toyota. Ben gapes at her in confusion, his palms upraised in question. Bet waves for him to go around her and keep driving. When he doesn't move it hits her, *he doesn't know where he is going.* She holds her hand up, urging him to wait.

"Barb!" she shouts. "Come back here!"

Barb is making remarkably good time, wobbling all the way. Bet gets back in the driver's seat and throws the car into gear. Barb keeps staggering forward. Bet accelerates around her and pulls the car sharply to the right to cut her off. Barb staggers around the car.

"Barb!" Bet yells. "Get in the car!"

She tries the move again, but Barb descends off the shoulder and into a ditch that Bet can't get into without getting stuck. Barb's shoes are muddy and ruined but she obviously doesn't care. She stomps back out of the ditch and onto the shoulder, moving steadily away from Bet.

"Get the fuck away from me!" Barb shouts. "You made me waste my time. You probably helped kill Mom with your fake suicide bullshit."

Bet leans her head out the window. "Barb, get in the car!"

She pulls the car to the right again, nearly hitting Barb.

"Go ahead, hit me!" Barb pounds the hood hard with her fists. "Kill me, like you did Mom!"

Bet is tempted. She could probably make a good argument that it was an accident, although the guys in the car behind her might contradict her story. She slams on the brakes and shoves the gear into Park so hard she almost tears the gearshift out of the floor. She opens the door in a fury and howls at her sister.

"Fine! Walk home! Make this all about you, you selfish bitch!"

Barb turns to glare at her.

"Oh, now I'm—"

Bet slams her door, moves the gearshift violently again and stomps the accelerator. She doesn't even look if the lane is open as she hurtles back into the road. Gravel slings behind her and rattles off the grill and windshield of the Sable.

"You are no longer my sister!" Barb shouts after her.

CHAPTER THIRTY-TWO
THE INTERVIEW

Rolled Cuff

Pod

Is there trouble in paradise? Rolled Cuff magazine caught up with Barb Deener to get her thoughts on Pod's forthcoming new album, "Sixpence Sortie." What we got was an earful. The lovely Barb, who we readily admit can drink us under the table, doesn't sound like she'll be saving space in her music collection for her band's latest record.

"It's more of the same," she said, beer mug halfway to her mouth, which is how she spent most of the interview. "If you liked the earlier stuff, you'll like it. If you're looking for artistic growth or new musical horizons, you should look somewhere else."

We did happen to note that Ms. Deener, who has been working on becoming a songwriter, has no actual tunes on the album.

"Crash said another songwriter's product would mess up the album's flow," she said. "Having songs about actual human beings might get in the way of songs about British werewolf fighter pilots."

For the record, the title tune is about just such a creature, which might be unusual for another band but not for Pod. We asked what kind of songs she would like to see on the album, but Barb had a mouthful of foam and declined to answer.

So, what's it like working with Crash?

"The trains run on time. You get a clear sense of his vision. You know what he expects of you. That's about the best thing I can say about it."

And what about Ben and David?

"They enjoy not having to think too hard, so they don't mind giving Crash the lead. They're good soldiers, they'll play what he wants them to play."

This is sounding more and more like a band in trouble, or at least a band with one very unhappy member. Given that this unhappy member is also one of the band's stars, Rolled Cuff has to think that Pod may not have a bright future. Lots of other bands are already borrowing from their playbook, adapting their typical fast/slow quiet/noisy harsh/beautiful approach. Pod makes sweet and sour rock songs, but Crash Pavement tends to write them about zombies or British werewolf fighter pilots, which can limit their appeal. Other bands are adapting the Pod style to straight-ahead rock and roll, and laughing all the way to the bank. Pod may be chuckling all the way to the grave.

BARB SITS IN A TOO-HARD CHAIR WHERE POD IS GATHERED IN THE basement of Beastie Sound in Armonk, New York. They're putting the finishing touches on the third album.

"What the fuck is this?" Ben stares at the white instrument, which Barb has to admit looks like the love child of a piano and a vengeful computer from a 1950s sci-fi movie.

"I just showed you," Crash says.

"I don't get it. It's a keyboard," Ben says.

"It's not a keyboard, it's a sampler."

"I just hit the drums once?"

"Right. Don't you pay any attention to what's going on?" Crash says. "You play each drum once into the sampler, then you can do whatever you want with it. You can speed it up or slow it down or change the scale."

He demonstrates, with the thump of the bass drum that Ben recorded, under his tutelage. The sampler begins issuing a steady thump. He twists a knob and the thump sounds like a snare. Crash looks up at David and Barb, a goofy grin on his face.

"Isn't this great? It's like music as plastic."

"But, why now?" Ben complains. "I know about Kraftwerk and New Order and all that shit, but why are we doing this?"

Crash steps back and trips over the pile of cables emanating from the keyboard. His face looks like he swallowed a lemon.

"Yeah, Crash, I mean, we're a rock band," David says, arms crossed. "Guitars and drums. We said no pianos. No disco thump bullshit."

Crash puts his hands on his head, as if holding it together lest it explode. "It's not disco. Give me some credit. It's just a good way to be different."

"Different?" Barb says. "*Everybody* is doing this. We're being different by doing the old-fashioned thing."

"They're doing the wrong thing," Crash says. "All the other bands are trying to use synthesizers just to play regular music. But these things can make sounds like you never heard. It's a way to take our music to a new level of unreality."

"I can't believe this," Barb says. "The record is nearly done,

Crash. We have done the whole thing without this sampler. Why do you need to bring it in now?"

Ben issues a few good steady thumps from the bass drum, as if to show that a fake one is unnecessary.

"I don't know," Crash says, then casts Barb a dirty look. "I guess I thought it would help us find new musical horizons."

"And new artistic growth?" David says, tossing a dirty look of his own. "I'm all for that, Crash, but I don't think this is the way to do it."

So, they all read the article. She should have expected that. "Look, they caught me at a bad time. I had too much beer." If they want to translate that into an apology, that was fine with her.

"Anyway," Crash says, "I listened to the tracks again last night and I thought they sounded too much like what we've done before. Barb is right about that. I thought I'd remix it."

"You thought *you'd* remix it," Ben says. "What about *us* remixing it?"

"Yeah, exactly," Crash says, then smiles back. "We'll re-record some of the bits with the sampler and layer them over the top. It'll make it sound more artificial, more hollow."

Barb runs a hand over her face. Her fingertips are creased and calloused from the guitar strings. She didn't get those callouses playing artificial, hollow songs. Or maybe she did. But now it's time to stop.

"That would be preferable to you?" she asks. "That's what you want?"

Crash's smile falters. "Well, yeah. It's disorienting. It'll put our listeners off guard. It's fresh."

"How is being artificial and hollow being fresh?" David asks. He shoots another nasty look at Barb. "I know that I'll just do anything you want, Crash, but this just sounds like a stunt. The album is good as it is."

Crash tugs at his black hair, as if he wants to pull it out by the roots. "It's not bad, but it could be better. I think this would be better, it would make it different."

"What's wrong with being intimate?" Barb asks. "What's so great about artificial? Why can't we include songs about real people?"

"Oh, please." Crash rolls his eyes. "People don't listen to rock and roll to hear about real people. They want to escape. They want to explore, go new places."

"That's bullshit," Ben says. "Look back at the great rock songs. They're all about people. People's feelings."

"But they're just rock songs," Crash says, exasperated. "We're going to do something new."

"Why are you so afraid of human emotion?" Barb asks. "What's so wrong with including a little of it in a Pod song?"

Crash glares at her. "Barb, look, I am so sorry about your mother. I know it upset you, and I know you and your sister are on the outs. But that doesn't mean you should drag all that baggage into a Pod album."

"Excuse me for having fucking human problems," she spits back, trembling with rage. "And for dragging that baggage in here where it might upset a werewolf or something. Because Pod is yours, right? It's your band?"

"No, it's *our* band. All of us. It's like a ship."

"And you're the captain," David cuts in. "I tell you what, Crash, it's not feeling like our band at the moment."

"Well, someone has to lead. Someone with a coherent vision. That's what's selling these albums."

"You want something different, Crash, why don't you put one of Barb's songs on the album?" Ben asks.

Barb's surprise pokes through her anger. He's never stood up for her before, and she's not the only one feeling pushed aside by Crash.

"Just put it on there, maybe without even a name," Ben says.

"Like the Clash did with 'Train in Vain,' on 'London Calling.' That didn't sound like a typical Clash song, and it became one of their biggest hits."

"But it would still interfere with the overall sound," Crash says. "Especially after I remix the album."

"So, you're going to remix the album, like you said a while ago," Barb says. "*You* are going to remix it."

"Well—yes. I'm going to remix it. With help from all of you."

"So, we all say don't remix it, and you say you're going to remix it," Ben says.

"That's right." Crash says. He stands up a little straighter. "And you're right, Barb. Pod *is* my band. People buy our albums because they want to hear songs. I'm not going to apologize for that anymore. You don't like it, get some kind of side project going."

She could work with Rebecca Hannifin and she has some money in the bank. Barb can afford to skate a while. "How about this for a side project?" she says. "I quit."

They all look at her blankly, and no one says anything. Ben's mouth hangs open.

"So, goodbye, then." She jumps to her feet and fights her way across the shag-carpeted studio floor.

"Barb—wait!" Crash rushes toward her with a burst of speed. He reaches for her arm, but she gives him a chilling glare and he backs off. "You can't break up the band!"

"I'm not breaking it up. I'm just quitting. Replace me." She struggles to keep her voice calm, to sound unconcerned. She also struggles not to cry, and her anger helps her succeed.

"But—I can't do that. We're a *band*. We're a team. You're popular. If you leave, then it's over."

She looks at Ben and David. They walk up behind Crash and shake their heads.

"Then make it a team," Barb says. "Put one of my songs on the album. Uncredited, whatever, like Ben said. Just one."

"Do, it, Crash, it won't kill you," David says.

"And put one of David's on the next album," Barb says.

"I don't write songs," David says.

"Well, if you happen to write one."

Crash's face gives her answer before he speaks.

"I won't do it," Crash says. "I've done what I think is best. You won't blackmail me."

David and Ben tense up, gearing up to beat Crash lifeless right there. Barb can see they hold back only by sheer will.

"Jesus, Crash, if you don't do it, I will," David says. "Barb, your song will be on the album."

"I don't think so," Crash says in a menacing voice Barb wouldn't have thought him capable of. "Check the contract. I approve everything on the album. I made sure of that."

Barb never read the contract, and she bets David and Ben didn't either. Crash could be bluffing, but she doubts it.

"You made your choice then, Crash," Barb says. "I'll see you around. Good luck with the record."

She's makes it halfway up the stairs before she startles a baffled studio tech at the top. Crash runs to the bottom of the stairs like a jilted lover.

"Barb, don't go now! The album is about to come out. Tour with us. Just tour to support it."

"Which version?" Barb asks. "The one we did, or the remix? Just replace me with a machine, Crash. That'll make it more remote and impersonal."

She steps outside, the late afternoon sun is bright and blinding. The world is composed of swirls and vague shapes, like through a window on a rainy day. She's crying, the tears falling as the doors shut behind her.

She stays in Armonk for the night, too tired and upset to get a bus ticket out of town. She lies on the hotel bed and scans for meaningful patterns in the ceiling. Going home to Percival would be an admission of defeat. Bet is there, and she doesn't want to see Bet. And her mother isn't there. The Outer Banks and her place in St. Louis are too far away. Calling Jack means she'll have to call his tour manager, and that number is in her suitcase. An overpowering weariness seizes Barb and she closes her eyes. She'll call him tomorrow.

When she opens her eyes it's dark. A dog-like howl pierces through the wall from next door. She sits up and is raises her arm to bang on the wall when the muffled words come through the wailing. Crash's room is next to her. She puts her ear to the wall. Crash is sobbing.

"It's over, mother, it's over," Crash cries.

He's wailing it, crying the way Barb always imagined a Russian would cry.

"What will I do, mother? It's all over."

It's a chilly evening, but Barb gets up and turns on the room fan full blast.

CHAPTER THIRTY-THREE

Jack walks to the beach house railing that overlooks the ocean as it pounds away at the shore just over the dunes. Barb watches him, a beer in hand. He's rugged in his denim jacket, framed against the dunes, and his longish brown hair whips in the wind. A cowboy lost and discovered on the edge of the world.

"So, what do you think?" Barb asks.

"Very cool."

"Of course the ocean's cool. What do you think of the house? I can't believe I haven't been able to get you here until now."

"You know the touring life," he says. "Dingy clubs, bad sound systems. No time for fancy beach houses." He pushes back from the railing and steps back inside through the sliding glass door. He looks around, making a show of assessing the place. "It's a little spare, kid. You need some furniture. My voice is echoing in here. Helloooooooooooo. Helloooooooooooo."

Barb giggles. "It's not that bad."

"It's pretty bad. Look at the furniture in here—oh, there isn't any."

"There is too. Right there." She points at the TV on a stand against the wall to the right.

"A TV doesn't count as furniture."

"I have a bed." She drops onto the mattress near the wall opposite the TV.

"You have a mattress. A mattress doesn't count as furniture either. It's something you're supposed to put *on* the furniture."

"Well, whatever. I'm happy. Come sit with me."

"Hang on a second. I need to get something you *do* have. Beer. Want one?"

"Got one." She hoists the brew in her hand.

"Want another one?"

"Sure. Save me having to get up."

He clomps into the kitchen and opens the refrigerator, which is only there because it came with the house. His voice doesn't really echo in the living room, but his footsteps do. He comes back and sprawls on the mattress next to her, then hands her one of the beers he's holding.

She takes the bottle, sets it on the mattress to her left, then rests her head on his shoulder. She likes the smell of salt on him. "So, do you like my house?"

"I do like your house. I like it even better than the condo. I'm curious, though. Why did you buy it here? Do you know anybody here?"

"Well, I met—what's her name? Tricia from Chapel Hill?"

"The one in Mudslinger?"

She nods and takes a pull on her beer. "That's right. The bass player."

"One of the sex symbols of alternative rock. After you, of course. But I don't think Chapel Hill is anywhere near here."

"No, I guess it's not."

She bought the house on a whim after her father asked what she planned on doing with her money from Pod. Reading about mutual funds was boring and she didn't want to waste it on cars. The condo in St. Louis wasn't enough. Pod played in Virginia Beach and she traveled south and fell in love with the Outer Banks. An alien landscape in North Carolina, with sand dunes so tall you could bound down them and feel like you were on the moon.

The three bedrooms, two and a half bath is big, but nothing fancy. It's rugged-looking house made of tan-painted wood. She has to cross a sand-strewn road to reach the beach, but she's seen enough hurricane news videos to know she does not want anything closer. She can see the ocean from her deck, and that is good enough for her.

"I just like it here. I'm going to fix it up now that I have some down time."

"You're not going to form another band right away?" He sips his beer.

She rolls the cool bottle across her forehead. "No, I don't think so. I want to rest a little bit. I've been talking to Rebecca Hannifin about doing something, but she's on tour right now, so I'll wait. I thought maybe I would buy some furniture."

"I heartily second that."

"So, how long can you stay, Jack?"

He finishes a sip of beer and gives her his famous sidelong glance, the Woody Harrelson one. "Oh, I see. I'm here just to move furniture, is that right?"

"No, of course not. But, you know, since you're here...."

"Uh huh, that's what I thought. Too bad I only have my motorcycle."

"Too bad I bought an old pickup."

He makes a face like he's eaten a sour candy, and Barb laughs.

"No, I can wait on furniture moving. We can just walk on the beach. And I can show you where the Wright Brothers flew the first airplane, if I can find it. And I think there are some good seafood places around here, or there should be."

"Barb—I don't think I can stay very long."

She sits up. Jack stares out at the ocean, or the sky, or something equally distant.

"But I thought you weren't hitting the road for another three weeks."

The Furians' new album is nearly out, but they aren't planning to start touring behind it until their single, "My Space," shows up on the Beverly Hills Cop IV soundtrack. At least, that's what he said when she called to tell him that Pod had broken up.

"That's right," he says. "But I need a little time to get ready and, you know, clear my head."

"Clear your head? Jack, you're in a rock band. You're not supposed to have a clear head. Didn't you get the rule book?"

He doesn't laugh. Suddenly the emptiness of the room, its lack of furniture, becomes ominous.

"What's going on, Jack?"

"I like your house, Barb. I just don't think I'm going to be seeing much of it. We're going to be on the road for a long time, and I don't think it's fair to make you wait." He takes a swig from his beer.

She's tempted to smack the beer out of his hands, send it skittering across the floor, make a scene, but she'd just have to clean it up after he leaves. His eyes are already gone.

"It's not fair to make *you* wait, you mean," she says.

"Maybe so."

"Is there someone else?" she asks, stupid for having to ask it, ashamed for sounding like the aggrieved wife on a soap opera. "Got some roadie on the hook?"

Jack snorts. "Of course not."

"Looking to get one set up?"

"A roadie? I don't think so."

She glares at him. *Was that supposed to be a joke?*

"No, I mean, no," he says, staring at the horizon. "There's nobody."

"So why not me?"

He glances her way and then looks away again. "I just think... we're two different people."

"Oh, Jesus. What breakup book did you get that from?"

She scoots away from him. He reaches out a hand, but she pushes it away with her knee. She's glad he brought her the extra beer because she could use it now.

"I suppose you want to be friends too."

"Well, yes," he says. "If you'll let me."

"Forget it." Her anger at the situation boils under her skin. It's such a cliche conversation, but all the words make sense. A real-life country song.

"When did this happen, Jack? Why the sudden interest in freedom? Not too long ago, you chased me over half the country."

"I know. But I can't keep up with you. You're on the road all the time. I'm going to be on the road too. We're not going to have time to be together."

Barb stares into the distance. "But I'm not going to be traveling now. And you're not going to be traveling for a while. This is the first time we could be together for more than like a fucking day. And this is the time you decide you want freedom?"

He shrugs. "It's just that I've just now realized what I want. What I need. This isn't really a choice."

"Not a choice."

"No. I mean, I need this time. To focus on the music. This could be our chance. You should understand that."

"I think I do understand, Jack. Do you suppose that the fact that I just broke up Pod has anything to do with this?"

He gives her a look intended to convey shock or surprise. He's a bad actor. "What are you talking about? Of course not."

"So, I break up the hottest alternative band in the world, I think that's fair to say, and an aspiring musician who was once all anxious to be with me suddenly decides he needs to focus on his music?"

"That has nothing to do with it."

"Are you sure? You know, if you wanted some of that Pod glory to rub off, maybe you should have been fucking Crash instead of me."

He stumbles to his feet, spilling beer. "That is ridiculous. You're just using that as an excuse to fight with me."

"Am I?" she asks. "Is that what I'm doing? I think I'm making perfect sense. You think I'm going to fail, don't you? You don't think I can survive without Pod."

"Of course, you can." He still isn't looking at her. "You can do anything you want, and I hope you do and do it well."

"But you're not going to be around to see it."

"Well—maybe. I did hope we could be friends. But what we had is over."

"You're damn right it's over. Get out of my house. Lose my address. If you want to find Crash so you can crawl into bed with him, I'll be glad to give you his number."

He gives her a glare of indignation. "Good luck to you, Barb." He stomps out the sliding glass door onto the balcony.

"I bought that beer!" she shouts. "You leave that here!"

He leaves his half-empty beer on the railing where she can see it. Barb sits and stares at it for a long time, finishing her own beer. Tears burn the corners of her eyes. *Jack's beer can stay on the railing. Forever.* It'll fill with rainwater and snow. Sand will encrust its mouth. Archaeologists will dig it up in thousands of years and wonder if it has some special meaning. Maybe they'll it was left there by a dumb son of a bitch.

After about half an hour, Barb walks to the beach to go for a swim. She wades into the surf. Swimming in an ocean is harder than she expects. The Atlantic is vast, uncaring. It sucks her in so fast she scrambles to stay upright. She's tired by the time she gets to where the water is over her head. She treads water and after drinking a couple of waves, learns to move to their rhythm.

She looks up and down the beach. It's a pretty day, clear and blue, only a few puffy white clouds showing off their feathery finery. From the sea, her house appears to hide behind dunes with a few of its multi-story friends. A few vacationers sit under umbrellas. A man in a white T-shirt plays fetch with a black dog, sending it into the surf again and again with a stick. The man shouts encouragement, and the dog barks as it bounds into the water.

Barb's jeans and shirt tug on her like weights. She should just shuck them and swim naked, but she has to emerge at some point, and people wouldn't like that. Plus, in "Jaws" the woman at the beginning was swimming naked and got eaten by a great white.

The ocean pushes and pulls her and she feels connected to everything, the people under the umbrellas, the man with the stick, the dog. When she gets back to the beach that will fade and she'll again be an aging rock star walking back to a completely empty house, where a half-drunk beer drips condensation onto her railing.

Her mother never went far from her home and was surrounded by the same people for much of her life. Barb has been everywhere, has friends everywhere, although she would have to stick pins in a map to be able to locate them. Her mother wore her friendships and family like a cloak. She hardly ever asked for anything. She died too early. And Jack didn't come to her funeral. Storm or not, he should have been there.

Her arms ached. *I could just stop swimming.*

The Atlantic would have its way with her. It might keep her

head up for a little bit, but then it would pull her down. Barb already feels herself giving in to the pull.

What would I find? My mother? Would she tell me that reading the Bible and being a good person was all a big waste of time? Or would she say, sorry, dear, I was right after all and you're going to Hell? Or would I just fade away? What's the point? It's all going to end. This must have been what went through Bet's mind. No wonder she couldn't really explain.

Barb is tired. She isn't going to stop swimming, she knows that. Her time to explore the infinite hasn't yet come. She still has a band to form, a sister to forgive. She takes a couple of deep breaths and starts moving to the shore, heading for a house that isn't a home.

CHAPTER THIRTY-FOUR
INTERVIEW

Short Takes
Barb Deener

As we look back on all the bands we lost in 1993, Short Takes talks with Barb Deener, former guitarist/vocalist for Pod, the most influential alternative band since—well, since probably forever. We reach her at her North Carolina home (and no, we won't give you the number). Even though it's late afternoon, Deener, a notorious late sleeper, sounds groggy.

ST: So, Pod broke up.

BD: That's what they tell me.

ST: You only recorded three albums, all brilliant. There was no sign you were losing steam. So, what happened?

BD: People change and move on, that's all.

ST: Little birds say you and Crash weren't getting along.

BD: Little birds get things right once in a while.

ST: That's too bad. We're hoping for a reunion.

BD: Don't hold your breath.

ST: It sounds like the rumors are true.

BD: I'm just talking generally.

ST: I don't know if you read the interview, but Crash said you were getting too dark after your mother died.

BD: That sounds like something Crash would say. I don't want to talk about that. Let's just say that you can't sing about spaceships and enchanted forests forever. At some point you've got to address things that are real.

ST: Shall we put it down to artistic differences?

BD: Art imitates life, so everything is artistic differences.

ST: What kind of music can we expect from Barb Deener in the future?

BD: Good music, I hope.

CHAPTER THIRTY-FIVE

"I was wondering if you had this in an extra-large," Barb says.

It's been two years since Bet has heard that voice and she looks up from the table of t-shirts she's straightening. Barb is holding a black dress she must have taken off the rack behind her.

"I don't think you wear an extra-large, ma'am."

Barb smiles. "Well, so you do know how to win friends and influence potential customers."

Bet smiles back. "I'm sure I could interest you in something much more expensive."

Barb hangs the black dress back on the rack. Bet feels certain the dress isn't something Barb would ever really wear. It has too many ruffles and isn't made of denim.

"Hey, Bet. How are you doing?"

"Just working. How are you?"

"All right. How's Dad doing?"

Bet shrugs. "He's doing okay. Not great, but okay. He bought a pool table."

"A pool table?"

"He always wanted one and mom didn't. But he has one now, a nice one."

"Can he beat you?"

"No. You should come by."

Barb nods. "I will."

"When?"

"I thought I would tonight."

They look at each other tentatively, eyes locking and then sliding away.

"I didn't know you were in town," Bet says.

"I wasn't. I came back."

"I heard that you broke Pod up. Is that true?"

"Yeah, I guess." Barg shrugs. "I had a good reason."

"Lack of artistic freedom?"

Barb gives her a crooked smile. "What have you been reading? But, yeah, something like that." She looks around the store. Faint music chimes from overhead speakers, an old song by Led Zeppelin, redone with cellos and flutes, all hard edges stripped away.

Bet watches her sister's face. Barb is a stranger here. She's dressed like half the people in the mall but there's an exotic air about her, as if her frank and fresh appraisal is what makes her different now.

"I'm sorry," Bet says, not sure what words apply when a band dies.

"Don't be."

"So, are you done with that now?"

Barb snaps her head around in surprise and smiles again. "Done? Oh, no."

"What are you going to do?"

"I'll tell you tonight. Does Dad let you drink in the house?"

"No."

Barb nods. "The spirit of Mom lives on, I guess. Can you sneak something in?"

"Of course."

HER FATHER LOOKS WELL AND HAS DONE A COUPLE OF NICE THINGS WITH the house. Barb suspects he's in no hurry to go to sleep, where there's just him and his dreams in the same old bed. So, they play pool. The old man is pretty good, nearly running the table on them a couple of times.

"All right, that's about enough of that," he says after the seventh game. "Some of us have to work in the morning. I'll see you both tomorrow. Barb, do you know how long you'll be staying?"

"Not sure, Dad. Probably a couple of days."

"Stay as long as you like. Stay all summer." He gives Barb a hug. He's thinner now, it's easier for her to get her arms around him.

Bet brings out the beer after he's gone.

"Glad to see your taste hasn't improved." Barb holds up the Old Milwaukee's Best.

"Perhaps the rock star in the family could have bought the beer."

They play another game of pool. Bet is the dominant player. She squares off regularly against their father, and it shows.

"I need to get one of these things." Barb lines up her shot.

The only furniture in the basement are the pool table and half a dozen barstools. Barb perches on a stool and watches her sister try to make a complicated shot. It's like looking in a mirror. Bet's hair hangs low across her shoulders and she's beefy without quite being fat. When she's not shooting, she holds the cue stick low across her hips and she walks with a bit of a swagger.

She could do it, Barb thinks.

"Bet, I don't suppose you ever looked at my old guitar books, did you?"

"No. I think they're still in your room."

"You haven't learned to play guitar or bass by any chance, have you?"

"Not that I noticed." She misses an easy shot, and scratches. Bet holds her cue upright beside her like a walking stick and looks at her. "Why do you ask?"

"I was just thinking about something. You know Salvation?"

"The going-to-Heaven kind, or the band?"

Barb laughs. "The band."

"Sure. They're all right."

"Well, the bass player is Rebecca Hannifin. I've been talking with her about forming another band."

"You should."

"And I've been talking with a drummer."

"This is all very fascinating, this look into the bowels of the world of rock and roll. Barb, it's not that I'm not glad to see you, but the last time I saw you, you were screaming at me. Now you're here talking like I know what you're talking about."

Barb sips her beer. From force of habit, they stash the empties in a plastic bag that they'll hide in the trunk of a car to dispose of later. They have also cracked the basement windows so they can smoke. It feels almost like old times, hoping their mother won't come down to check on the laundry. They don't have that problem now, but Barb still feels guilty and holds her cigarette in her palm, ready to hide it. She finishes the beer, crushes the can, and tosses it in the bag.

"You're right. I'm sorry. Let me start different. Bet, I'm sorry I was so angry with you after Mom died."

Bet looks at her quizzically.

"I'm serious," Barb says. "After Jack left me, I went swimming out in the Atlantic. For just a second there, I thought about what would happen if I stopped swimming."

Bet's eyes widen. "Jesus. Why didn't you tell me?"

"Why didn't I tell you? Why didn't you tell me?"

Bet looks at the table, as if planning her next shot.

"I didn't tell you, Bet, because I was ashamed. I felt what you felt. I think. It was just this weird feeling, like everything would go away. It was the first time in my life that anything like that ever felt like—I don't know—"

"Like an option?"

"Yeah." Barb nods, and Bet joins in, moving her golden head slowly up and down. "That's it. Like an option. So that's why I didn't tell you. And it occurred to me that that's why you didn't tell me. If I had been in your shoes, I would have done exactly the same thing."

"I don't know. I've thought about it a lot since then." Bet slides her cue over in front of her and grips it with both hands. "I think I went too far, letting it drive a wedge between you and Mom. I shouldn't have done that. It's one thing not to want to tell you about my suicide attempt, but that was too much. And I should have told you about Mom, even though she told me not to."

Barb's hair gleams in the harsh overhead light but her eyes are deep in shadow.

"I was jealous of you," Bet continues. "Still am, really. That was another reason I didn't want to tell you, and that's one reason you don't have."

"Jealous?" Barb frowns.

"Of course, jealous. You're a rock star, Barb, sort of. You're in a band the press just loves. You've sold...I don't have any idea how many albums you've sold, but a lot, I think. I've never left my hometown and you've gone out and become an international celebrity."

Barb grunts with surprise. *Not the sort of response one would expect from an international celebrity,* she thinks. She knows her lifestyle could be seen as glamorous by someone who never spent time in the back of a van out on tour, but she didn't realize her own sister could share the delusion.

"So, you're mad at me because I'm in a band."

"I don't think I'm mad at you. I think I'm mad at *me*. I never amounted to anything. Never really tried, actually. I was just disappointed in myself because I'm such a loser. I didn't want you to think I'm a loser too."

"I don't think you're a loser. You've known some things I've missed. You have friends here. I've moved around so much I've lost touch with everyone."

"You have some friends, though. Like that person you mentioned from Salvation."

Barb shrugs. "Yeah, I guess. But I feel dislocated. Like I'm not from anywhere. I don't think that feeling is good for me."

"But why would you want to be from here?"

Barb pauses. "Anyway, I think I have a solution to both our problems. You feel like you're not going anywhere, right? And I need to get a new band started, but I also want to connect with my roots, or something like that. So, I want you to join my new band."

Bet leans against the pool table, eyes wide with surprise. "What?"

"You heard me. Join the band. It'll be great. We'll be playing and singing together, just like we used to do."

Bet leans the cue against the table and runs a hand through her long hair. "We used to sing together, but I never learned to play anything, like I told you. And I never sang professionally."

"I don't care. Come with me and do this. We'll hook up with Rebecca and have a great band. I'll teach you to play guitar."

"But—I have a job."

"You have a job at the *mall*, Bet," Barb says, annoyance creeping up. She didn't expect to have to badger her sister to join the band. "If it doesn't work out, you can come back here and get another job at the mall. If the mall isn't hiring, maybe you can get on with Target or Wal-Mart."

"All right, all right, I get your point."

"So, will you do it?"

Bet studies her. "What will we call it?"

"I don't know. Nothing with the word Pod in it, that's for sure."

"Maybe something with 'death.' Like Death Vomit or something."

"Now you're getting it," Barb says. "That's too good, though, it's probably been taken. Actually, I had an idea. Remember what Mom said her friends used to call us after you were born?"

"Pains in the asses?"

"No. Well, they probably did. But she said she'd walk us around and they would call us the Delicious Twins. Because we looked good enough to eat. What do you think of that?"

"I think Mom needed new friends." Bet frowns. "You want to name the band the Delicious Twins?"

"Sort of. Then I thought we could shorten it to the DTs. No one will ask us what it means, probably."

"That reminds me, I need another beer." Bet deposits her dead soldier in the bag and fetches another and uses the palm of her hand to muffle the sound as she cracks it open. "I like that better," she says after a couple of sips. "The DTs. Gives us kind of a hard-living, hard-charging feel."

Barb nods. "That's right."

"What kind of music are you wanting to make now?" Bet asks.

"Stuff that's less weird than Pod. Just straight-ahead rock and roll. That's why I thought the name might work. Look, it won't be easy. You're going to have to really practice and work. But we could have fun too. And I know Pod's fans would love seeing you and me together."

"They'll probably get all kinds of weird porno ideas."

"I'm sure they will. But that can sell. So...are you in?"

Bet takes a deep swallow and wipes her mouth with her sleeve. "I'll probably regret it, but I'm in."

CHAPTER THIRTY-SIX
INTERVIEW

Score Magazine

DTs

SCORE: WE ARE HERE WITH BARBARA AND ELIZABETH DEENER, generally known as Barb and Bet, the leaders of the DTs. They are—

BARB: Who's we?

BET: Yeah, what's this we? It's just you.

SCORE: I'm representing the whole magazine, so it's sort of the royal 'we.' It makes the reader at home feel like part of the interview.

BARB: Well, that's nice, I guess.

SCORE: We're in the back of a little club in Columbia, Missouri, called the Blue Note. People are looking at us with envy because we are in the presence of two tall, beautiful blondes.

BET: Aw, go on.

SCORE: Your first album is about to come out. How do you feel about that?

[They trade glances.]

BET: It's old hat for Barb. It's exciting for me.

BARB: It's not old hat for me. It never gets old. I'm looking forward to this one being out there more than I have...in a long time.

SCORE: Barb, the new record—and folks, it's titled *Making Music with the DTs*—is obviously going to be compared with Pod.

BARB: [Looking irritated.] I know. But it sounds a lot different.

SCORE: It does indeed. For one thing, I can understand what some of the songs are about. It's less—

BARB: Weird?

SCORE: It's still kind of weird. But it sounds like you're having more fun.

BARB: I am having a LOT more fun.

SCORE: So, you don't miss working with Crash Pavement at all?

BARB: [Looking even more irritated.] I wish Crash well. That's all I'm going to say. I want to talk about the DTs album, not Pod.

SCORE: But being back here in the Blue Note must bring back some memories. This is where Pod got its start.

BARB: I do like being back here.

BET: Can we talk about me for a minute? [Shows a big fake smile]

SCORE: Sorry. What's it like for you to be in the band?

BET: I always thought Barb was having too much fun, so I figured somebody needed to keep an eye on her.

SCORE: It's rumored that you actually don't know how to play the guitar very well.

BET: I can play okay. I'm not as good a natural player as Barb is. But I'm learning.

SCORE: You've played a few live shows in California and New York. How did the crowd react?

BARB: Pretty well. There were a couple of yo-yos yelling for Pod stuff, but for the most part, they seemed willing to give the DTs a chance.

SCORE: I want to ask you about that name. The DTs. Are you making any references here?

BET: You mean, are we saying we're a couple of drunks, Mr. Whole Magazine?

SCORE: Well, the name *is* DTs ...

[They share a long look.]

BARB: Shall we tell him?

BET: Might as well. It's short for Delicious Twins.

SCORE: Not Deener twins?

BET: No. When we were little, somebody saw us and said we were just delicious. We thought they wanted to eat us. Our mother said they were just being nice, and then we thought it was funny.

SCORE: But you're not actually twins.

BET: No, we just look a lot alike.

SCORE: Barb, you're the eldest, right?

BARB: That's not a very nice thing to ask.

BET: Because she is. Two years and four months.

[Laughs. The Deeners have loud laughs. Donkeys would complain about the noise to hear these laughs.]

BARB: But which of us is better looking?

SCORE: You're both tall and blonde. Physically imposing. Striking would be a good word.

BET: Striking?

BARB: That's just another way of saying we have good personalities.

SCORE: We just don't want you to think we're hung up on your good looks.

BET: Apparently, you aren't!

SCORE: Uh, back to the music. Barb, your musical history is well known. Pod's three albums are considered some of the most influential music to come down the pike since the Velvet Underground.

BARB: Whew! I don't know about that. But I read somewhere that everyone who saw us went out and formed their own band.

SCORE: I think you read that in Score.

BARB: Maybe. You didn't say that all those bands went on to outsell us!

SCORE: But they didn't get as much respect.

BARB: You can't eat respect.

SCORE: Anyway, Bet, you're more mysterious to us than your sister. Have you always been interested in music?

BET: I have—we have. We've always sung together since we were little. We even used to make tapes. But I wasn't thinking of it as a career. Like I said, Barb's a better natural musician than I am. She came here, met Crash, and Pod got started. Then they took off and traveled all the time.

BARB: I had always thought it would be fun to get Bet in the band. Then Pod fell apart, and I thought, well, now's the time.

SCORE: We've heard a tape of the album, but we didn't have any liner notes or anything. Do you two share songwriting duties?

BET: No, not really. Barb and Rebecca wrote most of the songs. I haven't tried that yet.

BARB: We all had a hand in it. Rebecca Hannifin is the bass player and wrote five of the twelve songs, and Tom Singer is the drummer.

SCORE: You know Rebecca from Salvation when they used to tour with Pod.

BARB: Right. They haven't broken up. She just had some time available to work with us.

SCORE: And Tom drums for the Bouncer Boys.

BARB: Tom drums for everybody. He is solid.

BET: Although he really should do vocals with a name like that.

BARB: Or change his name to Tom Drums.

SCORE: Speaking of vocals, Barb, you were famous for your voice in your Pod days. That sort of raspy Southern drawl could suddenly sound so sweet, like the voice of an angel. Bet, upon listening to the DTs album, we notice you've got the same voice.

BET: We both smoke too much; that's why we've got that rasp.

BARB: And we're from Southern Missouri, which is why we sound Southern. It's kind of Southern-ish.

BET: And, of course, we're both angels.

[Laughter that could knock satellites out of the sky.]

SCORE: You must have come from a very musical family.

BARB: Ha.

BET: Hardly.

BARB: An anti-musical family, maybe.

SCORE: Anti-musical?

BARB: Oh, not really. It's just that nobody played music.

SCORE: Were you encouraged?

BARB: Not to do this for a living, no. Our parents, particularly our dad, did not think it was a viable career alternative. Still don't, actually.

[Barb flashes an odd look on her face indicating a sore subject, so we decide not to press our luck and to return to safer interview waters.]

SCORE: Who are your musical influences?

BARB: A lot of gospel, actually. That's the stuff we first listened to when we were young.

BET: Not black gospel, not the kind of thing Aretha used to do. White gospel.

SCORE: White gospel?

BARB: Hymns. Baptist church songs. With a band and every-thing, but more of a country sound. That high lonesome thing, almost bluegrass.

SCORE: We thought we detected a whiff or two of country on "Making Music."

BARB: There's more than a whiff. Aside from that, we liked everything from early Stones to the Sex Pistols.

BET: Mostly the Pistols. I'm also influenced by the guy we saw in California riding around on rollerblades and playing a portable electric guitar.

BARB: He *is* pretty good.

BET: I aspire to be that good.

[We have other pithy questions, but a large man who owns the club comes over to say it's time for a sound check, and then the Delicious Twins are to relax until the show. They utter some more laughs and bid us goodbye. "Enjoy the show," Barb says. We do.]

CHAPTER THIRTY-SEVEN

Bet waits in the wings of the Memphis Antenna Club. The whole place stinks of smoke as she sucks down her thirty-second cigarette of the day. Music blasts through the whole building. The band plays, some notes are missed, but the audience doesn't mind. The audience shouts out song requests, most of them for a band that no longer exists. Barb laughs them off. There's a request for something she wrote, and then the band gives it a go. The tempo is a little shaky, and Barb forgets some of the words. Bet can tell when that happens, even though the audience doesn't. Barb's voice gets blurry and imprecise, fuzzy.

Barb looks at Bet and the guitar strapped to her. Bet's heart begins to race. Barb makes a face. She smiles and waves. Bet's heart pounds twice as fast as the drummer's sticks. Barb's outstretched hand flashes in the stage lights. Red, green, then yellow, like some exotic fish.

Bet steps onto the stage, cigarette still between her lips.

"Ladies and gentlemen, if there are any here, I'd like for you to meet my sister," Barb says into the mic.

The crowd roars. A spotlight sweeps across the audience and

reveals the ghouls with their mouths open, and dark eye sockets, shouting for blood. The scary moment passes. The crowd looks from Barb to Bet, from Bet to Barb.

Barb cocks her head and gives her a smile, then faces the crowd again. "Here's another new song," she says, then mouths to Bet, "Monkey Business."

This song starts with a G7 chord. And it's up to Bet to play it. The band watches while Bet picks up the guitar from its stands near Barb, then removes her freshly lit cigarette from her lips and inserts it between the tuning pegs, Keith Richards style. Tom twirls his sticks and waits, his face as impassive as an Aztec carving. Bet turns her back to the audience, moves her fingers for the chord, then turns around. She strums the chord, Tom bashes the cymbal, and Rebecca's bass throbs. Barb could probably play all the guitar parts by herself, but she wrote this little bit just for Bet. Barb sings, her voice clear above the churn. She also plays guitar, and her guitar part is complicated. Bet doesn't have time to ponder this. It takes all her concentration to move her fingers. Tom and Rebecca pump away, steady as a train, and she doesn't want to mess up.

The crowd shouts along. Bet looks sideways at Barb. Barb finishes a verse, throws back her head, and flashes an experienced show smile. The chorus arrives. Tom pounds a backbeat Bet can feel in her chest, Rebecca plays a complicated series of descending notes, and Barb's guitar shimmers like a harp. Bet's part is just a series of flat strums, but she also must sing. *Monkey, monkey, monkey go home.*

It's no "Amazing Grace," but she finds it hard to play and sing at the same time. Her singing veers off-key. She hauls her voice back in line and misses a strum. The song sputters. Tom and Rebecca try to stay in line with her, which throws the whole piece out of whack. Barb notices but laughs. She starts belting out the next verse, Bet gratefully stops trying to do two things at once, and Tom and Rebecca get back on track.

The next couple of songs are more manageable. She only sings or plays, but not both at the same time. The crowd yells and throws their hands in the air.

"We're the DTs," Barb says. "I'm Barb."

The crowd shouts its approval for her being Barb. A couple of people take the opportunity to request Pod songs, but she ignores them.

"This is Tom on the drums."

Modest applause for Tom.

"Rebecca, on bass."

Rebecca folds the top of her body over her guitar, which is almost as tall as she is. She's short and lean, with spiky hair and eyes so big it looks like she stole them out of a bad children's painting. There are lots of shouts and whistles from her own fan base.

"And on rhythm guitar and backing vocals, my sister, Bet Deener."

Despite Bet's mistakes and lack of contribution, she gets the biggest applause. She waves, smiles, and lights a cigarette.

"We are the DTs," Barb says again. "We're working on an album now. Y'all be sure to watch for it."

They file offstage, and before Bet clears the wings, the crowd cheers, and claps for an encore. Rebecca and Tom disappear, heading for the green room and beers. Bet bumps into Barb in the low light. Their guitars clank together.

"I wasn't sure you were coming," Barb says.

There is an orange glow near her face. Bet should have thought to look for the cigarette.

"I wasn't sure I was either. I drove around. Got lost."

The clapping and stomping from the fans make conversation

hard. They stand close together. Their guitars continue to bump, the strings issuing screeching sounds of mild protest.

"You got lost? You're a woman. You're allowed to ask for directions."

Bet pops a cigarette in her mouth. Barb gives her a light. Bet gets a waft of beer, and the pang of thirst rocks her. Earlier in the night, she spent a large part of the evening communing with some marijuana and lost track of time watching cartoons.

"Like I said, I was driving around. I wanted to be here, but I was so afraid."

"Afraid," Barb says. Her voice loses some of its edge. "It's been so long I've forgotten what it's like to be afraid."

"I haven't. But then I thought about it and realized this is my chance. You've done this for me. I had to be here."

Barb sucks down the last puff and tosses the butt on the ground. She stubs it out with a black sneaker. "You gotta think about it, though. If you're in, you've got to be in all the time. No more coming late. No more mishing practices."

Slurring, the first sign that Barb is drinking.

"I won't miss anything. I'm in."

"I'm serious, Bet. This is professional stuff. No fooling around."

"I'm not fooling around. I'm in."

"All right. That's good enough for me. I'm glad."

"Me too."

"Now, let's get some beer and get out there and give 'em a great encore."

They head down the hallway and push through a faded and scuffed door. The green room for this place is not exactly luxurious. There is no telling what color the walls are painted. Decades of posters and flyers cover every inch of space, even the windows. None have been torn down. They've just been pasted over. Hippie bands peek through rips in punk posters. A folding table holds plates of chopped vegetables, which are largely untouched. Bags of chips are strewn around as if bears ravaged the place. Five coolers line the far wall, lids open. The supply of beer is low.

Tom sits propped against the wall, and Rebecca slouches in a folding chair. Bet steps around her to get to a cooler.

"Nice of you to join us," Rebecca says.

"I'm sorry," Bet says.

Barb pushes past, forcing Rebecca to swivel her legs out of the way. She gets two beers and hands one to Bet. Barb pops the top of hers and pours half the beer down her throat.

Barb and Rebecca are dressed as if they are in two different bands. Rebecca wears a crisp green T-shirt, tight black jeans, and pointed black boots. It looks like a uniform, something a new-wave band would wear. Barb's gray T-shirt is flecked with sweat. Her wet hair sticks to her shoulders like twining snakes. She wears loose-fitting jeans. Her face, Bet notes, is more rounded than it used to be. Her chiseled features are beginning to fade under a layer of chub.

"This isn't a job where you can just call in sick," Rebecca says. "You can't just roll in when you feel like it."

"I'm sorry. It won't happen again."

"And it would be helpful if you would actually learn to play," Tom pipes up. "This isn't a training band." He follows the same stylistic muse as Barb, but there's no chub. Countless hours of drumming and sweating have left him as spare as a spider monkey.

"I talked with her about it," Barb says. "It's cool."

A roadie opens the door.

"They're really making a lot of noise out here," he says.

The sound follows him. *Thump thump thump.* A few whistles ride the din.

"We'll be right there," Barb says.

Rebecca stands up, a head shorter than Barb. Like a fierce small dog, she's not limited by her size.

"All due respect, but it's not your call if it's cool or not. This is everyone's band, unless I missed something. If one of us isn't pulling her weight, it hurts all of us."

"It won't happen again," Bet says.

"There's more to it than just that," Tom says. He looks up from his crouch. "You were terrible tonight. My dog could play your parts and do a better job. And he doesn't have opposable thumbs."

"Look, lay off her," Barb snaps. "Give her a fucking break. So, she doesn't play in a dozen bands at once."

"She barely plays in *one* band," Rebecca says. "That's the problem. And it doesn't matter who she is."

"It does matter who she is," Barb says. Her accent comes through like an FM signal on a clear night when she gets mad, and it's clear now. "She is my sister, and *she is* a part of this band."

The club manager sticks his head through the door, eyes darting from one band member to the next. The audience waited for an encore from the cult band. Even super-famous bands like the Stones probably didn't make people wait this long.

"Is there a problem?" he asks. His long, wispy gray hair is matted with nervous sweat.

"No problem." Barb keeps her eyes on Rebecca. "We'll be there."

Rebecca doesn't wait for the manager to leave. "So, you're saying that she can do whatever she wants because she's your sister, flesh and blood of the great Barb Deener? Or make that *not* do whatever she wants? She can blow off practice, contribute nothing to the songwriting, miss most of our debut, and yet she is an equal member of the band?"

Barb tosses her beer at the wall. Suds darken the fading image of the lead singer of the Blow Monkeys peeking through the poster montage. "I told you, I've discussed this with Bet, and things are cool. But, yes, while we're at it, I am saying that whatever she has done up until now, she is a full member of the band. Full. No discussion. Do you get that?"

Rebecca's eyes widened but not in surprise. In anger. Bet looks from one to the other, then to Tom, and he looks away.

"I get it," Rebecca says. "You're the star, Barb. You run the show."

"I don't want you to feel that way," Barb says.

"As of right now, I do."

"I hope to change your mind."

"I hope you change your mind," Rebecca says. "I play in this band because I get enough bullshit in Salvation. I don't need it here. Do you remember what we used to talk about on the bus, Barb?"

"I do."

Rebecca holds her gaze. "I'm not so sure."

The manager pops his head through the door like a cuckoo clock. "Guys, are you—"

"Turn up the house lights," Barb barks. "We're done."

His head pops out again.

"Are you saying I'm acting like Crash?" Barb demands.

"You're acting like Crash *and* Todd."

"Fuck you, Rebecca. Part of what we talked about was giving people a chance and having fun." She waves a finger in Bet's face but keeps her eyes glued to Rebecca. "That's what I'm doing. I'm giving my sister a chance. And you will too. And if you think that means I'm pulling rank here, then fine."

Rebecca turns and stomps out the door leading to the alley. Barb follows, stopping to fetch a beer. Tom unfolds himself from the floor and reaches into the cooler. He gets himself a beer and hands one to Bet. She takes it, even though she has barely touched her first.

"A fucked-up night," he says. "Welcome to rock and roll.

CHAPTER THIRTY-EIGHT

Bet isn't impressed with her first sight of the Netherlands. She slumps in the passenger seat and stares out the window, hungover and jet lagged as the van heads away from Schipol Airport.

"It's flat," she says. "Just like Missouri."

"Missouri?" says Jan, a local heavy metal band member.

Tattoos crawl up and down his arms and the sides of his head, where his mohawk shows them off. He would be cute if he hadn't stuck so much metal through his face, if he didn't have a mohawk, and if he didn't have the tattoos. He would be cute if you could start over again from the neck up. Jan drove the van to pick up the DTs.

"Where we're from," Bet says. "In the middle of nowhere. It's flat, just like this."

"Oh," Jan says, offended. "We have many good museums."

Bet imagines Jan in a museum, quietly studying paintings. His tattoos include tidal waves, dragons, and women with big boobs. She doesn't trust his taste in art.

"Well, you have us beat, then," she says.

The other members of the DTs sprawl across the three back bench seats, asleep. Barb is upright, dead to the world, mouth agape, snorting like a pig. The band is playing the EuropeFest tour with other U.S. groups, but they were invited to play a heavy metal concert in Amsterdam with bands like Jakkyl and Clawface. The show fell during a five-day break, so instead of resting and doing laundry, like the intelligent bands, they hop a jet to Schipol.

Storm delays and one missed connection have them ten hours late. Boredom kept the alcohol flowing at the airport and at thirty-one thousand feet. Bet struggles to keep her eyes open.

"We'll have to go straight to the stadium," Jan says. "I hope that doesn't cause you any trouble with your hotel."

"I'm not sure we have a hotel, we're so late," Bet says miserably.

"Are you feeling okay?" he asks.

"I'm exhausted, and my head hurts really bad. Other than that, I think I'm all right."

Jan drives on in silence for a few minutes. Bet watches the green and flat landscape whiz by. It's well before noon. The DTs aren't a big draw at this festival, so they play early.

"I can give you a little something to pep you up and make you feel better if you like," he says.

"You can? What have you got?"

The chains clink against each other as he digs in his black leather vest. He pulls out a small packet, holds it in front of his face to ensure he's handing over the right one, then slips it to her. White powder.

"I assume this'll do the trick." Jan gives her a smile. "Oh, yes. Only the best. Don't do it now. Wait until we get there, maybe half an hour before you play."

"But my head is hurting now."

"Well, maybe a little bit now."

Bet taps some of the white powder into her palm and inhales.

She snorts a couple of times and wipes her nose. "Thank you, Jan."

"You are quite welcome."

"What do I owe you?"

He waves her offer away. "My pleasure. I'm a fan of the DTs."

She looks at him. "You are?"

"Very much so. I have all your records."

"We only have one."

"I have multiple copies of that one."

Jan is slicker than he looks, she thinks.

"Fair enough. I appreciate it."

"Have you heard my band?" He flashes a smile. "The Wolves of Fate?"

"I have heard of you," Bet lies, then says, "I have not heard you."

"Oh, you will tonight. I was hoping maybe I could give you a copy of our demo tape. We're popular in Amsterdam, but we'd like to expand."

"Oh, okay," Bet says. "That would be cool." He'll have to give her more cocaine before she listens to any band called The Wolves of Fate.

The show is full of kids with hair longer than Bet's, and those are the guys. The opening bands are loud and fast. The audience is in danger of spraining their index fingers and pinkies as they wave them in the air. The DTs have never played a crowd like this, a crowd so hyped.

"Oh, god." Bet peeks at the crowd from the edge of the stage. "We're never going to survive."

She dips into the stash from Jan, a little harder this time. She does it surreptitiously, like she's just wiping her nose. Her head clears. Her nerves settle and she even bobs her head a little bit.

"I've seen worse." Barb walks up to stand at her shoulder. "We could rile 'em up more. We should play nothing but Motley Crue covers."

"We don't know any Motley Crue covers."

"That's true."

"Maybe we should play Pod covers. The faster stuff. They might like that."

Barb looks at her. "I will not play Pod covers. Not even to save my own life."

They laugh, and Barb wanders off in search of beer. Bet feels another presence at her elbow.

"They're going to love you," Jan says.

Bet looks at him. "That's what we were just saying. You have any more of that stuff?"

The DTs songs are slower and quirkier than anything that's fueled the mosh pit, but the exhausted, muddy Dutch head-bangers welcome the break. The DTs play the heaviest songs they have and play them as loud as they can. The few boos get lost in the din. Tom pounds away at the drums. Rebecca points her instrument's neck at the crowd like it's a weapon and she's shooting bass bullets. Barb is at home on a stage in front of any crowd. She flirts with the muddy guys who whip their hands back and forth in the air.

Bet's fingers find the proper places on their own. Barb smiles at her, and the smile lingers in the air and drifts out over the crowd. Bet smiles at the crowd and they smile back. The guitar strings dazzle like little rivulets of fire.

Was it only cocaine in the baggie that Jan gave me? Bet wonders.

The DTs don't push their welcome. Just half an hour after they take the stage, they're done. They play half their album and toss in a Jethro Tull cover. Bet plays along as best she can and even thinks up a couple of good riffs on the spot. Barb nods her appreciation.

"Nice job," Rebecca says as they file offstage. That's the most praise she has ever given Bet.

"Thanks," Bet says, overcome with gratitude for the compliment.

"Yeah, not bad." Barb gives her an impromptu back rub. "Remember how you used to say Def Leppard sucked? But now you're a headbanger after all."

Bet laughs so loud she startles Barb and some of the backstage crew. She feels like she's vibrating, and at any second she'll shake apart.

"Hey, have you guys seen that guy, Jan?" she asks.

"Jan with the van?" Tom says in Schwarzenegger style, *Yon with the von*. "He's over there, talking to that guy with the muscles."

Jan is indeed deep in discussion with a guy who has muscles. The guy looks like he has auxiliary muscles to go with his main muscles, both sets heavily tattooed.

Bet walks over to them. "Hey, Jan," she says.

"Oh, hey."

"I saw your gig," the muscle man says. His voice is high-pitched. "I don't usually like chick bands, but I liked you."

"Thanks," Bet says, barely looking at him. "You got a second?" she asks Jan.

"Sure. Talk to you soon, Gunter."

"All right." Gunter turns to Bet and shakes her hand. "Rock on."

"You know it." She waits, rocking on her heels until Gunter leaves.

"You seem a bit jittery," Jan says.

"I wonder why? Why do you suppose that is?"

Jan shrugs. "Nervous from the show?"

"Nervous from the white. As in cocaine. I'm up too high. I need to come down."

Jan looks around. "Don't talk so loud."

"We're in *Amsterdam*," she says in a sort of whisper.

"So, I'm careful. You want to come down?"

"Yes! I'm driving myself crazy."

"I don't suppose you'd like to get big and ripped." He pretends to flex his muscles. "I could sell you what I've been selling him." He nods back at the muscle man hulking off in the distance, still visible in the crowd, as wide as any two other people.

She shakes her head. "Not what I had in mind."

"I didn't think so." Jan reaches into his pocket. Bet watches his pocket like a hawk eyeing a rabbit hole. "It'll still be free. But I was wondering if you'd be willing to listen to our demo."

Bet realizes the hidden cost of what she's doing. But having to listen to lousy music couldn't be that bad. She's heard bad music before. She wants to relax.

"I got something that can make you relax for sure," he says.

"Let's have it. The demo tape too. I've heard a lot of great music here today, and I'm ready for more," she lies.

Jan flashes a genuine smile, visions of a deal clearly dancing in his head.

Bet smiles back. He's not so bad looking when he smiles. The hand returns from the pocket bearing a small paper packet.

She frowns. "What's this?"

"The good stuff. The stuff all great rock stars use. Keith Richards liked it. Sid Vicious liked it. You're in a great band. You need it."

The packet is heavy in her hand. "Oh, geez."

"What's the problem?"

"I don't know how to use it. I don't have a needle or anything."

"You don't have to have a needle. You just need your nose. You can snort it."

"Really?"

"Really. Or smoke it. Unless you'd rather use a needle."

Ideally, she thinks, *just to do it right. Whoever heard of sniffing heroin? She should do it like the pros.* Richards, Vicious, Lowell George.

"Are there any—I don't know—instructions?"

Jan laughs. "Lather, rinse, repeat. That's all you need to know. And don't hoover it all at once."

"All right. Thanks, Jan."

"Aren't you forgetting something?"

Jan's other hand disappears into another pocket. It reappears with a cassette. He holds it out like a weapon, which Bet figures might be appropriate.

"Oh, right. I'll listen to it."

"It might be good to do them together. The music and the— you know."

"I'm sure that's a good idea."

Jan waves. "Goodbye. Enjoy. My contact information is in the cassette box."

Bet waves back. She turns and looks for her fellow DTs. They are all gone. Barb is in search of beer. Tom checks a spreadsheet to see when he's supposed to play with one of his other bands. Rebecca jams out to the music. The noise in the venue is like thunder. Barb smoked pot, but Bet wasn't sure how her sister would feel about the real hard stuff.

Bet decides this is exploration she should try on her own. They have guards on the important things here, the bathrooms and the free beer. The concertgoers make do with porta johns and plastic cups, but in the sprawling backstage area it's all glass bottles and real restrooms.

Bet finds a backstage bathroom and shows her plastic pass. She locks herself in and unwraps the package. It's tiny. Just some brown powder. She shakes some into her palm and snorts it before she changes her mind.

She sits still for a few minutes. The buzz of the universe, the constant awareness, movement, and life just beyond the senses, shuts off. Bet floats in a sea of calm. An angel floating outside heaven. The mad scramble of life on Earth is an abstract concept, something to study with dispassion. It takes thirty-seven minutes to blink an eye. She's encased in glass. Her skin is a concrete barrier against the world, a buffer against the universe.

She throws up and hangs onto the wall. Someone far away bangs on the door, maybe the guard, a nice young man with yellow teeth and a shaved head. But the guard doesn't exist, the door doesn't exist, the bathroom doesn't exist. The entire universe fits in the palm of her hand. One sneeze could destroy it all. She looks at the tiny packet in her hand and knows it won't be enough. She wonders if Jan plans to give them a ride back to the airport.

CHAPTER THIRTY-NINE

ALBUM REVIEWS

Breather

The DTs

AFTER YEARS OF LISTENING TO POD'S THREE GROUNDBREAKING ALBUMS, taking in last year's "Making Music with the DTs" felt like knocking back a couple of shots of whiskey after eating three pints of ice cream. Pod, for all its musical adventurism, essentially was art-rock weirdness reborn for a crowd too young to remember the original Pink Floyd or Genesis. After making her famous break with Pod and its charismatic/psycho lead singer Crash Pavement, guitarist Barb Deener seemed hellbent on going in a different direction. The DTs' sound was leaner and meaner but also looser.

Pod, for all its singing about UFOs and inflatable love dolls, put out carefully crafted albums with few sounds or snorts out of place. Rock and roll hasn't always been carefully crafted, and Deener obviously is a student of such famous slap-dashers as Crazy Horse and the Replacements. She dispensed with the sci-fi and went for the gut on songs like "Ebenezer," about an old man's regrets about not spending enough time with his family, a song as angry and lyrical as a Dylan Thomas poem. Rebecca Hannifin, one of the stars of the far more conventional Salvation, nearly matched her song for song, particularly with "Walking Your Ghost," about a dog park romance gone bad. The DTs were a breath of fresh air. Dropping the needle on the record—and even with the domination of slick and soulless CDs, that remains the proper way to hear this music—was like wandering into an unfamiliar bar only to encounter long-lost friends.

All of this is just a prologue to the sad news that must be delivered. "Breather," the not-long-awaited follow-up to "Making Music," is a disappointment, and suggests the band should have taken a longer one. All the things that made the DTs' first album so enjoyable have been taken to excess on the sequel. The band is sloppier. Bet Deener was notorious for her inability to play guitar when she joined her sister's band, but what was goofily endearing then has become tiresome.

The younger Deener demonstrated a near-genius ability to craft simple guitar loops on "Making Music," but she just apes them on "Breather." She hasn't spent the intervening touring and recording period honing her chops, and her acknowledged drug use hasn't helped. If anything, she has actually lost ground as a guitarist. The overall band's general sloppiness has become downright slovenly: there are pauses, noises and laughter between songs and even in songs. That can work once in a while, but on this record it sounds like the band checked themselves into a studio with a couple of cases of beer and just fooled around for a while, managing to accidentally record an album in the process.

Worse still is the loss of "Making Music's" emotional core. The third track, "Again Next Time," comes close. It's about reincarnation, but reincarnation as a way to get a second chance with a loved one who is gone, and it alone would be worthy of inclusion on the band's debut disc. On the rest of "Breather," the band showcases its versatility. Hannifin has earned her own place as an innovative bass guitarist, and Tom Singer's metronome-like drums anchor and uplift some of the best bands playing today. When they take on reggae, as they do on "Still Smokin," and country, as they do on "One Last Mile," the DTs are as technically proficient as any musicians anywhere (with the noted exception of Bet Deener, the Sid Vicious of the band). What's missing is the heart. Hannifin only contributed three songs to this disc, none quite as good as any of the ones she chipped in for the first effort. Barb Deener carried most of the songwriting burden and just wasn't up to the task or didn't care. "Breather" may be breathing, but it doesn't show signs of life.

"Is that the worst fucking review of an album you ever read in your life, or what? Jesus, they loved us last year." Barb tosses the "Rolling Stone" on the table and it slides into the two chili dogs she got at the 7-11 along with half a case of Pabst Blue Ribbon. "I mean, we barely missed getting on the cover last year. Now they say we're crap. Worse than crap. We're shit. I'm lazy, and—"

"And I'm incompetent." Bet cracks open one of the brews. "Isn't that great? They at least think you have talent."

"You have talent," Barb says soothingly.

"Whatever," Bet says. "Just don't let Rebecca see that."

"Let Rebecca see what?" Rebecca says as she enters with perfect comic timing.

The green room at Slick's, a club in Birmingham, is smaller than the clubs they played last year. The heat keeps them inside, avoiding the feast of visual wonders of central Alabama, while they wait the couple of hours before showtime.

"Nothing." Barb hides the magazine.

Cough it up. What is it, a bad horoscope?"

Barb hands over the magazine, avoiding Bet's gaze.

Rebecca flips through it. "This thing about college radio?—Oh, no, I see. The review." Rebecca moves her lips as she reads, and she isn't a fast reader. The Deener sisters wait in strained silence as Rebecca slogs her way through the article. "Brilliant." She throws the magazine on the floor.

"Hey, I *bought* that," Bet complains.

"You should have stolen it," Rebecca says. "I don't know if you noticed, but your crappy playing was singled out as one reason our second album sucks." She glares at Bet, hands on hips.

Bet abandons the magazine, letting the floor's mixture of beer, gum and unidentified particles claim it, and glares right back. "I can't help it if they don't get what I'm doing," Bet practically spits at her. "They didn't exactly love your songs. And they called you and Tom 'technically proficient.' You know what that means? Boring!"

"Who's boring?" Tom asks as he walks into the room.

"We are." Rebecca reaches down, and with Hulk-like strength, liberates the magazine from the goo, and hands it to him. "And Bet is incompetent, and Barb is lazy. And our new album sucks."

Tom skims the article, holding the filthy magazine by the edges. Mercifully he reads fast and doesn't move his lips to do so. "Sid Vicious," he says with a faint chuckle. "Two stars." He drops the magazine. "That's terrible. That's the same as Belinda Carlisle's solo album."

"Well, the article makes it pretty clear who the leaders of the band are, since we barely rate a mention," Rebecca says. "So, if the album sucks, we know who has to fix the problem."

Barb stands up fast, the metal legs of her chair shriek in protest against the concrete floor.

"Fuck you, Rebecca. You were in the recording studio the whole time. You knew what we were doing, and you said it was good."

"I know that I had ways to make it better, too. And you ignored most of my suggestions. You're as bad as Crash. All that stuff you said about us really working together as a band is bullshit. This is a solo project. For you."

"It is *not*," Barb says.

"It is *not*," Bet echoes. "I'm in the band, too, in case you didn't notice."

"I *barely* noticed," Rebecca says. "You've never fucking around when we rehearse and you're barely around when we record. When you are around, half the time you're fucked up on something. They didn't call you Sid Vicious for nothing."

"You have no right to say that," Barb says. "I don't know if you've noticed, but the crowd loves her. They're not looking at you. They're looking at her."

"They're looking at her because they can't believe what a shitty guitar player she is," Rebecca snarls. "They're looking at her because she's a minor rock star with no talent. She's a freak."

Before Rebecca can flinch, Bet smacks her hard across the face with her right hand, which is still holding a half-full can of beer. Foam flies and Rebecca lurches backward and trips over a cooler. She releases a howl of anger and frustration and pain.

"Knock it off." Tom jumps between Bet and the prone Rebecca.

Bet backs away, hands to mouth, shocked at what she's done.

Tom and Barb lean over Rebecca. Blood from her nose and tears have joined the beer foam froth on the floor, and she pulls herself through the muck like a wounded soldier. She lets out another deep groan.

"Are you hurt?" Tom asks.

"My shoulder." She gets the words out between muffled sobs. "I think I dislocated my shoulder." Rebecca's left arm juts out at an odd angle.

"Can you move it?" Barb asks.

Rebecca wiggles her fingers. "Yes. Oh. But it hurts."

"It doesn't mean anything if she can move her fingers," Tom says sharply. "We've got to get her shoulder back in its socket."

"Does—does anybody know how to do that?" Barb asks.

"I saw it in a movie once," Tom says.

Rebecca shakes her head. A door opens on the other side of the room. The sound guy, Jack, sticks his shaggy head through and does a left to right sweep before he spots them. His bush of hair rides atop his tattooed head and falls over his eyes..

"You guys okay?" Jack asks.

"We may need an ambulance," Tom says.

"No," Rebecca says.

Jack brushes his hair aside. "Oh, shit! What happened?"

Rebecca eases up and sits, her hurt good arm holding her up in the sitting position for support. "I don't need an ambulance. Just take me to a doctor somewhere so he can pop it back in."

"But, Jeez, can you still play?" Barb asks.

"I don't know." Rebecca stares at the floor. Her nose stopped bleeding but sweat drips down her face. "I can move my fingers."

"I doubt you can play," Tom says. "But if we go now, we can get back in time, and maybe you can play. We're always late going on anyway." He turns toward Jack. "Where's the nearest place?"

An hour later, a doctor rolls Rebecca down a corridor in a wheelchair, her left arm crooked into a bright red sling.

"They gave me Demerol," Rebecca says to no one in particular, her glassy eyes revealing that her pain is but a distant memory. The sentence comes out at half her usual speed. "And liquid Valium. He in-jected it."

"We had a time getting her arm back in place," the doctor says, following with a nervous chuckle at Rebecca's announcement.

"He put me on the floor and stood on my shoulder," Rebecca says, as if recounting an amusing event from a first date. "The Demerol just made my eyeballs heavy."

"Ummm, yes," the doctor says. "I've given her a prescription for some painkillers for later. There's an all-night drugstore just down the street."

"This is going to sound like an odd question," Tom asks, "but is there any chance she'll be able to stand up on stage in about half an hour and play bass in our band?"

The doctor issues a sharp little laugh. "I doubt she'll be able to watch TV in half an hour."

Bet grabs the prescription and sneaks a quick look. *Percocet. Not bad.*

Back in the hotel, she gives an exaggerated yawn, hoping to encourage Barb to turn off the TV and go back to her own room. Barb doesn't take the hint.

The Percocet makes Bet sleepy and antsy at the same time. The world is a little bit removed, which is all right with her. It's not heroin but it's all right.

"Bet, did you get some of Rebecca's drugs?" Barb demands.

"What? No!"

You picked up the prescription at the pharmacy. It was open when you handed it to Tom."

"So? It must have just ripped in transit."

"If I go next door and count what's in the bottle, will it match what's on the label?"

Bet assembles her face into what she hopes will pass for a face of outrage. "Of course it will. Unless Rebecca took some. What are you going to do, pump her stomach?"

"You know she won't take drugs."

"She looked pretty drugged up to me."

"And tomorrow she won't even take an aspirin. Bet, I think you need help. You drink too much. You take too many drugs."

She rests her hand on Bet's knee. For just a second, an electric jolt shoots through Bet's spine. Her fingers tingle as it dissipates. The hand-on-the-knee move is exactly the gesture their mother used to make.

"I don't want you to be the *real* Sid Vicious in this band," she says. She looks into Bet's eyes, but Bet keeps them moving, sliding out of reach. "You know what happened to Sid Vicious."

"He was a junkie," Bet says. Her voice is a little happier than she intended. "I'm not a junkie."

"Aren't you? Junkies steal drugs from their friends."

"Fuck you. Get out of my room."

Now the outrage is becoming real. Barb is bringing her down. *Harshing my mellow.*

Barb shakes her head. "No. I won't. I'm going to stay here tonight. Bet, you tried to kill yourself once and I didn't know about it. I'll be damned if I'll let you succeed right under my nose."

"Oh, please. Like you care."

Barb tenses up and balls, then unballs, her fist. "I do care, even if you don't. I'm telling you, you won't do this on my watch."

"You didn't even stick up for me tonight." Tears well up behind Bet's eyes, peeking around the anger, and she doesn't want them, doesn't want to seem weak.

Barb frowns. "What do you mean?"

"Rebecca and Tom were saying I'm not any good. No talent. Sid Vicious. You" –

the tears make their way to the front but she chokes them down—"you didn't say I was any good. You just said people come to see me. Like Rebecca said, because I'm a freak."

"Oh, please," Barb snorts. "I didn't say that. I said you had talent."

"But you didn't mean it."

They glare at each other for a long while. Bet defeats the tears, slays them, throws their skeletons away.

"Well, Bet, maybe Rebecca's words hurt you because you know they're true."

"See? You don't defend me."

"And you don't show up for practice, like she said. You don't help write songs. You haven't learned to play hardly anything beyond what I've taught you."

"I wrote the riff for 'Hold On,' and that's the only thing about that song anyone remembers."

"That's bullshit. You wrote a catchy riff that a dog could play. The song would be fine without it."

"Get out of here."

"I'm not going, I told you."

"Then I'll go to your room."

Bet rises from the bed and Barb rises to intercept her. Bet stomps for the door but Barb is there, leaning forward like a linebacker.

"Are you going to take me on?" Barb asks, her face a mask of anger and irritation, all bloodshot eyes, and yellow teeth. "Are you going to dislocate my shoulder like you did Rebecca's?"

Being face to face with her angry sister makes her realize again that they are both large women. Evenly matched. If they fight, it won't be pleasant. If they fight, someone is going to call the front desk. If someone calls the front desk, they might call the police. They might find a small bag of pot. They might find half an ounce of cocaine. They might find trace amounts of heroin. They might make an already bad day much worse.

"No," Bet says. She looks at the floor, a primitive show of deference. "I'm not going to dislocate your arm."

"Not that you could," Barb whispers.

"I'm going to go to bed," Bet says. "And get some sleep. And get up early tomorrow and practice."

"And you're not going to take anymore drugs either," Barb says. "You just leave your bags alone."

CHAPTER FORTY

"Holy cow, look at that line," Barb says. "I didn't think Crash would pull that many people. Do you think it'll be sold out?"

"That's the line for the bathroom," Bet says. "The club's upstairs."

They pass a line of surly, smoking young men waiting for the bathroom as they head up the stairs. They pay fourteen dollars per ticket. They're wearing their hair tucked into blue floppy hats as a disguise, but the goateed guy that hands them the paper stubs doesn't look up.

"Were we ever this young?" Bet asks.

"You still are," Barb replies.

"I don't feel like it. You can hear my knees popping."

The opening band has come and gone. The upstairs concert area is a big open room with a bar on each side, and there's plenty of room in the back.

Barb heads for the bar and comes back with a beer in each hand. The club is stuffed with smoking, inattentive kids. Barb and Bet smoke too. If they are ever to be recognized anywhere, it's in a club like this, but there's no danger of that happening.

Barb pours about a quarter of her beer down her throat. Bet takes a slug of hers. She mellowed out on something stronger, courtesy of an extra-long bathroom stay in the hotel before they came to the club. Barb still doesn't know.

Roadies appear on the stage like dung beetles, rolling away the opening band's instruments. The crowd unleashes a few hoots of excitement. The roadies reappear with Crash Pavement's instruments, and Barb recognizes his favorite guitar.

"How many people are in his band?" Bet asks.

"Three or four. He used to have some guy who projected slides behind the stage, but I read that he's stopped that now."

Three guys walk out onstage. Two are clad in thrift-store suits, but one, the drummer, wears only shorts and a T-shirt.

"They're just kids," Bet says.

"Right. Easy to push around. They won't push back."

The lights dim, and the kids in the audience shout and suck on their cigarettes with greater fury.

"And now the man of the hour, the man of any hour," an announcer says from somewhere, the voice echoing around like a bat in the rafters. "Crash Pavement!"

The cigarettes arc to Earth like falling stars as the kids put them out to cheer and clap their hands over their heads. Crash lurches in from stage right, hunched over like Quasimodo. He grabs the microphone like he's hanging on, and the band tears into the first song. It's loud, fast, and unfamiliar, but the crowd dances along. Bet dances listlessly in place, but Barb doesn't move. It sounds like a Pod song without her vocals, only not as good. The song ends. Crash doesn't thank the audience and doesn't even seem to see them.

The second song is "In the Mix." The crowd takes a second to recognize it, then the club erupts in cheers.

"A Pod song?" Bet asks, and Barb nods confirmation. "The second song is a Pod song? That fucking loser."

Crash's solo album, recorded with a group of studio musicians he dubbed the Ikons, hit the alternative charts but didn't clutch the bottom rung for long. Rolling Stone gave it two stars and said it sounded too much like Pod and lacked Barb Deener's sugary vocals to offset Crash's trademark screech. Barb agreed with that assessment and, hearing the song now, agrees with it still.

However, Crash knows how to keep the crowd going. Up, down, up, down, excitement, calm, excitement, calm. It reminds her of Pod's first show in England almost a decade ago. The bad thing for Crash and the Ikons is the downs come when the band plays original songs from the solo album. The ups come when they play Pod songs, which means Crash is cheating. Almost every other song is a Pod tune, with the bass player singing falsetto in Barb's place. It's not the same, Barb thinks, but the crowd cheers with gusto.

She watches Crash closely. He still does his twitching dance. He does everything he used to do, but with less energy. In between songs, he clutches the microphone stand for support. His hair is a little thinner, too, and his stomach a little bigger. He evens has a bit of a tan, but it's hard to tell under the green and red lights.

Brash, arrogant Crash, the phony mad Russian. Barb never thought she'd feel sorry for him. But she feels sorry for anything trapped in a cage, and Crash is trapped in a cage of his persona, the cage of himself.

"I don't like them," Bet says after a while.

"Yeah, let's go," Barb says. "I'm kind of tired, anyway. Let's go see if there's something good on TV."

CHAPTER FORTY-ONE

ANTS EAT BET'S FLESH. TINY BITES ARE EVERYWHERE. THEY NIP AND PULL without mercy. Her stomach is full of cement that threatens to force its way up her throat. Some of it has already succeeded. Chunks are evidence on her cheek. She's lying in the chunks on a cold floor, resting in Hell, unable to move. One hand is tucked underneath her like the broken wing of a baby bird that's been pushed out of the nest. The other is a splayed starfish pushing against a chilly, smooth surface. Hell is a small, dark place with bad music playing far away. Now and then, other tormented souls try to invade her personal corner of Hell. Something pushes against her foot. A door? Cries of disgust sound off when she doesn't respond or move. Then they go away. At one point, long ago, her eyes were open. The place was green, and she recalls a toilet and a sink. She remembers trying to get to the toilet, but she didn't make it.

If I open my eyes the light will tear through my lids and try to rip out my brain, shred it into tiny pieces, she thinks. *If I move, the remaining cement in my stomach, a supersized McDonald's No. 1 combo meal with extra salty fries, will attack again.*

It tasted good going down but was painful on the return journey.

She would like to move. She would like to get up and straighten her jeans and walk back into the club. She would like to smile at the people and see them smile back. They are so young, with young faces. No experience rests upon their brows to cause wrinkles, no laugh lines are etched at the corners of their mouths. Their smiles are open and unforced, even on the smooth faces of the ones with metal studs through their cheeks or tongues, even on the ones with cigarettes permanently perched on their thin lower lips.

A nice cool glass of water would do worlds of wonder for her. But then again, she's in Hell. The Bible story of the man who lifted up his eyes in torment and asked for but a single drop of water to cool his tongue had the right idea. With a glass of water to drink maybe she could get up and go into the club, smile, and get another glass of water. Then she would be ready.

The band is supposed to play, but she can't move. She doesn't play all that well even at the best of times, but at least usually she can move, which helps. Maybe she can pull through this and pull herself off the floor. It won't matter if she looks a little ragged, she's in a rock band. She's not doing her job if she doesn't look a little ragged.

The song playing leaks in from the other room. It's the bumper music between bands, pumped out over the loudspeaker. This club likes to play bad songs from the Seventies between acts to show the kiddies how fortunate they are to be able to listen to good music. Typically Bet hates it, but it's the music of the angels. It's a love song of a man on the road who misses his woman at home. She would cry if it wouldn't hurt. So she listens to the wan, distant sound of the song and wishes she could get up, brush herself off and walk into the club.

I'm going to lie here on the floor just a bit longer, no more than an hour, then I'll get up and brush myself off and put on a good show. I'll drink a lot of water because I'm very thirsty. Maybe take up jogging, start eating right. I'll feel great and look great.

The audience will eat it up. But she'll do it for herself, not for the fans.

God, that song is so sad. Why didn't I ever like that song before? It's beautiful. It's a masterpiece.

Bet falls asleep for a while, not that she notices. There isn't a big change between sleeping and waking. An angel comes to visit her, an angel in black, with bright blonde hair. She squints at it but then the light tears under her eyelids and starts ripping up her brain, just as she feared, so she shuts her eyes again. The visitor isn't an angel of mercy. The angel hits her with the door a few times and calls her some names she doesn't think angels are allowed to use.

"Look at you," the angel says. "Is this what you want? Is this rock and roll to you?"

The angel speaks with the voice of Barb Deener, which means it is no angel at all. "Get up," Barb orders. "Goddamnit, we're supposed to be on stage in half an hour. You're hogging up the bathroom. All the girls are going into the boy's bathroom."

Bet does not, and cannot, move.

"Bet, this is such bullshit. You are the most irresponsible person I have ever seen. We are supposed to play, what you get paid for, and you are fucking passed out in the bathroom. High school ended a few years ago, honey."

A witty reply hovers just on the edge of Bet's consciousness.

"And now you need to get the fuck up. You're going to sleep in the fucking bus, and we're going to play."

Barb hooks her hands under Bet's armpits and heaves.

"No," Bet protests, but it's too late.

Her supersized No. 1 combo meal with extra salty fries, or what's left of it, makes for the exit.

"God DAMN it!" Barb shouts. "Give me some fucking warning, will you? Are you okay?"

Bet spits and heaves. Her throat feels like she's been gargling Drano. For some reason, she nods that she's okay.

"We're going to have to pay for the cleanup," Barb mutters. "We're going to have to shell out to clean up the bathroom in a dive! I hope you're happy."

A crushing wave of guilt and nausea overcomes Bet. "I'm sorry," she says, barely able to form the words. Her voice warbles all over the place. "I'm sorry." Her chest rocks with sobs. She covers her eyes with her cold, wet, and sticky arm. "I'm so sorry."

"All right, all right, you're sorry. You're going to be real sorry tomorrow. Now, come on. Do you think you can walk?"

Bet can't convey to her sister how sorry she is. She wants Barb to understand. She regrets her selfish actions and is turning over a new leaf.

"I'm sorry, Barb." Her sister's name comes out as "Bob."

"It's all right, honey, it's all right. You can be sorry later. I just need you to walk with me now, all right? Can you do that?"

Barb steers Bet toward the door. Bet extends her hand and touches the wall to steady herself. Barb pushes the door and they step outside. A small crowd stands by the door, lined up for the men's room next door.

"Sorry," Barb says. "Those double shots are worth every penny."

A couple of people chuckle. Bet keeps her head down. Her hair hangs in front of her face, sticks to her face. A couple of the women head for the now open bathroom, only to recoil in horror once they look inside.

"We'll get someone to clean it up," Barb says over her shoulder as she hustles Bet along.

Bet shuffles and stumbles like a zombie. Rebecca and Tom stand near the door. Rebecca's expression is close to the looks from the women who tried to get into the bathroom, only her expression is angrier and more disgusted. Tom looks amused. Bet is not sure which is worse.

"Don't worry about us," Rebecca says as Bet shambles by. "We'll do all the work."

"Shut up," Barb says. "Later."

"There may not be much of a later at the rate she's going."

"You shuddup," Bet retorts.

Five days later, Bet sits in the sterile lobby of a residential treatment facility, clutching a battered pamphlet explaining the Twelve Steps. The facility is in the burbs of St. Louis, four hundred miles and a state of mind away from her close encounter with a filthy bathroom floor.

"Ms. Deener?"

A thin, young man walks out of a back hallway and extends a hand. He wears khakis and a blue shirt, both pressed. His hair is conservative, short and moussed into place. He has a pleasant smile and is pale. He's carrying a manila folder in one hand. Bet is bored just looking at him. She can't imagine him ever tossing back anything harder than a wine cooler.

"Nick Drake. It's nice to meet you. All your things are here. Come on back, I'll show you around."

Bet has read the pamphlet about sixty times. She believes in God, despite all evidence to the contrary, so she figures she's well on her way to recovery. She's willing to turn her life over to a higher power. Most of the time.

The DTs had a serious meeting two days after what she likes to think of as her "incident" at the club. She was in no condition to meet the next day, which forced the band to play without her again. They have already replaced her with a friend of Rebecca's. The DTs press ahead.

"You're not fired," Barb assured her, words that still ring in her head as she follows Nick down the hall. "But you have to get better. In all senses of the word."

She had to create a list of her shortcomings for the clinic. That's not what they called it but it's how she thinks of it. In the past six months, she has passed out or blacked out six times, the most spectacular also being the most recent. She consumed five beers a day, most days. She snorted heroin sixty-eight times and cocaine seventeen times. Heroin was the big winner, as she doesn't like things that wake her up.

She hears an odd tinkling sound as they walk down the hall. It calls to mind a memory she wishes had perished, but which sticks in her mind. Nick is talking, pointing at various attributes of the facility, but she's not listening, she's remembering.

She had sex with a roadie who gave her some heroin. He wasn't a bad-looking guy, a little scruffy. They started talking and the subject of drugs came up, as it often did, and an hour later Bet was hunched over the railing outside one of the entrances to the football stadium while he pounded away at her from behind. She remembers the tinkling sound her necklace made as it clinked on the railing, and the ragged sounds of his breath. She doesn't remember his name. They never kissed. She is only grateful he gave her the dope first.

Bet keeps her list folded in her Twelve Steps pamphlet and touches it as she follows Nick. She wonders if he has a copy in his little manila envelope. It's not too bad, she thinks. She's in a rock band, for god's sake. She didn't shoot heroin or do it every day. She isn't Sid Vicious, no matter what Rolling Stone said.

Someone sent her father the Spin brief about her passing out in the club. Sent it anonymously, with the relevant portions underlined so he couldn't miss the news. They wrote in the margin, in a crabbed hand that had pushed down so hard it smeared blue ink across the gossip: *"You must be so proud."*

CHAPTER FORTY-TWO

"This is kind of what I pictured this would be like," Bet says.

She sits on the grass outside the Breyer Program lawn, holding a well-worn acoustic guitar. Next to her sits Dwight, a drug addict and alcoholic with a squat torso and stubby little fingers. He's not bad looking, with his sheaf of unruly blonde hair and lopsided smile. And his stubby little fingers can play anything with strings.

"What, sitting outside on a nice green lawn, playing an acoustic guitar and singing folk songs?" he says.

"Yep. Just like that."

"And, instead, they make you come to group therapy and spill your guts out and cook and clean and not drink and not do drugs," Dwight says, smile firmly in place.

"That's right."

"And it's only now that you're able to come outside and enjoy a sunny day with a remarkably handsome young man, to receive your first guitar lesson."

Bet smiles too. It's the kind of blue day that would make a serial killer relax and enjoy nature. "Most of what you say is true."

"Surely, you don't question the part about the remarkably

handsome young man?" He feigns a hurt look. Bet is betting it's the look he's employed dozens of times to try to cadge drugs from hard-hearted dealers when he was out of money.

"Of course, not that part. The part about it being my first guitar lesson. I'm a professional rock and roll musician, I will have you know."

"Not from what I hear."

She takes a mock swing at him with the guitar.

"Hey! Watch out!" He caresses the guitar. "It's not much to look at but it plays well. I've hocked nearly everything I've ever owned, but I never sold that guitar. I've laid on the floor for two days sweating and shivering and touching that guitar, but it never occurred to me for a minute to sell it."

Bet nestles the guitar back in her lap, sorry she took the risk of damaging it.

"Actually, I've heard your stuff. You've got good tones. You really bite down on a string sometimes, and not everybody does that. You know how to get a clean sound when you want it. You just lack—some of the basics."

Bet gives the guitar a gentle strum. "Dwight, I lack virtually *all* the basics. I've only learned what I needed to know to be able to contribute some identifiable sounds to my sister's songs. And what I would be able to play drunk or stoned. The average tuna fish commercial has more musicality than anything I've done."

Two weeks ago, she would never have been able to admit that. The clinic—the facility—has been painful. She hates going spelunking in her emotions, but Breyer made her. She came in as a rock star with the usual rock star baggage. Now, she's a young woman from a small town with a drug and alcohol problem. She's a woman first. The rock star thing is way down the list, well after sister and daughter and human being. It's a job.

It's a job that gives her many temptations and many excuses. It's also an opportunity. And she sometimes blames Barb for things, but she also realizes it's a job Barb gave her and Barb can take away. Sitting on the lawn under the blue sky, with Dwight's battered wooden and metal soul in her hands, she knows she very much does not want that to happen. She was given an opportunity before. Now she must earn it.

"You know a few chords," Dwight says. "Your fingers go right to them. I can tell."

She strums an A, then a G. "Yeah, I know a few."

"But you don't really *feel* them. You know them in your head but not in your heart."

"Yeah, I know."

Rebecca used to say similar things, and Rebecca was right. Rebecca is a prissy little snot, but she is right about that. Barb would say the same thing. Barb feels the chords. Anything with strings speaks to her. She can play a guitar as easily as she can whistle. To Bet, a guitar is a machine. She doesn't feel it. She's a little afraid of it.

"You feel that way because you don't really speak the language," Dwight says.

"Oh, all that sheet music just blinds me," Bet says. "I see those little black squiggles and they just look like sperm or something."

Dwight looks at her in amazement and she laughs.

"Well, I knew rock and roll was sexy, but I guess I never understood why," he says. "No, I don't mean you have to learn to read music. Paul McCartney doesn't know how to read music, and he did all right. I mean, you just need to understand every sound the guitar neck can perform. Know where they are. And you need to know the names of the chords."

"I know some of them."

"E6."

"What?" She frowns.

"E6. Play it. Right now."

"Um," she says, as her fingers claw their way across the strings.

Dwight makes a honking sound. "Too slow. You fail. We hire another guitar player."

"But that's like reading music!" Bet protests.

"No, it's not. Looking at those little sperm on paper is reading music. Being able to know how to play a chord, any chord, instantly, is what you need to do. Paul McCartney can't read music, but I guarantee you if you shouted out 'E6,' he'd be able to play it without thinking about it."

"But he plays bass."

"He plays guitar too."

"But he's a—"

"He's a what?" Dwight cuts in.

"He's a professional musician."

"I thought *you* were a professional musician. You told me you were, just a few minutes ago."

She pushes the guitar neck down and looks across the green expanse of lawn that flows down to a dilapidated brick fence. "I'm not, though. I'm just the kid sister of a girl in a rock band, and she gave me a job, and I fucked things up and now I'm here." She bites her lower lip to keep it from trembling.

"Hey. Look at me. You know what I am, Bet? I'm a very talented musician. I know enough about music to know that for sure. I used to play sessions in Nashville and L.A. and now I'm sitting here right next to you on this grass and I'm here for the same reason you're here. I can guarantee you that nobody I used to work for will hire me again. I'm too unreliable. I stole stuff from a studio where I was working once in L.A., got several guitars and amps, sold them for drugs. You want to see somebody who fucked stuff up, you look right here at me."

Bet does. She looks into the eyes of a man who knows himself.

"You've got a chance," he says. "You're still in the band, right?"

Bet remembers the disgusted look Rebecca gave her when she announced she was going to dry out. Tom's face was harder to read, but he probably was just calculating which of his other bands he was scheduled to practice with. If she was going to get back in the band, it was her sister who was going to have to let her.

"I think so."

"So, what you need to do is show them you're good enough. You're not good enough now. You know that."

His words don't even sting. They're just true.

She nods. "I know."

"You won't be here much longer. If you like, I can teach you. Maybe two or three times a week. I know in the program here they don't want us forming attachments, but this would be a professional thing. I can play, Bet, you know that."

He can play, that's for sure. She heard him playing Spanish classical guitar, then segueing into "La Bomba." He can play better with one hand than she can play with two.

"I think that would be good," Bet says.

She won't have much time to prove her worth to the DTs. Dwight is here now, ready to go. If she were more religious, she might think it's a sign from God.

"Just one thing," Dwight says. "Don't tell me where you live."

"What? Why not?"

"Just don't. I don't want to know. I don't even want to know the town. We can meet in St. Louis three times a week. Can you do that? Can you get to St. Louis three times a week?"

"I—I think so." Her Toyota should be able to trundle that far.

"Good. Five hundred a week sound fair?"

"Five hundred?"

"Does that not sound fair? Five hundred for three sessions a week, maybe a couple of hours per? And some homework assignments?"

Bet has no basis for comparison. Barb never shelled out a nickel for lessons, unless you count her Mel Bay songbook, and Bet gave her that for Christmas. But then that's the whole point—Barb didn't need them. And here is good old booze-and-drug-addled Dwight, sent here by God to teach her how to play guitar. It's probably the only thing that's keeping him alive, fulfilling his divine purpose.

"All right." She nods. "Five hundred a week."

She is a rock star, of sorts, and rock stars have money, at least part of the time. Barb has spent most of hers on a North Carolina beach house and a condo in St. Louis. Bet has spent most of hers on drugs and on the Breyer Program, so she can sit on this grassy hill next to Dwight and learn to play guitar. She looked at several new cars, but now she'll buy musical ability instead.

"First lesson free." Dwight extends an arm to show how magnanimous he was being.

"First one's always free," she says.

CHAPTER FORTY-THREE

"You should put a revolving door here," Bet says.

Her father laughs. "Feeling some *déjà vu*, are you?"

"A little."

He grabs another box from the car and carries it into the house. It is something he has done before.

"I just feel a little odd coming back. Again. But thanks for letting me," she says.

"I don't mind at all."

This is the easiest move she's ever made. She shipped most of her stuff before she went to the Breyer Program, so all that's left are the clothes and books from the program. She is *reading* the books.

She feels like a yo-yo. This is the third time she's moved back into her parent's house. She moved back after she failed to kill herself, and then again after her mother died. Twice because of her own weaknesses and once because of someone else's. Barb left and never came back or never came back for long. Bet used to envy that.

"Place looks pretty good," she says, bobbing her head slowly as she surveys the living room.

"Thanks, if you're serious," her father says.

"It does, it looks nice."

"What were you expecting, a frat house?"

The house welcomes her like the old shoe it always was, although her father doesn't quite maintain her mother's fanatical level of cleanliness. But no deer heads have sprung from the walls, no beer can pyramids erupt from the tables, no moldy pizza boxes come to life on the carpet.

He made some improvements. The National Geographics that ate an entire bookshelf were gone. Her mother liked them, and he would leaf through them now and then, and Bet figures he couldn't dispose of them completely. They are probably in storage. He has also moved the host of ceramic figurines that dotted the tables and mantlepiece. They were cute little cows, angels, and dogs, but they collected dust like their sole purpose was to intercept it before it could touch wood. Bet suspects the figurines now live in the basement with the National Geographic magazines.

The house looks like the house of a man whose wife died five years before and has kept it as a shrine with his own stamp on it.

"The rest of your stuff is in your room," he says. "Let's put this there and then you're moved in."

"Again."

"Again. And, like I said, welcome back."

Her room is the same. She should just seal it up and declare it a time capsule.

Bet learns from a short article in Rolling Stone that the DTs are on hiatus. Rebecca Hannifin has joined another side group, the

Monkey Traders, and Tom Singer is busy with his usual variety of musical pursuits. Barb Deener is said to be cooking up a side project of her own, but she's at her beachfront house, doing hardly anything. Barb could come home, of course, but she doesn't want to. She fears the house now that her mother is no longer in it. Instead, Barb offers empty invites to North Carolina with no date attached and the excuse of no furniture, like beds.

The band's hiatus, though scary to Bet, gives her time to practice. She watches TV, of course, and plays pool with her father in the basement, but she practices guitar a lot while he's at work. When the DTs do reform, she'll be ready. She'll outplay Rebecca, outplay her own sister. She even writes songs.

Dwight tells her she's making good progress. They sit by the river where tourists line up to enter the arch. She plays and he critiques and then thinks of something harder for her to play. He doesn't look as good as he did at the Breyer Program, and he didn't look very good then. But he's always there on time, early even, and she's learning under his direction.

He never comes onto her, or flirts, He never touches her, only his guitar. She bought the same make and model, a Fender, figuring it would sound the same. It does when he takes it from her to demonstrate, otherwise his always sounds better.

Bet's eyes snap open and she sits upright in bed. A crackling sound pulls her attention from half-dream to full awake. She slides to the edge of the bed and listens hard. The sound is from downstairs, a tinkling sound.

Someone is breaking in.

She pictures a big guy with a mask and a gun, moving through the darkened house like a shark. Her heart pounds so hard, she can hardly hear anything aside from the beats.

She takes slow, deep breaths to calm herself. She needs to hear to track the shark. She doesn't have a gun and never has. Uncle Reggie has one, a rifle longer than her arm, but that won't do much good at the moment.

She needs to call the police. Muffled footsteps shuffle in the dark. The shark is in the house and on the move. She can almost feel his presence, an alien invader that makes her skin crawl from hundreds of feet away, through plaster and wood and metal.

Her door is open, just a crack. Her father snores a bit, and she and Barb never let him forget it, so he keeps his own door closed. She eases out of bed and crawls to the door. Carefully, she pushes her door open a bit wider, holding her breath and praying the door won't squeak. She peeks her head through the threshold, brushing her hair back over her ears. Her father's regular breathing, snoring, comes from behind his door. An army could invade the house and set up a USO concert and he would snore right through it.

A drawer rattles open, then shut. A robbery is underway. Maybe the intruder wants only a TV or a VCR and then he'll go away, but she saw "In Cold Blood" and she's not counting on that. She pushes the door open more and crawls across the hallway carpet in her pajamas. More thumps as drawers and cabinets open and close. The shark is still in the kitchen, so she crawls faster, trading noise for speed. She's a few feet from her father's door when the footsteps move to the stairs. Her heart hammers out of control.

She wants to scream, pound on her father's door, but she can't move. She's frozen. She is going to die outside her father's door and he'll wake up and find her bloody body here in the morning. Footsteps pound up the stairs, no longer trying to be quiet. Bet sits on her butt, facing the stairs. She still can't scream but she'll fight. He stands before her in the darkness and she flexes her legs, ready to kick him down the stairs.

"Bet?"

She knows the voice but can't place it. It is familiar but out of context.

"Bet?"

"Dwight?"

"Bet, I don't want to hurt you. You're supposed to be asleep, go back to bed."

"Dwight, what the fuck are you doing here?" She doesn't loosen up. She's still prepared to kick him. His voice sounds higher than usual, strange, as if he's speaking through a straw.

"I—I—just get back to bed and leave me alone. Please, Bet."

She slides backwards until her back rests against her father's bedroom door.

"Leave you alone? You broke into my house! You don't even know where my house is! How the fuck did you get here?"

Dwight sniffs, like a dog taking a scent. "I followed you. I told you not to tell me where you lived but you were too easy to follow. You should be more careful, Bet."

"Dwight, what the fuck is wrong with you?"

He sniffs again. "I'm in trouble. Nobody will hire me. I've stiffed everybody, and nobody will sell me anything. I don't have any money, I spent it all on the Breyer thing and now nobody will hire me."

"I pay you, Dwight."

"I-I know, and I appreciate it, I do. But it's not enough. It's just not enough, Bet."

"So why are you here?" she demands.

"You have money, Bet. You're a rock star. You told me yourself. I just want to get a couple of things that you won't even miss, and then I'll be out of here. Just consider it a loan, I'll pay you back."

"I thought you were going to clean up," she shoots back. "You went through the program."

"Nothing works," he says, not self-pitying, just honest. "That was the third program I've been in. I've got to have it, Bet."

"Where's your guitar?"

"I sold it."

"You sold your guitar?" She can't believe it.

"I don't have any money. I sold the guitar."

"You said you would never sell the guitar."

"I know. But I did."

Bet keeps her legs flexed, ready to strike. Dwight has hit rock bottom. His guitar is gone, his anchor. There is nothing to tie him to the Earth.

"Come on, Bet. Just go on back to bed. I don't have time to talk to you anymore. I'll be out of here before too long and you won't have to worry about me again. Don't bother about coming to the lesson on Monday."

"Don't worry about that," she snaps, angry now.

The door behind her gives as her father cracks the door open and Bet nearly falls through.

A crack of light beams through, catching Dwight square in the face. He throws his arm across his eyes and hisses like a vampire. Bet looks up, a dark cylinder pokes through the crack in the door. Her father bought a gun at some point.

"What are you doing in my house?" he asks, his voice calm and lethal.

"I'm a friend of your daughter's." Dwight lowers his arm.

"Did my daughter invite you here at three in the morning?"

"No sir, she did not," Dwight replies. "I just need a little money. Bet will vouch for me, I'm a good person. I'm just having a little trouble right now. Just go on back to bed and I'll be out of here in a few minutes."

"Minus my TV and my—whatever else," her father says. "I don't think so. You need to go on out, right now, empty handed. I will shoot you, don't think I won't."

Dwight squints at the gun barrel.

"I'll shoot you right in the middle of your head and nobody will think twice about it. You broke into my house, it's my right."

"All right." Dwight puts his hands up, palms out.

"You're going to leave this house empty handed."

"All right."

"Go down the stairs."

Dwight takes a step backwards and nearly falls down the stairs.

"Careful," her father says. "Turn around and walk down. Slowly."

"What, you don't want me to break my neck?"

"Not before I shoot you, no."

Dwight turns and takes the first step. "I'll go on down now. You two can go back to bed."

"I don't think so," her father says. "Just walk slow."

He steps into the hallway, holding a long copper pipe. If Bet wasn't still so scared, she would laugh out loud. He glances at her briefly but keeps his eyes on Dwight. He touches Dwight in the shoulder with the pipe, just to remind him it's still there.

"Nice and slow," he says, and follows Dwight down the stairs.

Dwight is deflated by the whole thing. Bet follows, and Dwight just slogs along, head hanging low. Her father marches him to the door.

"If you come back, I will shoot you as soon the second I see you," he says.

Bet peeks out the window. Her father can't very well follow Dwight outside, in the streetlight. Dwight meanders, head down, into a battered Pinto, without a single look back at the house. He just drives away.

Her father sags against the door. "Friend of yours?" he asks, his voice shaky.

"He teaches me guitar. Or did. Dad, that was amazing! I really thought you had a gun."

He crosses the room and collapses on the couch. "I was wishing I did, to be honest. I was looking around for anything, and this is the only weapon-like thing I could find, some tubing left after we had the plumbing redone. Pretty sad. I've never been so scared in my life."

"I couldn't tell." She flips the switch for the living room light and the lamp in the corner flares to life. "You were like Dirty Harry or something."

"Was I?" Her father wipes a sheen of sweat away from his forehead, but a faint smirk appears. "Once I figured out he wasn't a raving lunatic, I guessed I could bluff him. So, this is the guy you met in the program? The one you've been driving to St. Louis to see?"

"That's him. I guess it didn't take. That's too bad, he's really a nice guy."

"He did seem sort of harmless. I guess if your house has to be broken into, he's the guy you'd wish for." Her father drops the pipe on the carpet and yawns.

"I think I'm ready to go back to bed. Are you okay?" she asks.

"I think so. My blood pressure is coming back down."

A wave of tiredness washes over her. Her father yawns again. Sadness washes over her.

He locks eyes with hers. "Is something wrong?"

"No. Well, it's just that I've lost my guitar teacher now."

"I feel bad that you have to put yourself at the mercy of lunatics like that. Business is kind of slow right now, and I'm thinking of winding it down. I could teach you."

Bet laughs. "First, you've got a gun that turns out to be a pipe, and now you're going to teach me guitar. You're full of surprises, Dad."

"I'm not kidding."

She lifts a brow. "Since when do you know how to play guitar? You hate music."

"Since before you were born. And I don't hate music. I *love* music. It just didn't love me back."

"What the f—what are you talking about?"

"I used to be in a band. We were pretty good. But we kind of—ran into difficulties, and it never happened."

She stares at him as if he just announced he was going to go live in the jungle with the apes. "You were in a band?"

"I was."

"What kind of band?"

He looks a little miffed. "Rock and roll, of course."

"Let me get this straight. You, who discouraged anything having to do with music, were in a rock and roll band."

He thinks about it for a second. "That's right. I know firsthand how hard it is to make a living making music, so I didn't encourage it."

"I'll say."

"I'm not going to apologize," he says, and she detects no apology in his tone. "It's a hard life. You know that. I'm proud you've done as well as you have with it. But I didn't want you to think for a moment that it would be easy."

"I'm not the one who's done well with it. Barb is the one who can play. I wouldn't be in the band if she hadn't asked me to be."

He stands, wraps his arm around her shoulder, and they trudge toward the stairs.

"Don't kid yourself. You bring something to the table or Barb wouldn't have asked you. She's a professional, I've watched her more than you know. She knows what she's doing. That's why she wants you in the band."

"Thanks, Dad. So, you'll teach me guitar?"

They start up the stairs.

"I'll try. I haven't played in years. I haven't played for most of your lifetime. But I was pretty good and I think I can pick it up. We'll have little jam sessions."

"Just don't try to be cool. Or try to rap, or anything," she says.

"Rap? What's that?"

Her laugh echoes off the hallway walls. "Exactly. Does Barb know you were in a band?"

"No. And I'd rather not tell her."

They stop at Bet's room. She's so sleepy now she's swaying and fears she may fall over. "Dad, you've got to tell her. There have been too many secrets in this family. It doesn't matter now. You should tell her. All these years she's thought she was some kind of freak, a musical deviant. I mean, we come from what, a line of farmers?"

"On my side, yes."

"And then grandpa didn't want to be a farmer anymore so he went into insurance. And grandpa Black worked in some kind of factory. But there was no music in there, until Barb came along. Or that's what she thinks."

"She's right, in a way. I was the first one interested in music in my family, as far as I can tell. And I haven't played a note since before you and Barb were born. As far as I'm concerned, Barb is a self-made woman."

"Still, Dad. You should tell her. I'm sure she'd like to hear about it."

"I'm sure she would. All right, I'll tell her."

"And don't make me tell her. *You* tell her."

"I'll tell her, I'll tell her. Don't worry. And in the meantime, I'll teach you how to play. I probably won't be as good as Dwight. But I think I can still remember the chords."

The next day, her father buys a Fender like Bet's in St. Louis, which she bought because it was just like Dwight's. True to his word, he's not as good as Dwight. But he's good enough.

CHAPTER FORTY-FOUR

"It's time for dinner," Margaret says to John. "Where's Barb?"

"I think I saw the back of her head disappearing into the play-house," he says.

He sits on the sofa with his feet propped on the wooden coffee table. Walter Cronkite is on the newest, twelve-inch color TV a man can buy in nineteen seventy-nine—but even color can't hide the fact that nothing much is going on in the world today.

Margaret sticks her head around the kitchen wall and frowns. "Can you go get her?"

The small wooden playhouse he built for the girls in a fit of industriousness last summer, spurred on by plans printed in Popular Mechanics, sits in the backyard. The red wooden sides, black tar-paper roof, and white-trimmed windows give it a quaint appearance, but inside it's just a small square room. It's also sweltering in the summer, even with the window open. John supposes to the girls it represents freedom and autonomy, but to him it's just a hot little box he shouldn't have built.

"Bet, go get your sister!" he shouts. "Bet!"

Margaret's reappears, leaning around the wall. "John, she's

not feeling well. She's asleep, I told you that. Keep your voice down and go get Barb. We'll feed Bet later."

"Sorry, sorry. Long day."

He slowly shoves himself upright from the couch. He could just yell from the door, but Margaret doesn't like that. He slips on his shoes and goes outside. Despite the fact it's twilight, it's hot. The porch light illuminates the flat backyard, which is home to a clump of pine trees clustered like teenagers. The playhouse sits smackdab in the middle. Bad music gets louder as he draws closer. Guitar chords fling into the night air by slender female fingers.

Her uncle Reggie bought her a guitar for Christmas. John wasn't at all pleased about it, but Reggie almost dared him to complain. John said nothing, and for a while the guitar lived underneath Barb's bed, untouched. But she rediscovered it, along with the Mel Bay songbook Bet gave her.

He nears the playhouse, and calls, "Barb, come on, it's time for dinner,"

The door and window are open and Barb hunches inside the house. Her head is down, her golden hair hanging over the guitar neck. The yellow light from the back porch hits her fingers. She's working on a G7, a tricky chord that requires a lot of strength in the index finger and flexibility in all the others. She hits it again and again and it sounds different every time, not the intended result.

"Barb," he says, louder, steel in his voice. "It's time for dinner."

She looks up, her eyes intent and focused, almost angry. "Give me five minutes. I've almost got it."

Everyone has argued with him today. He doesn't need this all day long. "No, come on. Your mother has dinner ready."

She strums the strings again and a near facsimile of a G7 rings out, amplified by the wooden walls of the playhouse. "Five minutes, please. I've nearly got it."

"Barb, you don't seem to be hearing me. You put that guitar down and you go inside right now, and you eat your dinner. It's getting late and we don't have time for you to learn how to play that thing right now."

Her eyes glow underneath the strands of her hair, yellow in the porch light. She looks demonic. "When am I supposed to learn how to play it?"

"Look, you get out of that house right now. You shouldn't be wasting time on that thing anyway. I don't know why your uncle gave it to you. You put it down right now, young lady, and come in this house."

"If I quit now, I will forget what I just figured out," she says, her voice as serious and flat as his own. "It'll just take me five more minutes and then I can eat dinner. By the time you get back in there and wash your hands I'll be done and ready."

She turns her head back down again, blocking him out. He steps into her light so she can't see what her fingers are doing.

"You will not tell me when you are ready to eat dinner and when you are not, young lady. You put down that guitar right now or you will never touch it again, I can guarantee you that."

"But daddy, you don't understand," she says. Now the resolve is gone from her voice, replaced by the whine of a little girl. "I played with this for a while after Uncle Reggie gave it to me but I didn't really understand it, but the other day I pulled it out again and it really sort of worked. I don't want that feeling to slip away again. I'm afraid I'll *lose* it if I stop."

He steps away from the light and looks at her again. *No, not demonic. She's a determined little girl with a new guitar and nothing else.* It'll never be enough to play a good G7 chord, to play "Kum Bah Ya," to play like Segovia. Never enough.

"You won't lose it, honey. It's just a guitar. You'll put it back under the bed and forget about it and move onto something else."

"No, I won't. I like it. You don't understand, you don't like music. You and Mom never listen to anything. I like it. I want to learn how to play it."

"Honey—it's not like that. I like music, your mother and I like music. I'm sure we don't listen to it as much as you and your friends do, and I'm sure we don't like the same kind of music, but that doesn't mean we don't like it. It's just—it's just that it's too hard to make a living at it. It's not something that's worth spending a lot of time on."

She cocks her head to one side, like a dog trying to understand his language. "I just want to learn how to play it. Don't people know how to play guitar without making a living at it?"

"Yes, of course they do."

"And I'm just a kid. I'm not planning to make a living at it. You aren't going to put me to work yet, are you?" She gives him a wicked smile, and he chuckles.

"No, I guess not. Not just yet. I just mean that—creative things are very hard. They can sort of wear you down. I don't want you to get hurt."

"I won't get hurt."

"And you're not going to take lessons. I am not going to pay for any music lessons."

"I don't need any lessons. I just want to learn it myself."

It's not like the lessons with Mrs. Ludvigsen. The girls didn't take to the lessons, and a piano is big and expensive. A piano he can fight. Guitars are something else. Guitars are small and sneaky and seductive. Barb doesn't just hold it, she caresses it, and you have to caress it to play it.

"All right. Come on now, let's go eat. You won't forget what you've learned."

She hesitates, then agrees. She lays the guitar on the small wooden bench inside the playhouse.

"Go on, now," he says. "I'm going to check on the back gate. I'll be right behind you."

She runs toward the porch light, her gangly form silhouetted in the light. John waits until Barb is in the house and picks up the guitar. It's a nice Gibson, Reggie wasn't cheap. John holds it, realizes how difficult it must be for Barb to play.

His fingers effortlessly form the G7 she was trying to play, and he gives the strings a light strum. The guitar is out of tune and with a sharp, metallic cry the E string breaks, bringing back awful memories. John puts the guitar down in disgust. Reggie gave her some extra strings. He'll have to replace the string, so she doesn't know he broke it. Once it's on, he'll have to tune the guitar. Once it's tuned, he'll need to play a little song, just a short song, to make sure it's right.

The guitar is seductive.

CHAPTER FORTY-FIVE

WHILE ON HIATUS FROM THE DTs, BARB's skills scored her guest appearances on four albums by three bands before she made the rare appearance in Percival to see her sister. She finds Bet sober, running three miles a day, and with a decent command of basic music theory. She's more surprised to learn that her father once was the lead member of a rock band, and a locally notorious one at that. He sat her down in the kitchen one night and told her the whole story.

Barb spent the rest of the night and part of the next day re-examining incidents in her childhood, reinterpreting them in this new light. The times he yelled at her about how music was a waste of time and all the times he discouraged her were different.

Bet walks Barb through the chords of one of her father's favorite songs, "Pearl of Great Price." Barb expects it to suck, but it doesn't. It's at least as good as the best songs she's written, and better than a lot of them. It's better than a lot of Crash's stuff, too, and, although it doesn't have the weird tempo and key changes Crash likes, it's more difficult to play than it sounds.

"That's a really tricky chord change," Barb says.

"Yeah, it is," Bet agrees.

"And this is Dad's song, huh?"

"Yep. An antique."

Barb gives her head a small shake. "I thought all those Fifties songs were easy to play. But this one's tricky. You can lose the rhythm right here and you'd have to wait to the chorus to get it back."

"It's not a bad song."

"It's not bad at all. I'm still just surprised. The old man was holding out on us all this time. Are you sure he doesn't have a tape of this somewhere?" Barb asks.

"He says no. He says they never recorded it. He didn't even write the music down."

"He's kept this thing in his head all these years?"

"Apparently."

Her father couldn't remember their phone number half the time. Her mother did most of the bill paying because the first of the month always rolled around and took him by surprise. No wonder, he carried a concert's worth of music around in his noggin.

"Did he teach you any more?" Barb asks.

"A few. I'm trying to write the music down."

Bet reads and writes music, in a rudimentary way, thanks to the efforts of their father and Dwight. Barb never learned how. She tried, but most of the time she just learned the chords and then did everything else by ear. Barb watches her sister closely while Bet stares at her fretboard. Her face, once rounded and slightly puffy like Barb's own, is thinner, with cheekbones showing through. Her pants are baggy, not a problem Barb has. Barb's gut, a doughnut-shaped roll, accompanies her sizable breasts. Bet just has the breasts.

Bet is sharp and fit, and while Barb doesn't envy the process that got her to this point, particularly the daily three-mile runs, she's jealous of the result. The sense she missed something, once again nags at the back of her mind. She missed out on the chance to spend a lot of time with her mother. Now she's missing out on the chance to spend more time with her father, to learn what other secrets he's kept all these years. But she feels the road calling again.

"Bet, I'm ready to get the DTs going again. I was thinking we do a little quick tour and then get back in the studio."

"That's good."

Barb keeps her expression neutral, but a mixture of hope and fear surge through her. "I want you back in."

"What do Tom and Rebecca think?"

I haven't actually talked to them. But I know Rebecca's free. Tom is never free, but I think he'll come back if I ask."

"That's not what I mean. What do they think of me being in the band again?"

Barb shrugs. "They'll have to like it, or they won't be in the band themselves. I learned one good lesson from Crash. I've got control of this band. I want you in, and that's all that matters."

"Barb, I appreciate that, but I don't want to be in the band just to be some kind of welfare case. I want to be able to hold up my end."

"From what I've been hearing from you, you can. I think you're playing better than I am, right now."

"Oh, please." Bet rolls her eyes. "No, I'm not. I don't think I ever will. It's a natural thing for you."

"But you can read music now, and I never learned to do that. I'm telling you, Bet, I need you in this band. If you don't come back, the DTs will cease to exist."

"Well, I don't want to be the one responsible for that," she says with a twisted grin. "Surely, the earth would stop turning."

Barb grins back. "That's right."

Bet's expression sobers. "And after talking to Dad, finding out about how he gave up and how he thought about his music all these years, and kept those songs locked up in his head so he was the only one who could hear them—I don't want to do that."

"Neither do I. So, are you in?"

"I'm in. Where should we get together?"

"I don't know, I'll have to call around and see where people are. We're going to be really good this time. I can feel it." She looks at the squiggles Bet has made, black ink sperm swimming across even, orderly lines. Glad, at least, Bet can understand it and explain it to her.

CHAPTER FORTY-SIX
REVIEW

City Paper Reviews
The DTs

Thursday night, the 9:30 Club

The DTs, true to their name, have had something of a rough time lately. After a successful debut, driven largely by the songwriting skills of former Pod guitarist Barb Deener, they hit the proverbial sophomore slump particularly hard with the album "Breather." Barb's skills seemed rusty and there were rumors that founding members Rebecca Hannifin and Tom Singer were unhappy with her leadership. Adding to the band's woes was sister Bet Deener's insistence on sprinkling some Keith Moon/Brian Jones/Sid Vicious spice into the mix. Perhaps keeping her sister away from booze and drugs took too much of Barb's time to allow her to actually write better songs.

Needless to say, when the DTs came to the 9:30 Club, this reviewer had lowered expectations. Thankfully, they were exceeded. Bet is out of rehab now and has erased the biggest complaint against the band—she can play. In fact, she's able to play better than her sister. She also has a refreshing stage presence. She and Barb trade good-natured barbs with the crowd, leaving Rebecca Hannifin and Tom Singer as the official wallflowers of the DTs.

Your reviewer is a male, and it must be said at this point that Bet Deener looks great. The Deeners have always sported a sort of rounded, party-girl look that no doubt contributed to the band's name. Barb retains it, but Bet, off the sauce and whatever else she was on, now has a lean, chiseled physique and a cheekbone-centric face to match. The crowd still loves Barb but now they love Bet too.

The show was mostly a greatest hits rundown, which is a little disconcerting for a band this young. If they managed to sneak in a new song, Barb didn't tout it, and I didn't hear it. Even so, the show was a hoot. The DTs are now more musically solid than ever, they have two talented front women and more good songs than most bands can ever produce. Some of the lackluster tunes from "Breather," particularly the faux-country romp "One Last Mile," benefit from the band's newfound energy. A song that once sounded like a cheesy, lazy country-punk knockoff had the crowd singing along as shamelessly as if they were at an Alabama concert. Whatever it is that Bet Deener isn't taking anymore, maybe the rest of the DTs should lay off of it as well.

THE NEW YORK CITY STUDIO ISN'T IN A TRENDY PART OF TOWN. THE graffiti on the door is ominous, a threat instead of a decoration. Inside, a bank of large, gray fans flank the far end of the room. Lights on stands, and lights mounted on racks flood the space with bright, daytime-style light. People mill about, but the photographer and his assistant groan over coffee. The assistant pops a couple of pills and readjusts her sunshades.

The photographer isn't famous, but he's scored covers with a couple of shots for National Geographic Kids and Teen Beat and is "up and coming," according to the label's publicist. His eyes are losing a battle against encroaching wrinkles, his head is undergoing a rapid deforestation, and his oversized black glasses are thicker than bulletproof glass.

He's probably relieved at the advent of autofocus, Barb thinks.

"You're all beautiful, beautiful," he says, using one of the large fans to create a fake breeze. "All right, we're going to move a couple of you around, now. Tom, I know you're taller than the rest, but I still want to get you in front here. Get some dynamic tension going. Now, you two, I want to sort of have you standing behind him, like you're peeking around his shoulders. Like you're at a club, you know, and he's some tall jerk in front of you and you're trying to see who's on the stage."

He grabs Barb's and Rebecca's shoulders and moves them into place. Bet watches with some surprise. The assistant, a young woman with straight hair and bangs, lounges behind the fan, slowly eating a doughnut as if absorbing it by pressing it to her lips.

"And you, dear, we're going to put you in front here, sort of like he's your boyfriend, so he's blocking these other women so you can see. Doing a little play acting here, you see." The photographer gently grabs Bet by the shoulders and pushes her to Tom's side.

"I'm going to be here?" she asks.

"Of course," he says. "It'll look great."

It is an unusual place for her to be. She has never been in the front of a DTs photograph before. It was always Barb or Rebecca, or Barb and Rebecca, with Tom and Bet hovering in the background, out of focus more often than not.

"Maybe his hands on your shoulders," the photographer says.

Tom puts his hands on her shoulder, the roughness and weight a surprise to Bet.

"No funny stuff, Tom," she jokes, and he snorts out a laugh.

"Vivian! Move that fill about a foot to the right," the photographer calls.

The assistant moves and holds the doughnut away from her mouth as she pushes a large square light.

"Such cheekbones you have, my dear," the photographer says. He stands right in front of Bet and she stares into his eyes, tiny and far away. "Yes, we need to show those cheekbones."

Barb issues a low grunt behind her. Barb doesn't have cheekbones, or not ones a photographer would highlight, and Bet never used to either. Replacing gin and beer with water and Diet Coke had brought them back, and now everyone will see.

At least, everyone who buys the "Radio 24/7" soundtrack. If they turn past the picture of Christian Slater on the cover, open the CD case and look at the pictures of the bands whose songs have been selected for the movie, they might see this picture of the DTs. It will be about the size of the viewer's thumb. If the viewer squints, they could possibly make out Bet Deener's new cheekbones and maybe see Tom Singer's hands on her shoulders and wonder if they are lovers, together for the moment in the heat of some wild rock and roll lifestyle.

It is not the cover of Rolling Stone, or Spin, or Blender or anything else. The DTs are past the point of scoring a cover, at least until they issue an album the critics like and the public buys. But they will be inside the CD, and possibly on posters, if the photo is good enough. It is not much. But it is the first time Bet's been in front, so it's enough.

CHAPTER FORTY-SEVEN

Barb looks up from where she sits in a plush chair in the Big Farm Studios as Bet walks in. They're in Kansas City and it's chilly inside the sparse rehearsal space, which is why she's wearing a scarf and what she attributes her bad mood to.

"You're late," she says.

"Hi, to you, too, Barb. I'm not late. There was no set time to be here, so I can't be late," Bet retorts.

Barb rolls her eyes. Tom and Rebecca stand behind their instruments, fiddling with tunings and have been for half an hour, ready for a much-needed rehearsal. There're a dozen new songs to work through for the album.

Barb's exhaustion is soul deep. She's too aware of the bags and dark circles, darker than usual, that weigh down her features. Her eyelids are alert but are slow to open when she blinks. Her work on the songs is a monumental effort to recapture the spark of magic she felt a lifetime ago when the DTs recorded their first album. The magic was with her still until she read the reviews of the second effort. Before, she skated on instinct, but now that failed. Now it's work. And she can't work if her sister, the late-blooming star of the band, is late.

"Tom, did I, or did I not, say we should meet at eight?" she says.

"Actually, Barb, I don't think you did. You just said after dinner."

"Well, fine. But, Bet, we are going to have to be knuckling down now. Everybody is here but you, even if maybe there wasn't a firm time."

"Well, I was giving an interview, if you have to know. Getting us some good press."

"An interview?" Barb frowns. "With who?"

"None other than the *Percival Junction.* I didn't say big press, just good press."

The Percival Junction consists mostly of classified ads and notices of missing dogs, but Barb grew up with the paper. Several of her pet hamsters were dispatched to the afterlife wrapped in it. In all her years with Pod and the DTs, her hometown paper never ran a word about her, but they saw fit to interview Bet.

"I did us proud, don't worry," Bet says. "The reporter was Rick Welker. He said to say hello."

Barb doesn't remember anyone named Rick Welker. Bet probably went to school with him, which is why the *Junction* wanted to talk to her.

Bet unwraps her scarf from around her neck like she's pulling off a boa constrictor. Frost creeps around the edges of the outside windows. You can not only see your breath, you can almost see your frozen words in the air.

"I hope you had something to eat, Bet. We're probably going to be here for a while."

"I had a little bit. If I had known you were planning an all-nighter, I would have had more. Maybe we'll get bored, and it won't last so long."

Tom bunkers himself behind his kit. Rebecca adjusts the settings on her full stack, both of her bass guitars on stands flanking each side of the amp has two basses, neither large enough to hide her petite frame.

"I told you, it's crunch time, Bet," Barb says. "You need to show some enthusiasm."

Bet claps her hands together to warm them. "I'm just so enthusiastic I could puke. I'm sure I'll be even more enthusiastic when I see the song list you've proposed."

Barb hoped to play everyone through the songs so they could see how they fit together. She wanted them to feel the rhythm, the pulse. It's the best song planning she's ever done. It's just perfect. And now her sister, her sister who didn't even want to be in the band, is going to complain about it.

"I guess what I'm asking is, is my song on your list? Or Rebecca's songs?" Bet studies her.

Rebecca's head pops up from behind the amp like a prairie dog.

"Well, of course they're on the list. I thought I would run us through some of the other songs first."

"But are they on the *album* list?" she says.

All eyes are on Barb. Tom, who doesn't write songs, peers out with bemused detachment. Rebecca and Bet stare at Barb, awaiting the answer. Bet's best song, cleverly entitled "My Song," took her weeks to nail down. It's not that bad, but it's also not that good.

"They're not on the tentative list I submitted to the label."

"Oh? And how tentative is that list?"

"Let's talk about this after the run-through. I think you'll see what I have in mind."

Rebecca steps around in front of her equipment in one ungraceful step, bumping her equipment as she does. "Geez, Barb, I can't believe you're doing this. After all those times we bitched about how the guys weren't letting us in. Now you're doing the same goddamn thing."

"It's not like that. You don't understand. I'm the one feeling the heat from the label. I'm the one everyone blames for fucking up the last album. If this one sucks, are they going to blame you, Rebecca? Are they? Or you, Bet? No. They're going to blame me."

It feels good, cathartic, to let them know the burden she carries. Barb's courage rises, and she continues, "And the critics may carp about some of your songwriting or playing or whatever, but if the album is no good, they'll blame me too. Not you. Not you. Not you." She points to all the band members, then to herself. "*Me.* So, I need to have a say in things. I need this control. I looked at the songs and arranged them in a damn good order. And your song doesn't fit the mood, Bet, it's as simple as that. I can't fit it in. And your songs don't work either, Rebecca. Same thing.

"I don't want to put them on as hidden tracks because everybody knows about those, and it'll still mess up the feel. Maybe we can put them on as single B-sides if we release any singles. But the label won't do any singles at all if they don't like the album, and if they don't like the album they'll blame me and they may very well drop us altogether. So, I have control. If you don't like it, there's the door."

The silence is so deep that Tom's Adam's apple moving in his throat is the loudest sound in the space. Barb is shaking. Her vision blurs and small stars burst in her eyes, pinwheeling around like tiny fireworks.

Rebecca's right, and she has lied. She's doing the exact thing Pavel Karash did, and for the same reason. Except Pod was on a roll, Crash could have afforded to experiment, but he never would. The DTs are in a different boat, and it's sinking. She needs to keep it floating, whatever it takes.

"Why don't we vote?" Bet says.

"What?" Barb snaps out of her daze.

"I said, why don't we vote? Let's play everything and see what we think. We're in this band, too, I don't care what the label thinks."

"I agree," Rebecca says. "You've heard all the songs. We haven't. You may be right, maybe ours don't work. But then we'll all know."

"It's only fair, Barb," Bet says. "We all need this record to work as much as you do. It's not yours alone. Don't make all this pressure for yourself."

Barb sees the spots again. She's never felt like this before. She got into music to *avoid* stress. "Bet, I hate to break it to you, but this is my band. I have to feel the pressure."

"*Your* band?" Rebecca says. She picks up one of her basses and holds it like a club. "I thought it was *our* band. We talked about forming it together, remember? Do you remember that?"

"I do. But you've also gone off and worked with Salvation again. And, Tom, you work with everybody."

"Tom, don't you want to chime in here?" Rebecca asks, her voice sharp and hot.

"You know, I really don't," Tom says, remaining behind the wall of drums. "I will just point out that this is the least professional band I'm involved with."

"Thank you for that vote of confidence," Barb says. "Look, I know we started this band together. We all know that." She is trying to keep her own voice level and reasonable, calming, like her father's when he's selling insurance. "And I brought my sister into the band. But I want you to know that I'm the only one who's been dedicated to the DTs full time. Rebecca, you're as much a part of Salvation as you are this band, and don't think I don't know that you're working on a solo album. And, Tom, if you could catch sexual diseases just from being in a bunch of bands, you'd be dead by now."

"And what about me?" Bet asks. "I've never done anything else. Ever."

"Oh, yeah? You go off and get hooked on anything that comes along and then go detox and then come back like nothing's happened, and suddenly you're trying to push me out of the way and get in front of the pictures."

Bet sucks in her breath. Barb realizes that was a run-on sentence that ran on a little too long.

"So that's what this is about, is it? You can't stand anyone else getting the attention, is that it?" Bet steps closer, right in Barb's face, hands on hips, muscles flexing in her forearms like Popeye.

Lean and mean Bet. I'm flabby and huge by comparison, Barb thinks.

"No, that's not what this is about. But I will say it's a little irritating for you to go flouncing around like you own the place when you came into the band like—I don't know, almost like window dressing. You can barely even play."

"That's not true," Bet says. A weird smile starts creeping across her face. "I can play now, Barb."

"Well, okay, you can play better—"

"No, I can *play.* I can play better than you. That's what this is about. You've been Little Miss Creative all this time, and now I'm better than you, and you can't stand it."

Rehearsal, and the space they're using, has become a waste of time and money. Rebecca sighs and leans back. Tom eyes the door. Barb glances at them both, gives an acknowledging nod, but can't let Bet's assertion go unchallenged.

"You are going to tell me that you can play better than me? Little sister, I've been playing since you were still drooling over that dumb basketball player, Stan. I've been playing while you were selling perfume and skirts and shit at the mall. I've been playing while you were sitting on your ass in Percival and it's because of me that you're not still there. So don't go telling me that just because Dad gave you a few lessons that suddenly you are better than me."

Bet's weird smile remains. She looks like some deranged person from a horror movie. "I won't tell you anything, Barb. I'll show you."

She walks over to where her guitars are arrayed and picks one up. She crams a cord into the socket, then stabs the other end into one of the Marshall amps.

"Get yours plugged in."

"What?" Barb blinks. "Seriously, we don't have time for this."

"We'll make time. I'm tired of you running me down. I know what I'm doing and I'm going to show you. Plug up, sister."

"What? Is this some kind of Western? We're wasting time here."

"Barb, pick up your fucking guitar and plug the fucker in and *play*!" Bet orders.

Rebecca crosses her arms, waiting. Tom's peeks out over the snare and fiddles with his bass pedal, also waiting. Bet's knuckles whiten as she squeezes her hand around the brown fretboard.

"All right, Bet, if it will make you happy, I will play with you."

Barb picks the middle guitar, her favorite of the three next to her on stands, an old Gibson. She knows every curve of its body. She can play it with her eyes closed, with one hand tied behind her back, with every cliche she can think of. She loops the strap over her arm and plugs into her amp. The two amps hum at each other, the electronic version of trash talk. She turns to Bet. Bet stands, cool and collected, with that same cocky smile plastered on her face. Rebecca and Tom are forgotten.

"So how should we do this?" Barb asks.

"Just play something you think I can't."

Barb looks at the guitar neck, the coiling of the strings, and begins a slow, chugging, rendition of "Smoke on the Water."

"Oh, come on," Bet says. "Get serious. Anybody can play that."

"I'm kidding. Get ready to eat my dust, little sis."

She cranks into "Dueling Banjos," sure Bet won't know the song. She bites into it hard, picking the notes like she's trying to cut the strings. To her surprise, Bet picks it right up, giving the call and response in notes equally crisp and clean. They carry it as far as they can, to the point where it would sound better with actual banjos, then Barb tears into "Sweet Home Alabama." Bet waits a second or two, long enough for Barb to suspect she has won easily, then chimes in with the rhythm guitar notes. When Barb switches to the rhythm notes, Bet takes the lead without missing a single one.

The song ends, and Barb says, "All right, so you've been practicing. I'm done with the easy stuff."

She switches to the guitar solo from "Hotel California." But there she is, plinking along as sure-footed as Joe Walsh himself. Barb switches to the solo from Pink Floyd's "Money," but Bet steps right into that one as well, making the eerie solo sound even creepier through two amplifiers. Barb hits a wrong note, made all the more obvious by the fact that Bet hits the right one.

Barb shifts gears. With as much gusto as she can, with a force that makes the muscles in her arms stand out against the skin, she plays the solo from "Holiday in Cambodia." Bet takes a second or two to recognize the Dead Kennedys and then chimes in again, her notes even brighter than Barb's. Barb realizes the truth with a sinking heart. Her sister can play.

"My turn," Bet says. "Follow this."

The sounds she pulls are amazing. It sounds like she's playing two guitars at once. Her fingers are splayed like spiders. A surge of panic washes over Barb. She recognizes it but it's alien territory, she doesn't know where to get in.

"Segovia," Bet says.

"I know it's fucking Segovia," Barb snarls. "I just don't know the song."

Bet smiles. She shifts to Dire Straits' "Sultans of Swing." Barb chimes in with relief but she's rattled and doesn't keep up with where Bet is in the song. She likes this song too.

"Fuck it!" she shouts. "You win!"

She unsnaps the strap and nearly drops the guitar. Rebecca laughs. Barb huffs, the blood rushing to her head. She holds the guitar by the neck and smashes the body on the ground. A chunk of metal whips past Bet's arm.

"Hey!" Bet shouts. "We're not The Who!"

"Fuck it!" Barb shouts again. "Rehearsal is over!"

CHAPTER FORTY-EIGHT

She floats face down in the water, her hair rippling with the tide like golden seaweed. A man looks, looks again, and looks a third time. A woman drowned or drowning. There is no lifeguard. He strips off his shirt, fishes his cigarettes and lighter out of his shorts, and drops then onto the sand as he races into the water.

He reaches her seconds later. She's dead weight. Her shoulder thumps against his thigh. The surf makes her body buck and fight him. He's breathing hard by the time he pulls her onto the beach. He drags her without ceremony across the sand and rolls her over. White female, long dirty blonde hair, black T-shirt, faded jeans. She'd be pretty, maybe, if she didn't look so dead.

He scans up and down the beach. No one is in sight. No doctor in the house, and she isn't breathing. He sucks in a lungful of air and blows it into her mouth, nearly gagging on the salt tang. He spoons one hand behind the other and pushes in the center of her chest...twice, three times. He leans in to impart another breath. The man has no medical training, but he likes doctor shows. A repeat of the breath and chest pushing doesn't revive her.

She's dead, Jim.

The woman sputters. She sits up and coughs out salt water.

"You're alive!" he cries, delighted that watching TV paid off.

She opens her eyes. Blue, he sees. Red and blue. She groans.

He sits back on his haunches. "I saved your life."

"I'll thank you later. Maybe."

She closes her eyes again. She *is* pretty, in a rugged way. Her T-shirt and jeans are not the usual outfit for swimming. Maybe she hadn't gone swimming. Maybe she'd gone drowning.

"All right, I'll thank you now," she says, eyes slitted. "Thanks. Now run along."

"I don't think I should leave you."

"I'm fine." She coughs.

"No, I don't think I should leave you."

"Then stay."

He folds his hands around his knees and looks at the ocean. She lies on her back, coughs with her eyes closed.

He returns his attention to her. "I have a cell phone"

"That's wonderful."

"Is there someone I can call?"

"No."

"You may need medical attention. I'm not leaving until you get it or give me someone to call."

More silence.

She coughs more, then digs in her pocket and pulls out a damp strip of paper. She hands it to him. A business card. "It's wet. Sorry."

There isn't much ink on the card.

The DTs

Everything, All the Time

And a phone number.

He looks at her. "The DTs. I've heard of you. You're a band."

"We are."

"You did that one song I like."

"Glad to hear it."

"Come to think of it, I saw something about you on TV just the other day. It was—it was—" He lapses into embarrassed silence.

"I know what it was," she says. "It was VH1. *Where Are They Now?* So now you know where they are now. Aren't you lucky?"

He dials the phone. "Who am I calling?"

"My sister."

"Right. Your sister in the band."

The phone rings for a long time. He pulls the phone away from his face to hang up when he hears a female voice. A voice he's heard before.

"This is Bet."

She sounds just like her sister. Looks like her, too, if he remembers the show correctly.

"I—"

"Who is this?" she cuts on.

"I'm with your sister. She was drowning. I think she needs medical attention."

"She was *drowning*?"

"Yes."

"Is she okay now?"

He looks to his right. The woman—he remembers now her name is Barb—has found his cigarettes and his lighter. She's struggling to get a flame.

"She's okay." He lowers his voice and turns his face away. "I believe she was trying to kill herself."

Silence on the phone, then a rush of breath. There's another rush of breath from his right as Barb finds the flame.

"It was her turn, I guess," Bet says. "Tell me where you are, and I'll be right there."

CHAPTER FORTY-NINE

Barb hugs herself, shivering in the front passenger seat. She pulls her cigarette pack from her pocket but it's all wet and ruined. She tosses it on the floorboard of the car in disgust.

"You want to tell us what this is about?" Bet looks from the road at her for a second, then returns her attention forward. "I thought we were past all this."

Thankfully, their father sits in the back and doesn't join in. Barb leans against the half-open passenger side window. The warm ocean breeze blows her damp hair into snakelike designs on the glass. "I was swimming," Barb says. "And then I just got tired of swimming."

Bet looks at her for a few seconds, then watches the straight, dull, and trafficless road. "That's the thing about swimming. You always have to keep swimming. How did you get all the way down the beach?"

"I don't know. I started out from my house."

"You don't look like you're dressed for swimming."

Barb looks down at her ruined jeans. "I'm dripping all over your seats. When did you get this car?"

"Don't worry about it, it's a rental. You weren't going swimming, were you?"

"No, not really."

"Why?"

"Why? Why not? I was just sitting around my house, and nothing is going on. My band—my second band—is over, and I didn't have a single good idea in my head for a good song. Not one. Do you know how long it's been since that happened?"

"Well, I can guarantee that if you had managed to drown yourself, you would never have written another one."

Their father sighs from the back seat.

Barb leans back and closes her eyes. "Whatever. I guess it's a good thing you guys came along when you did."

"You knew we were coming. I talked to you yesterday."

"I know. That made me depressed too."

"What, us coming to see you? You've been inviting us forever."

"No, you coming to see me to perform an intervention."

Their father finds his voice, although it quivers with emotion. "Barbara, you need one."

Bet parks the car in the driveway, a flat piece of tan pavement that disappears into a pile of sand. Barb's house isn't old but is weather-beaten. The screen door sags and has a hole big enough for a cat to fit through.

"This is my castle." Barb pushes her wet hair out of her eyes. "I need to do a few things. It's kind of a mess."

She stumbles out of the car, walks through the sagging door into the front room, and plops down onto a blue couch next to a red chair and a mottled yellow rug.

"Nice furniture," Bet says.

"Primary colors. Have a seat."

"We have something to do first. We're going to find your beer and pour it out. Liquor and wine too. If we find any drugs, we're going to flush them."

Barb reclines and stretches her arm across her eyes.

"Fair enough. Just don't clog up my toilet."

It takes Bet and their father a while to finish the job. Beer cans and liquor bottles sprout all over the house in various stages of fulfillment. They don't find any drugs. Bet finds a suspicious green plant product in the kitchen. It could be a spice, but she isn't sure, so down it goes. Barb sits up on the couch when Bet and their father walk out of the kitchen, staring at the far wall.

Bet sits next to Barb, who grudgingly moves a leg to make room. Their father perches on the chair.

"Now," Bet says. "Down to business. Everybody wants us to finish the record. But you've got to be clean to do it."

While Barb has crawled into a beer bottle next to the ocean, Bet has been taking the calls from the label, which are becoming rather insistent. Bet has a calendar full of little red marks, indicating when Rebecca and Tom, especially Tom, will be available.

"Steve Albini has agreed to produce, and Rebecca says she doesn't even care if you put one of her—"

"No," their father interrupts. "Elizabeth, you're going about this the wrong way."

Bet glares at her father, who has never been addicted to anything stronger than root beer. "Dad, I know what I'm—"

"Barb, you need to be okay as a person before anything else. The album doesn't matter. The band doesn't matter. What matters is that you feel positive about yourself."

"Well, that's true, Dad, but—"

"Listen, I think both of you girls need to get out of this business." Her father's voice is steady and urgent now. He's in selling mode. "Forget the band. Forever."

"What?" they say in unison.

"What are you talking about?" Barb demands.

"Look at you," He hops to his feet like a prosecutor. "Bet, you're a junkie and an alcoholic. And Barb, you're at least an alcoholic, and for God's sake, just a couple of hours ago you tried to kill yourself. All over music! It's killing both of you and I don't want to see that happen."

Bet glares at him. They agreed in the car on the way over that Bet would handle the mini-intervention.

"Dad, you don't understand. The music is a big part of her life, maybe even the major part. It always has been. If it wasn't, she would have given it up in the face of all your opposition."

Barb doesn't mind being the object of discussion. She sprawls on the end of the couch and watches her father and sister through half-open eyes.

"It's been a big part of my life, too, I just didn't acknowledge it for a long time. But—"

"Look, I'm not saying don't have anything to do with music." He shakes his head. "Just, you know, Barb, you could be a producer or something. You, too, Bet. Or session musicians. But all this responsibility with the band is going to put you both in an early grave."

Barb comes to life. "Maybe we could take over the family insurance business. Would that make you happy?"

He sits back down. "No, not really—"

"You're not being honest with yourself, Dad," Barb says. "Look what the music did to you. You felt the same way about it that we do, but you denied that. You didn't tough it out."

"Things were different for me—"

"No, no, they weren't. You know, Dad, you could have helped us through all this, but you forced us to keep things from you. You could have helped us." Bet looks at her father. "You know, Dad, you've never really seen us play, have you?"

He stares a hole through the floor, then shakes his head.

"Maybe you should see what it's like, if we can keep Barb off the sauce long enough."

Bet looks at Barb, struck with a brilliant idea. Barb senses it too. Barb laughs and lays her head back on the couch.

"What's so funny?" their father asks.

CHAPTER FIFTY

THE CROWD STAYED THROUGH THE TWO OPENING BANDS, THE BLUE Zombies and the Musical Spears. The DTs are back on the road, previewing songs from the third album, and the sizeable crowd is there for them. The crowd in front of the stage is twenty deep, at least.

A surge of pride bursts through John for his daughters. Many of those in the crowd are tattoo-slathered, chain-smoking ne'er-do-wells, but that's rock and roll these days. John is by far the oldest person in the joint, although some members of the crowd are older than he would have expected. There are plenty of skinny smokers and drinkers half his age, but there's the odd bald spot and paunch here and there.

The opening bands are nothing to write home about. They're all chubby and stuffed into black clothes and sing about cultural dislocation. John doesn't buy it. Why does popular music have to be so angry? The music isn't bad, and both drummers are excellent, he admits, but, in general, he's not impressed.

His daughters walk on stage and crowd gets rowdy. People who wandered off to the bar or bathroom come back and press as close as possible to the stage. Chatter about the band gears up around him as the band checks out their gear and sets up. The kids are eager to hear new music. Bet disappears offstage.

John smiles. His daughters persisted and succeeded, despite all the time he spent discouraging this, but part of him is glad they ignored him. Now they're on stage, loved by many, and both are clean and sober. Very professional.

"Dad! There you are. Come on." Bet pushes through the crowd and stops at his side. She tugs on his arm, pulling him toward the backstage ramp. She's covered up in a hoodie so she won't be spotted. He nearly doesn't recognize her himself.

"Where are we going?"

"Backstage. Come on."

"But I wanted to watch the show from out here. I've got a great spot."

"No, come on. We've got a better spot picked out for you."

He's half-pulled and half-follows her to the backstage door, where a thin man in a black jacket and a leopard-skin vest lets them through. Backstage is nothing like the Club Bandstand. It's dingy, for one thing. No broom has been seen in this place in quite some time, if ever, and the floor squishes as he walks through. Bet pulls him through the knot of opening band members, still standing around congratulating each other as they angle for the best beers in an oversized cooler.

"Hey, Bet, you want a beer?" one of the Blue Zombies asks.

"No, thanks," Bet says. She pulls John in front of her and steers him to an attractive young woman in a grey sweatshirt, her hair pulled into a ponytail. "Dad, this is Rebecca. Rebecca, this is my father."

"Very nice to meet you." Rebecca extends a hand.

John smiles and she smiles back. This is the Rebecca who fought with Bet, denigrated her playing skills. At least she didn't hit anyone on the back of the head with a guitar. He could live with his daughters thinking he was once an angry rock and roller.

"And this is Tom. He's a brilliant drummer."

The young man beside Rebecca smiles and shakes John's hand. "You have some amazing daughters, man."

"Thanks. I do know that."

Tom's got a beer in one hand, as do all the members of the opening acts. The backstage area reeks of beer, and not just from the current occupants. The smell is old, soaked into the wood. It's amazing anyone in this world can resist it. Rebecca isn't drinking. Barb and Bet clutch plastic water bottles so large that John doesn't see how they'll make it through a whole show without a bathroom break.

"Sit over here, Dad, we've got a spot for you," Barb says. She pulls up a ratty black bar stool with a plain wooden back.

He sits in it and smiles to indicate it's good, even though it's terribly uncomfortable. Barb smiles and wanders off to talk to a roadie. She points in John's direction, maybe at the array of guitars a few feet to his right. John readjusts himself in the barstool a couple of times, standing each time and looking around at the drinking crowd in the small space.

The crowd gets restless outside. Waves of chatter and shouts from the main audience space vibrates through the room. He closes his eyes, the energy of the eager crowd pulsing through his feet and hands, awakening memories buried long before his daughters were born. The familiarity of the mounting excitement triggers John's nostalgia, although he's never played crowds so big. *But dang they love to* smoke, he thinks. He always thought the kids he knew used to smoke a lot, but they were nothing compared with the chimneys that now wait to be entertained just a few feet away.

"All right, Dad, we're on," Bet says.

"I kind of thought that's why the lights went down," he says.

"Don't be smart."

"Break a leg."

Bet kisses him on the forehead and heads out of the wings behind her bandmates. The crowd hoots and cheers. The noise gets louder when Bet steps from behind the wings onto the stage. Barb waves to the crowd. Tom disappears behind the drum set. Rebecca gives a little straight-waisted bow, like she's one of the Beatles. Bet waves to the crowd, too, just like Barb did, the same arm, same queenly wave.

"Thanks for coming out, you guys," Barb says. "We've been taking a little break, but it's nice to be back."

Feedback squeals from the mike briefly, then the DTs launch into a song. It's a crowd pleaser. The shouting and hooting crests over the band like a wave and then settles to a dull roar as people sing along.

It's not really his kind of music. It's still rock and roll, still has drums and guitar and bass, but it's far beyond anything he knew back when he used to care. The songs seem patched together, Frankenstein sounds without any underlying rhythm. They're fast, they're slow, they're fast and slow. They don't make any rhythmic sense. John's not sure if the lyrics are any good, because he can't understand them. He prefers rock songs that make sense. He took pride in writing songs that used a standard verse/chorus, verse/chorus, bridge, verse/chorus scaffolding, but still managed to be original and surprising.

While he mulls the decline and fall of rock and roll, they end the first song. It sort of falls apart rather than stops, with lots of extraneous sporadic strums and drum hits instead of a clean power-chord finale. They show a little more discipline on the second one. It has a base of Fifties-style rock, with a layer of grungy guitar and his daughters' beautiful harmony laid on top of Rebecca's deft writing. They end the song as if the sound was cut off by a guillotine. They can do whatever they want to with this stuff. They're professional musicians.

Barb talks to the crowd to loosen them up. Something about beer. John looks around. No one is watching him. *Not really.* He shifts in the chair again, stands, then moves it over a bit before crossing his arms and staring at it. He could probably sneak out and get to the back of the club to watch the show. The door guy from would let him back in before it's over, and Barb and Bet would never know the difference.

"We have a special guest tonight," Barb says.

The crowd claps and cheers with such enthusiasm John could feel the sound booming through the walls. Barb could read a Chinese menu and get this crowd clapping. John wonders what it's like to have that much power.

"He's a rocker but he's been out of the scene for a while. He's written some beautiful songs, and we thought we'd like to share a couple with you. If we can get him out onstage."

John stiffens. He turns from the uncomfortable seat and faces the stage just in time for Barb to turn and look offstage, right at him. His heart pounds and he falls back into the seat. Barb smiles and curls her index finger, summoning him. John shakes his head and waves her off.

"He's a little shy, but if you make some noise maybe it will scare him out," she says, and the crowd obeys. The noise is thunderous.

John still shakes his head. The idea of standing before a crowd, *this particular crowd,* is terrifying. They won't like his old fogey rock, they'll eat him alive.

Bet puts down her guitar and sneaks around behind the drum kit into the wings while John sits, dazed and still shaking his head at Barb. Bet takes a few giants, exaggerated tiptoe steps and grabs him, her fingers snaking around his arm.

"Come on, Dad. You waited for this for a long time. You're going out there."

"Ladies and gentlemen, I would like to present to you John Deener, our father," Barb says.

The crowd claps and shouts. Like he was an actual rock star, and they actually want to see him.

Barb continues, "He's written a few songs, and we know how to play them. Would you like to hear them?"

John steps from the wings onto the very edge of the stage and waves limply to the crowd, both in greeting and to try to convince them not to request his songs, but it's too late. Tattooed arms pump in the air and pale faces demand music. *His* music.

A roadie straps a guitar around his neck. Almost in spite of himself, he gives it a quick strum. The guitar is in perfect tune, and the crowd shouts again. Either they really want to hear his songs or they are very easily entertained, or both.

"This is a song called 'My Angel,'" Barb says. "It's by a band named Percival. They're from Percival, Missouri, our hometown, just a ways south of here. Our dad used to lead the band."

John looks at Barb, looks at Bet. They beam at him and sneak pleased glances at each other like they are eight years old again and just baked him a cake. He beams back so big his cheeks hurt.

I have two beautiful daughters, tall and strong, and they're doing what they love and have an adoring crowd waiting to hear them do it.

Barb extends a hand toward him and gives a little bow, as if to say, take it away. He glances at Rebecca. She's smiling, too, like she's his third daughter. So, he takes it away.

And it sounds pretty good. It's a simple song, which is why he started with it when teaching Bet to play guitar. It's also a fun song, peppy with a good backbeat. Barb coddles the vocals like she wrote the words herself. The crowd shouts and whistles when it's over, loud enough and long enough that John waves at them, a little embarrassed.

"Would you like to hear another?" Barb asks, and the responding roar indicates the affirmative.

"This is a very special song. Another song our father wrote. It's called 'Pearl of Great Price.' Get us started, Dad."

The members of Percival could never agree on a bridge for the song, so they never put one in, but John and Bet worked one out that's perfect. He knows the rest of the song very well, it's burned in his bones, but he's worried he won't remember the bridge.

Barb steps to the mic and sings better than Al ever did. Her voice lifts the song to a whole new level. John sneaks a look at the crowd. The song isn't fast, not even as fast as "My Angel," and he thought they might have lost interest and headed for the bar, but they're as rapt as ever. John cranks it up a notch as he heads into the bridge, looks at Bet, and grins. She kicks into the lead. Any doubts about her ability are gone. She tears into it like she was raised in a roadhouse, her fingers finding the chords with no fumbling.

The crowd shouts approval when her solo is done. Rebecca is doing her part, too, sending out meaty bass notes with a precision Dickie could never match. Tom is amazing. Barb said he plays with half a dozen bands and John can see why—he's a metronome, pounding out solid rails of rhythm for the song to ride on. John realizes it's the first time he has ever played the song all the way through on stage, and "Pearl of Great Price" has never sounded so good.

He looks again at his amazing, flawed, talented, troubled, beautiful daughters. He realizes he is right, and Bet is right. It is important that they are good people, and it's important that they do the thing they love most. He and his wonderful, lost wife worked so hard to bring them to life, and now they're giving him a new life, letting him join in the thing they all love. He's making music with the Delicious Twins.

"This is what it's about, Margaret," he whispers. Then bows to collect his applause.

I FINALLY GET TO VISIT FRANCE

I did not know if I wanted to become an ace. I had one confirmed kill but to be an ace I would need four more, and now I was not sure that I wanted that tally against my soul, even if they were Nazis. My shoot-down of the German pilot did not gnaw on me. I did not lose sleep over it, I did not think about it that much. But, somehow, the dead pilot became a presence that would not go away. Sometimes while walking across the base, I would see a man move out of the corner of my eye, but when I whipped my head around, no one was there. Sometimes, I thought I heard a man trying to whisper an urgent message to me in German, but no one was there. So, it did not bother me, but it was also something I could not forget. One German ghost was bad enough. Four more might be a little bit much.

I wrote to Virginia, and she wrote to me. My letters were on cramped postcards supplied by the U.S. Army. They didn't let me say much, but I couldn't say much anyway. We didn't want to give anything away. Virginia's letters to me weren't much longer and were equally mundane. She was not a prolific letter writer, as it turned out, but I treasured each one she sent. We exchanged vows of love fairly early on in our correspondence, but after that we stuck to day-to-day topics, like what we had for lunch or whether we were sick or not. I didn't want her to know the reality of war; I kept my postcards as relentlessly cheery as a propaganda newsreel.

Our action stayed fairly heavy as the winter of 1944 lifted and spring began to spread across Europe. Men and women were dead everywhere, cities were ruined, great civilizations poked and stabbed blindly at each other, but Mother Nature did not notice or care. Blossoms poked around the ruined metal sculptures of destroyed tanks, vines curled around corpses, moving them aside, coming through.

We were steadily flying bomber escorts now, keeping the monsters safe as they pounded the guts out of Germany. We had a good reputation for a bunch of Race flyers. We had not lost a single bomber, and Colonel Davis intended to make sure we never did. "You stay with your bombers," he said, over and over. "Do everything by the book." So, we did, and the book was pretty good, because we never did lose a bomber to an enemy as far as I know.

We lost other things, though. We lost ourselves, sometimes. Hardcore, who had become my best friend while we were overseas, was shot down by an ME-109. It got on his tail and he could not shake it and his wingman could not get to him in time to save him. So, he died. And, like so many others, he knows more about life and death than I do. His real name was Walter Darby and he was from some nothing town in Texas, but for some reason he was eager to get back to it. I did not think there were any Race men in Texas, just like I didn't think there were any in Ohio, but he said there were, and he was one of them, and he intended to live there until the good lord called him home. The good lord called him earlier than expected.

Hardcore was the most restless man I have ever seen. He could not stand to be cooped up unless he was asleep or in the cockpit, so he wandered all over the base. He reminded me of something I read about sharks, that they have to keep moving all the time or they will die. Hardcore was the only one I told about the ghost of the German who tried to haunt me. I thought for some reason he would understand, and he did. Hardcore had shot down two planes. He figured the ghosts would be after him, too, but he never stood still long enough for them to catch up.

I lost myself on a sunny summer day in 1944.

We were supposed to escort some B-17s and B-24s to bomb the Herman Goering tank works in Germany. We had flattened pretty much everything else Germany had but they were still good at making things, including tanks, and the Allies really didn't want them to have tanks anymore. One thing they still had were guns and ME-109s, so we were going as heavy escort there and back. We didn't see a lot of action for a long part of the trip and I was getting kind of bored. We were observing radio silence and the bombers were responsible for all the navigation, so all I had to do was fly along with them, keep my eyes open and be quiet. I think I nearly fell asleep at one point. It was a bright, clear day, and the sun hung lazily in the sky, filling my cockpit with light and my head with thoughts of a nice long nap.

The buzz saw started up as we got closer. A flock of ME-109s rose from the ground like mosquitoes and headed for the bombers, flying in pairs just like we always did. Hawks and eagles might fly and hunt alone but that was deadly for fighter aircraft. We had to hunt in packs. We needed not only to protect the bombers but to protect ourselves.

Heavy shells from below started exploding around us, making a poom-poom sound like fireworks but releasing balls of fire and thick clouds of smoke. I heard the whine of the ME-109s and the ack-ack-ack of the big guns on the Flying Fortresses. The quiet of the day was gone. No more need for radio silence, everyone now knew we were there. I was the wingman to Bobby Masterson, a quiet man who turned up from Tuskegee just a few weeks before. I didn't know him well. He was from New York City but the vices of the big town had not rubbed off on him. He never drank, never cussed, seemed to smoke only grudgingly and absolutely refused to gamble. That meant he had more money than anybody else on the base, mainly because he never spent it on anything. He might as well have grown up in some small town in Iowa. He had a girlfriend who had already written him a sheaf of letters even though he had barely arrived in Europe. That didn't bother me now; I had my few letters, and to me they outweighed all of his.

"You got one coming on you, Bobby," I said. "I'll take care of him."

"'Preciate it," he responded, as coolly as if I had just offered to buy him a soda.

A cool head in a firefight. That's what you want to be around.

The ME-109 saw me coming and the pilot realized he wasn't going to be able to out-turn me, so he dropped down and broke off the engagement. More fighters were coming up ahead at 11 o'clock, so this freed Bobby and I to get after them and chase them away. The mission continued on for a while then, with the MEs circling warily and us swiveling our heads around constantly, trying to spot them while also trying to keep from getting hit from below. I know that in the movies the airplanes are dogfighting constantly, but in real life you are acutely aware that your one and only life is sitting in a very expensive airplane, and you are careful. But you can't be too careful. We were nearing the objective and the flak was getting heavier. We never lost a bomber to an enemy fighter, but we certainly lost some to ground fire. I looked out the right side of my cockpit and saw a shell from below hit one of the B-17s right in the middle. The wounded Flying Fortress slowly fell out of formation, its crew leaping out of every window and door like ants. Jumping out of a plane was nearly as dangerous as being in one. The rear gunner pulled his chute too soon and went limp in the harness just after he cleared the plane, probably dead, which was just as well because his body hit the wing of the bomber behind him. It was strange that here I was in my little tin can and I felt much safer than those poor guys in an airplane bigger than several buses lined up.

"Johnny, you've got a girlfriend trying to sneak up on your tail," Bobby said, with no more drama than if he was telling me my shirt was untucked. "I'll see if I can make her leave you alone."

"'Preciate it," I said, borrowing his phrase. It seemed like a good, economical thing to say in such a situation.

He passed over me and I turned to see the ME-109 go into a steep dive. Bobby went after it, the right thing to do because he had his speed up and could catch this guy. But the German plane was apparently going faster than both Bobby and I thought because Bobby wasn't able to catch him as soon as he hoped. And, as it turned out, as soon as I needed him to.

I had hardly turned my head back around before I saw two more blotches on the horizon. I thought they were puffs of smoke from ground fire, at first, but soon enough I saw the wings and the tails of approaching ME-109s. They were headed for a B-24 that had pulled up to replace the B-17 that was now smeared all over the ground. I wasn't going to let them have it, Bobby or no Bobby.

"Forget that girl," I radioed him. "We have a couple of new dance partners."

"On the way. Don't dance with them both by yourself."

I didn't have a choice. They were headed straight for the bomber, probably figuring that a lone fighter was not going to put up much resistance with a lagging wingman. I have said before that we had never lost a bomber to enemy fighters, and I was damned if it was going to happen on my watch. I figured my best defense was a good offense, so I charged right between the fighters. They broke off, one to either side. I cut a hard left, slamming my body against the Mustang's metal frame. The Mustang could turn better than most airplanes and I thought I might be able to pick one of them off and even the odds a little. The Jerries weren't fooling around, though. The other plane went into a steep climb, a gutsy move because it exposed him to more fire from the B-24. But he probably figured—correctly—that the bomber wouldn't fire because the crew was afraid of hitting me.

I wish they hadn't worried so much, because he got on my tail and I couldn't shake him.

"My dance card's getting full pretty quick, here, Bobby," I said, trying to keep my voice as cool as his always was, but I was sure the shakiness was evident.

"I'm hurrying," he said. His voice sounded shaky too, and I knew then that I was in real trouble.

The ME-109 was right behind me, sending bullets whizzing past my canopy. I couldn't go into a tight turn to the right because that would send me flying right into the thick of the bomber fleet. I would almost certainly hit something, or, at the very least, I would defeat the entire purpose of my being there by escorting a German fighter right into the middle of a herd of U.S. bombers. I couldn't do a tight turn to the left because the other ME-109 was there, waiting for me to do just that. I couldn't go up because the Jerry was behind me and could probably out-climb me. And going down was stupid because I'd be closer to the ground and the flak.

Sometimes you have to do stupid things. I punched the stick and went down. I almost wished I was in a P-47 Thunderbolt right then. They were fat things, but they could dive like meteors, from what I had been told. The Mustang could dive, too, but no better than the ME-109. We went down together, me whipping back and forth, trying to avoid his bullets. He wasn't all that good a shot, but he was right behind me and didn't have to be. I could feel the vibrations as his 20mm slugs dug into the back of my fuselage, which caused jolts of pain as if they were puncturing my own body.

"Hang on!" Bobby shouted into my ear, his voice having lost all traces of its famous cool. "I'm coming!"

He wasn't coming fast enough. Smoke poured out of my right wing, which was bad because the wings held the fuel. I wanted to be flying a North American P-51 Mustang, not a crop duster. The plane was still responsive despite the damage, and I continued to whip it back and forth, missing most of my tormentor's shells. I hoped the smoke would blind him.

"Almost there!" Bobby shouted.

A dizzying explosion felt like it was going to knock my teeth out, and then my world started to spin. Vomit rose in my throat, and I had never thrown up while flying, or even gotten a little green around the gills.

I had indeed gotten too close to the ground, and a patient gunner had just given me a nice little present in the form of a shell that blasted through my left wingtip and set my plane spinning like a top. I managed to stop the spinning without throwing up, but this just gave the ME-109 behind me time to perfect his aim. My plane shook with what felt like one hundred little explosions and now smoke came from the engine, too, blinding me.

I dropped even lower. I was not going to let this Jerry shoot me down, and if I got low enough, it would be hard for the ground gunners to get me, as they were used to shooting at much higher targets. I was flying not far above the trees now, which limited my mobility. I didn't want to be waggling my wings too much because there was a danger I could actually hit a tree, and that could do as much damage as any German shell.

The smoke from my beloved P-51 was getting thicker, which was good in a way because it did blind the ME-109. He had to fly off to the side to see where I was and then fly back into the smoke to try to shoot me, which gave me plenty of warning. All I had to do was jog off to the side a little bit and let him shoot the air.

The strangest thing happened then. After a while he got tired of sucking smoke and just settled off to the right behind me, out of the smoke but off to where he couldn't get me. We cruised above the forests of Germany together, not all that fast anymore. I looked back and saw his head in the cockpit and gave him a little wave. He gave a little wave back. Nothing personal. I guess he just wanted to get a confirmed kill and make sure he actually shot me down, but he wanted to be gracious about it.

Another odd thing was that my Mustang was actually performing pretty well, considering it probably had more bullet holes than fuselage and was on fire. I carefully tested the controls, without making any moves that might startle the ME. Everything responded fine, more or less. I probably couldn't do any barrel rolls, but I could land if I had to. As it was, I didn't need to do anything for a while. We trundled on across the landscape for what seemed like hours, my plane spewing ugly gray smoke across a nice blue sky. The flak and armadas of aircraft that I had left behind seemed like part of a different world. It occurred to me that my war was about to be over. There was no way in hell I could get back to Ramitelli; I was nearly out of fuel. I couldn't go back because the ME was right on my tail, ready to end my world in addition to ending my war. There was really nothing for me to do but relax and enjoy the ride. Maybe I would get lucky and the ME would hit a tree and crash and I could claim it as a kill of my own.

I was almost starting to get bored again when the ME began to pull away. He was probably running out of fuel, too, and couldn't wait any longer to claim his prize. He gave a little waggle of his wings and fired off a couple of shots into nothing and banked into a slow turn. I didn't try to follow him—I wasn't that stupid—so I continued on until I couldn't see him anymore. My fuel gauge was banging on empty. The fire on the wing hadn't helped with that situation, at all. I tested the controls again and everything seemed to be working okay. I was pretty sure I was on enemy territory, and I didn't want to deliver a partially functional Mustang to the Jerries. I needed to get up higher and bail out.

I started a slow climb. I got to about 12,000 feet when I saw a dot on the horizon. The bastard was back! The ME-109 had tricked me! He was coming on fast, determined to get his kill after all. I didn't have enough gas to dive again and try to pull it out again. I barely had enough fuel to try to turn and evade him that way, and the truth of it was that I was scared the plane would fall apart under any sort of rough maneuvers. I basically sat there and let his guns chew into the plane. He got off a long volley and shot past me, probably figuring one encounter would be all it would take. He was right. I waited until his plane flashed by and bailed out. I had heard stories about German fighters shooting U.S. troops who were parachuting, which was against the rules. I didn't want to give him the chance. I figured that by the time he came around again I'd be too low for him to bother.

He didn't bother, anyway. He saw my chute and saw my North American P-51 Mustang plummet to the ground, so he had his kill. A little American flag would go underneath his cockpit, and I hated that it would be mine. I watched my plane corkscrew into the green hillside and explode. I had just cost the U.S. taxpayers tens of thousands of dollars. As I drifted down, I saw a small crowd assembling below, apparently coming out of the trees. I got closer and saw a road and some slow-moving cars, as well as cattle in the field and tiny moving human shapes here and there. I was outside some small town somewhere, but I didn't know where, or even which country. I started to pay close attention because the ground was coming up faster now and I didn't want to kill myself by slamming into a tree.

I managed to avoid a couple of trees and found a nice open

field, coming to a textbook-perfect running stop. I dumped the chute as fast as I could and turned to face three rough-hewn women with knives in their hands. They were advancing toward me steadily, with looks of grim determination on their faces. I knew the Germans were tough, but I didn't expect to square off with three hausfrau the very second I hit the ground. I was tired and didn't want to deal with this, and I wasn't sure what I was going to do. The knives were a good size and the flight suit made it cumbersome to try to fight, but at least it might protect me from the blades and give me a chance to knock some good old American sense into them.

I was thinking that I should charge one of them, take the element of surprise, when suddenly they dropped to their knees and began sawing away at the cords of my chute, which was splayed out along the ground like a big dead jellyfish. They weren't after me, at all, with the knives. They wanted the silk from my chute. Things had been rationed so much that they needed the silk for clothes. One of them said she hadn't had a suitable dress to wear almost since the war began. I stood and stared at them, still in my fighting stance. Another, who was sawing away with some gusto, said she needed to make dresses for her daughters.

It took another few beats of my heart before I realized that I understood their conversation. I didn't speak German. They weren't speaking German. They were speaking French. I had flown over the border, somewhere back there beyond the trees. I had always wanted to come to France, and now my dream had come true. I thought of Dominique. She would have had a good laugh at this.

www.scarsdalepubishing.com